Anything

Mayberry University Series

Kristina Welch

Copyrights

Copyright © 2025 by Kristina Welch

All rights reserved.

No part of this publication may be reproduced, distributed, or transmitted in any form or by any means, including photocopying, recording, or other electronic or mechanical methods, without the prior written permission of the publisher, except as permitted by U.S. copyright law.

This is a work of fiction. Names, characters, places, and events are the product of the author's imagination or are used fictitiously. Any resemblance to actual persons, places, or events is purely coincidental.

Book Cover and Illustrations by Kristina Welch

With editorial contributions from Dori Harrell and Sally Apokedak

Unless otherwise indicated, Scripture quotations are from the ESV® Bible (The Holy Bible, English Standard Version®), copyright © 2001 by Crossway, a publishing ministry of Good News Publishers. Used by permission. All rights reserved. ESV Text Edition: 2025.

Scripture quotations marked HCSB are taken from the Holman Christian Standard Bible®, Copyright © 1999, 2000, 2002, 2003, 2009 by Holman Bible Publishers. Used by permission. Holman Christian Standard Bible®, Holman CSB®, and HCSB® are federally registered trademarks of Holman Bible Publishers.

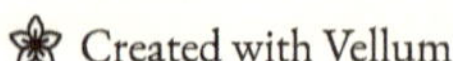 Created with Vellum

For Brit, my favorite overachiever, front porch buddy, and GIF giver.
I have a crush on you the size of Texas.

And for Roscoe, author of the sweetest boy cursive notes.
You're the best big brother a family could ask for.

Dear reader,
This story, full of sweet romance and encouragement, also contains themes of PTSD and the aftermath of a near-assault. There are no descriptions of sexual assault coming to fruition, but please proceed cautiously if this is a difficult topic for you. I hope I've addressed these important issues with the care and sensitivity they deserve.
Warmly,
Kristina

PROLOGUE

SAFE TO SAY a low-drama life of voracious reading didn't prepare me for the harsh reality that developing curves could lead to terrified sobbing in a gas station bathroom. "One thing led to another," as they say. But I have to stop dwelling and analyzing. I roll my shoulders to reset. Just pack.

I glance to my bedroom window, visible from the driveway. I'm itching to run up there and throw a few of my book friends into a box—Alina Starkov, Anne Elliott, Hazel, Lara Jean. Do I have human friends? Sure, but my book friends wouldn't judge me for packing three types of graph paper. Besides, they're the only ones who haven't let me down. Then again, maybe they have. For all their warnings and promises, they never prepared me for what happened last year. They led me to believe that a pretty face and a curvy body would make my life ten times better, even a hundred. But all that glow-up magic? It's a lie.

Mom emerges from the other side of the car with her telepathic look. "I'll bring you some water, sweetie."

The intense Colorado sun has me squinting like I'm in an old Western. I should grab my sunglasses, but any distraction right now is risky. There's too much to figure out, too much to avoid. I force myself to pace as I focus on the task in front of me. For once it's useful that I'm incapable of simultaneously walking and thinking hard.

A lady and her shuffling basset hound distract my manic steps to the sidewalk. "Aw, can I pet your dog?"

"Surely. This is Stella. And I'm Judy."

"I'm Kit."

Stella's long ears and droopy eyes make her a candidate for Monday morning's mascot, but her tail wags when I squat. She lowers to a sit and plops over to make her belly available to me.

I chuckle and scratch it. "Are you enjoying your walk, Stella?"

"We saw a mountain lion hiding in the red rocks on our last walk," Judy says. "She's still spooked."

"Poor doggie. That's so scary." Am I projecting onto this dog? I shake my head and pat her belly. "Don't worry, Miss Judy will keep you safe."

Judy's wise smile wrinkles her face. "Do you have a dog?"

"No. And I leave for college tomorrow, so—"

"Oh, honey, that's wonderful. Where are you headed?"

"This little school in East Texas." Beyond weird that I enrolled somewhere I hadn't heard of until a year ago. A full scholarship is certainly motivating.

"Well, enjoy the adventure."

I send a wave and a warm smile I don't feel. I'm not up for any more "adventures." Last year was enough of a roller coaster for a lifetime. I open the back car door to Tetris my things into Dad's Accord.

Mom's still gone and, yep, I see her through the office window. She bends over laughing, hand on Dad's stomach. With the pleased smirk of hitting his mark, he pulls her closer. My parents are disgusting. In the best way, of course. They're like real life versions of Prince Derek and the Swan Princess—if Odette was spunkier and a redhead.

I flinch at the low purr of a sports car and snap toward the noise. But it's not blue. Not even close. It's not him. And just like that, it's gone.

Mom reappears on the driveway and hands me a water bottle in silent communication. *Nope, still don't want to talk.* I thank her and gulp down most of it.

Maverick saunters out and relieves me of the bottle.

I tilt my head, amused in advance at my brother's forthcoming antics.

"You'll need to save room for one more in the car." He takes a swig.

Whenever I tell Mav he's bossy, he corrects that he has "leadership qualities." He and Mom both.

"Think you'll take care of all those driving hours in one trip?" she asks him.

Ah. Mav's license is now within reach.

"You know it, Mamacita." He drapes his arm lazily around me, rocks his hip out, and imitates us in a ridiculous high-pitched voice. "Road trip!"

This kind of class-clown behavior is exactly what I need right now. I bump his hip with mine, sending a message. He knows and bumps me back. My eyes fill, and I squeeze him into a side-hug. He's been taller than me for years and I'm still not used to it.

Take care of him, God? Both of them?

"Cool, guys. It'll be fun." He ambles toward the backyard, summer swag in full effect. Likely on his way to talk Grey into some mischief.

My crazy brothers. What a relief that they're dudes. If they were girls, I'd constantly worry—

A slam of the car door reverberates, shaking me, pulling me down a mental black hole. Every muscle tenses. My arms curl around me. My eyes squeeze shut against the memory. It's coming. Black clouds of fear pour in and cover everything with a vivid false reality. I smell rain. I hear the crunch of pavement. I feel the slosh under my feet. I'm living it again, running again.

The car door. Scrambling up. Forcing my legs faster. Lungs aching. Gas station lights.

I angrily paw at the tears falling and the wisps of fear that remain. Every time it's so real. Three long months ago, and it still isn't in the past. I crumple against the car and slide to the driveway, hugging my knees to my chest, as if making myself smaller could protect me.

Please make it stop. Please.

I'm always here, I feel God whisper.

"Oh, sweetie. I'm so sorry." Mom drops to her knees on the hot cement and cradles me. "The door. Was it the door again?"

I squeeze her arm. I hate that I'm like this now.

"Can we talk about it?" Quiet tears in her voice. "Are you okay?"

Under no circumstances will I talk about it. I know she loves me, but she can't understand this. She just can't. I shake my head and bury my face into her shoulder.

I want to pray, but I don't know what to say.

I'm always here.

This move couldn't come at a better time. Get me out of this town—to a place where memories are less likely, where my mind can start fresh. I need to be anywhere but here.

CHAPTER ONE

AFTER THE SUMMER of doom and gloom I had, this campus might just be the distraction I need. I enrolled before everything went down, so it's not a Jonah or *Forrest Gump* situation. More like *Alice in Wonderland*—I've tumbled into Mayberry University and its world of nicknames, traditions, and stories. Let's be real, change isn't my strong suit, but I'm so desperate for different that I'm not even mad about it.

"Do they really expect me to sit at the same table all year?" Sophie assesses the table of guys behind me. "What's with the cardboard sword fight outside? Are we supposed to know why the cafeteria is called Saga?"

"Frankly, I'm too scared to ask about the frog," I say. Oops—I'm not with my old friends. I have no reason to expect they'll recognize my *Tangled* quote.

Sophie claps with excitement. "Chameleon!"

"Nuance," Mia finishes.

I mirror Sophie's clapping. She's contagious that way.

Maybe these girls will be different. Last year, my old friends dropped me as fast as my new friends embraced me—and for all the wrong reasons. After only a week and a half on campus, it's hard to guess whether my suitemates will fall into one of those categories.

"I love inside jokes," Ayumi says deadpan. "I'd love to be a part of one someday,"

"Yes! Ayumi!" Sophie says. "You would be an *Office* fan."

"I heard the food service company was called Saga like decades ago." Mia is brand new too—a junior transfer student rather than a freshman like us—but she already knows all the things and all the people. "Administration's been trying to make the students call it the Corner Cafe ever since they built this fancy building. Clearly tradition trumps all around here."

"Clearly," I say, and pan the room.

It isn't quite the Great Hall at Hogwarts, but it's actually nice in here, carpet and stone columns and hundreds of gleaming wood chairs. No plastic seating or linoleum like the fluorescent cafeteria of high school. I can't blame Ayumi as she picks at the food on her plastic tray. Fancy vibes aside, nothing tastes quite like it did at home. The whiffs of antiseptic and fried food don't help.

"The sword fighters were wearing purple, no?" Mia asks. "That's Club, another dude floor."

I try to stay focused, but my attention drifts again to the students pushing through the doors, friends hugging and chattering, guys high fiving across a table. Students in red shirts leave the cafeteria line and head to the other red shirts. Purple with purple. Yellow with yellow. Every color marks a dorm floor, and while not everyone is wearing their floor shirt, enough do that it's easy to tell where each group sits. I'm at the G1 table—Griffin Hall, first floor—with black shirts. Floormates band together like schools of fish, often choosing to stay on the same floor all four years. The whole floor pride thing is weirdly cultish, but also fun. Like a never-ending summer camp.

I thought college was supposed to fill my mind with knowledge about the world. Maybe it will, but so far it's been more about learning the rules of this alternate universe—what each floor is known for, why guys spray paint their friend's stomach and throw him into a pond, when to use someone's floor name versus their real one. Still, it's comforting to be wrapped up in this foreign reality. I can choose who I am, have a fresh start, because not a soul on this campus knew me before. I can be the Kit I want to be and not the Kit from last year.

My attention narrows at a pair of broad shoulders gliding from the orange-dotted table attached to ours. Perfectly imperfect wavy blond hair frames a clean-shaven face. Like a Greek sculpture dressed in a GQ spread. He moves with a quiet confidence that should come with a theme song. With a flick of his wrist, he returns his tray and floats toward the door. The subject at my table has moved to classes this week, but my eyes are stuck. Upperclassmen have only been back a couple weeks, but I've already heard enough about Noticeable Guy to know his name— Levi Whitaker. Oddly, none of his fans have talked to him much. You'd think a guy like that would have a list of exes as long as Taylor Swift's.

The edges of my vision darken, snapping me out of my daze.

What is wrong with me? Drooling about the popular, powerful guy after last year? I know better. I hate that he's pulling my attention. I hate him and everyone like him. I cringe and rub my eyes. Not exactly the 'love your neighbor' thing I should be doing.

I squint, forcing myself to see him clearly, objectively. His haircut, manners, and clothes—bought with the money I've heard he has in spades. His fit physique—earned with discipline. So this guy made himself into who he is.

It's not fair. He can afford to position himself squarely in the spotlight. He's strong, not vulnerable, so he'll never have the consequences I did. He can protect himself. I hide my clenching fists before the girls notice. I beat back my attraction to him, angry that my body refuses to hear my mind. He's arrogant, well known, sought after—a walking, talking Nope. Guys like him cannot be trusted. I will never make that mistake again.

A guy from my differential equations class strolls in and claps Levi on the shoulder. Austin, I think. He's bulky but guileless, treats girls with respect, and hasn't paid me any attention. I'd guess he's more guy's guy than ladies' man—a relief considering we'll be in class together twice a week.

As they talk, Levi listens intently, twirling something in his hand.

Another guy walks by with fist bumps. "Samwise. Jeeves." His voice carries.

Those must be their floor names—nicknames that stick with them their whole time at Mayberry.

Two girls follow. One calls to Levi with a suggestive look while the other giggles. Levi replies impassively and turns back to Austin, questioning him without words. Austin shakes his head, and they continue their conversation.

That dude has more red flags than a bullfighter's arena. Sure, he has a spotless reputation, but I know better. Aiden's reputation was just as misleading, or I never would have gone out with him. That kind of power and popularity isn't put to waste. I stamp this verdict across the Levi Whitaker folder and slam closed the filing cabinet in my mind.

As if he heard the clang, Levi zeroes in on me. His lips part.

I whip my head away. Quick—what are my friends saying? If I could just make a relevant comment to look preoccupied. Something about the resident advisor on our floor?

"... so she somehow got her brother a spot on Flooders ..."

I force a casual nod, but there's no jumping in the middle of a Sophie story. Just one last peek? He's pushing the door open and stealing a last glance at me too.

"Not you too, Kit."

I yank my focus back to the table and contort my face to look innocent. "What?"

Mia snorts. "The young blond Tony Stark, I assume."

"Levi? He's a snack." Sophie's eyes scan the room and snag on the boys at the door.

I shift in my seat and suppress a head shake.

"His pecs are visible through his shirt," Ayumi says.

Sophie cackles. "I knew that was in there somewhere."

Ayumi bristles. "I'm not saying I like him."

"Sure you don't," Sophie taunts.

"I'm just saying ..."

Ayumi needs a subject change too. I break in. "So tonight—"

"Everyone says Levi is mission impossible," Mia interrupts. "But you're pretty enough to level a guy like that."

That's not how this works, I want to yell. My heart pounds, but I tighten my filter and study her silently across the table. Mia's rich brown eyes match her creamy skin. Tall, curvy, and fabulous —like a young Tyra Banks. She's clearly had a different experience with beauty than I have. Then again, maybe she earned her grit the hard way.

"And she's got that Miss Congeniality vibe," Mia says.

Ayumi nods along, but Sophie purses her lips.

Mia looks to her. "'She's beauty and she's grace?' What, no singing?"

My stomach drops at Sophie's expression. I can't bear to have a repeat of last year. Any of it.

"Anyway, maybe you'll be the one to catch his eye." Mia leans back and considers me. "All that shiny hair, big blue eyes. You two are some kind of match."

I bite my teeth together. Not a match. Not with him. Never.

"I've never heard of a guy shooting down so many girls." Ayumi is barely audible in here. "You really are pretty though."

I muster a polite smile. Most girls love hearing that kind of thing.

"Hair shmair." Sophie tosses her Blake Lively locks over her shoulder like it's a nuisance. "I'd kill for those hips. Must be nice."

So she isn't thrilled with the tall, thin, and athletic thing she has going. I wish I were surprised, but this is standard procedure. Girls don't value what they already have. And worse, the longer a girl has been gorgeous, the more she compares herself to others, like beauty is a curse that grows with time. Something tells me Sophie has been cursed since birth.

Suddenly loosening, Sophie breaks into "Hips Don't Lie" and draws glances from nearby tables. Her voice is so beautiful it pulls at the soul.

Mia moves her shoulders to the beat. "Something about that dude makes me want to knock him down a peg, prove he's not untouchable."

"How? Like play Hitch?" Ayumi nibbles a fingernail.

Sophie cuts her song short. "Ooh, I love *Hitch*."

"Yeah ..." Mia says. "Set him up to see what it's like on the other side of the swooning."

My fingers knot together beneath the table, squeezing until my knuckles ache. I hate being talked about like this. And I want less than nothing to do with that Levi guy. "You guys, just—no. I'm not going after him or anyone else."

Three sets of eyes lock on me.

"On a *boy*-cott?" Mia asks.

A bark of laughter from Sophie.

I straighten and take on a firm tone. "I had a bad experience." Maybe that will shut it down.

"Go on," Mia says.

"No. Thanks."

Ayumi graciously brings up G1's movie night, and the subject finally drops. I sink into Saga's hum of boisterous chatter, and my heart slows to a manageable beat.

I can keep myself safe this time. Step one is avoiding that Levi guy and anyone like him.

CHAPTER TWO

THE WEIGHT of heat and humidity feels like punishment as I rush northwest toward the auditorium for chapel. My linen dress flutters too high with each step, so I press it down with my book-free hand, avoiding a Marilyn Monroe moment. I could slip in a few minutes late—the girls are saving me a seat—but I can't stand being irresponsible. Sophie wouldn't think twice, bouncing around on her own timetable, untethered to schedules, rules, or expectations. She's blissfully free. But I have to keep my life in order. Now more than ever.

Mom's voice echoes in my head. *"Hurry must be fought."* I force myself to slow down and check my phone. My jog over here paid off—I'm fine on time.

The red brick auditorium sits proudly ahead. Nearly every building on campus is brick, as is most of the surrounding town of Pinecrest. Maybe it's a Texas thing. A concrete path winds through the trees that shade this part of campus. Plenty of lush oaks, but the pines are my favorite. Scrappy and heat-resistant, they aren't quite the towering ponderosas of Colorado, but close enough. Their woodsy scent reminds me of home.

What is that music? I'm nearing the doors when I see its source. A two-foot-long boombox next to a student I don't know. "Never Gonna Give You Up" blares as he gets his groove on eighties-style outside the auditorium. Oh, this is good. The vintage blazer over his faded-orange shirt must be sweltering, but he's the picture of cool as he moonwalks for his growing audience.

Yesterday I saw a freshman in the same shirt emblazoned with "Flooders." With a matching bandana around his head, he was rolling a massive tire to class. When someone asked him what it was about, he just shouted, "Woo, NASCAR!" in an exaggerated southern drawl.

I reach the auditorium doors and step inside. At last, a blast of blessed air-conditioning hits me.

Someone whirls around and bumps hard into my side.

Ouch.

Great, now I've dropped my books all over the floor. The girl calls a "sorry" as I crouch down, frantically gathering everything while trying to keep my dress in check. As I scan the floor for anything I missed, someone steps through the crowd and bends down to pick up a pen. Oh, that's Levi. He holds it out to me, his confident movements turning hesitant.

My heart pounds in my chest because I hate to make a scene in public and not because some guy is handing me a pen, right? My mind screams "run," but I try to act more chill than I feel.

He looks like Aiden the sequel. Please keep him away from me.

"Are you alright? Did you find everything?" Mesmerizing hazel eyes—I didn't need to know about those—sweep my face as if he's memorizing it.

Right, the pen. "Thanks, but that's not mine." With my best impression of an Olympic race walker, I high-tail it out of the lobby.

I squeeze past two of my girls in the G1 row and collapse into the flip-up seat beside Ayumi, still breathless. Mia and Sophie acknowledge me and continue belting out "Up Again" as it plays over the loudspeaker.

He's just a guy. I have to get a grip. I don't have to talk to him. He didn't even do anything. For that matter, Aiden would never bother to pick up a pen for someone. My throat grows tight. I try to swallow away the sensation with sheer will and end up in a choking fit.

Sophie is completely lost in her dramatic singing, and Mia's dark curls bounce as she sways, so maybe I'm safe from commentary.

Ayumi nudges me gently. "You okay?"

Mia stops mid-song. "She has the black lung."

Levi saunters down the aisle surrounded by an entourage. He'll pass immediately behind me. I grip the armrests and go still.

"When are you gonna knock Pretty Boy down a peg?" Mia leans around Sophie to tease me, her voice mercifully low. "I could arrange for you to save a dog from a taxi."

"No *Hitch* moves required, thank you."

Sophie jumps into "I Knew You Were Trouble." She has no idea how accurate her song choice is. My cheeks twitch at her enthusiastic rendition. She could pass for a young Taylor Swift, especially when she leaves her hair wavy. Full-on Fearless era.

Mia joins in to sing, thrilling Sophie. Ayumi's dark eyes and tight black braid usually give her a severe look, but when she brims with laughter, I break into giggles. Just what I needed. I shake my head at my suitemates. I haven't wished for my book-character friends once since I've been here. God wrapped up flesh and blood girls, complete with hilarity and movie quotes and songs for days, and dropped them into my suite as a beautiful present.

Thank you.

I elbow Sophie. "Your birthday's in a month, right? We need to get planning."

She sucks in a breath and strangles me with a hug across the armrest. "Yes!"

I rub the ear that is now permanently impaired. "I have an idea. Want me to run it by you or keep it a surprise?"

"I love surprises! Aw, Kit, you're the best." She hugs me again.

She twists around, and Austin throws her a little smile—they know each other?—on his way to the section behind us. Knowing Levi is back there makes me want to turn around and find him Where's Waldo style. To keep tabs on present danger. Not to catch a peek.

CHAPTER THREE

"KIT, get your juicy butt in here," Sophie says. "Mia's turn."

While my floormates were brainstorming a nickname for me, I've been sitting against a pine, catching up with my family text chain. What a bunch of nuts. Two empty benches nearby, but the smell of this tree is almost like home.

I brush pine needles from my shorts. "Coming!"

Mia gives a dramatic bow and takes my place outside as I squish onto one of the waiting room-style love seats in Griffin Hall's first floor lobby.

"Okay. Floor name for Mia." Zoe's still all business. "Suite D, talk to me."

Tradition!—cue Tevye's song from *Fiddler on the Roof*. I'm getting used to it all, drinking the Kool-Aid. The night of brainstorming floor names for new G1-ers is clearly a whole thing. The G1 upperclassmen rock their faded floor shirts as they chatter on the other sofas. Some of them contribute to the task at hand and many distract from it. We've gone full cult with the hubbub and matching outfits—even we newbies were instructed to wear black —but the giddy atmosphere is contagious.

"Merida," Sophie says. "Mrs. Weasley. Beyoncé. Ooh, on horseback. In the music video for 'Run the World.'"

"Love that, but there's already a 'Beyoncé' on campus. Mrs. Weasley? Merida?"

Casual disagreements bubble up around the room.

"Other thoughts." Zoe raises her voice over the chatter.

"She gets those care packages from her *abuela,*" Rosemary offers, barely loud enough.

"Good, good." Zoe stands in the middle of the room and stares me down. "Kit?"

We analyzed every detail for the other girls' names, but with Mia being the last, everyone's losing focus, eager to get to the Flooders' first intramural football game. They're the third floor of Albert Hall, renamed from A3 to "Flooders" after a failed prank years ago. The G1-ers say they're our "brother floor"—whatever that means.

Zoe doesn't wait. "You have a thought, Kit. Suggest a name."

The room quiets, and my skin heats at the attention.

"If not Mrs. Weasley, we need another character who's nurturing and sassy," I say. "Someone strong."

"Luisa Madrigal," Ayumi murmurs next to me.

I repeat it louder, pointing to give her credit. "Luisa from *Encanto* is perfect."

"Oh, totally," Sophie says.

The room hums in approval.

"*Luisa* for Mia. Any objections?" Zoe shouts.

None.

"All in favor?"

All the hands go up, and the meeting is adjourned. I nod to myself. Mia will love her floor name, and it suits her perfectly. We chose Luna from *Harry Potter* for Ayumi. Now that someone suggested the similarity, I can't unsee it. Not her appearance, of course, but her vibe. As for Sophie, we finally settled on Stevie Nicks. She was first, and we had everyone's participation. After tossing around countless singers, we decided Stevie's free spirit and whimsy fit Sophie best.

"Ki-it," Sophie calls from outside with exasperation.

Oh, everyone's left the lobby.

"A beauty but a funny girl, that Belle," she whisper-sings to Ayumi and Mia.

Mia sends her a look. Spilling a floor name before a newcomer reads it on the back of her first floor shirt is strictly against tradition.

Belle … I do love reading and *Beauty & the Beast*—and nearly all Disney princess movies. Plus, I have brown hair. I shrug. Works for me.

The relentless summer sun clings to the horizon, and our giggling pack navigates past the gym to the athletic fields where we watch the game in the grass. The girls gab about classes and gush about boys and giggle about which Flooders earn "cool points" for their performance on the field. Mia dances, like always. Sophie announces the game in a ridiculous voice between conversations. Ayumi lends her peaceful presence. All of us G1-ers cheer for the Flooders and revel in the time far from our homework, despite the oppressive heat. The scent of mud and leaves drifts to us from the pond nearby. No wonder the mosquitoes are eating us alive. I'll remember to bug-spray up next time.

The distraction of mosquitoes isn't enough, however, to keep me from oh-so-guiltily staring at Levi. As both a wide receiver and cornerback, his strong legs in running shorts carry him rapidly down the field almost every play. I'm winning a one-sided staring contest over here.

"She's living her best life," Sophie sings. "Wakes up before sunrise." It's almost the Ben Rector song. "Levi's more dreamy than Kit thought he could be."

I whip my head around, so busted. Sophie laughs proudly.

Thank you for this, for these girls. You know what's good for me. You know what I need.

I know the plans I have for you.

The Flooders win their game and, Sophie insists we make a Little League–style tunnel for the guys. Of course they love it. Female attention is catnip for the male ego.

We all head back to the north side of campus where our dorms sit—the guys to Albert Hall, across a field from our Griffin Hall—and I catch Levi watching me on the other side of the group. No. I know better than to want attention from a guy like that again. As if to remind me, my memories send a shudder racing down my spine.

CHAPTER FOUR

THE QUAINT, charming Arma Chapel has redefined sanctuary for me. Its warm lighting and high wooden beams wrap me in a sense of peace. But even here, I can't fully relax. My guard never lowers. I'm always scanning the room for danger, like I'm the Black Widow or something—especially when I spot him. Every Sunday night, around thirty of us gather here to sing worship songs and pray while most students rush to finish homework. It's nothing like the big, formal services in the auditorium. The worship is intimate here. I savor every minute.

We learned in our hoo-rah freshman orientation that it's the only original building still standing from the school's beginnings a hundred years ago. Back then, buildings were made more like art —clean lines and simple beauty. I've always loved the classic— minimal, graceful, and elegant—whether in buildings, art, algorithms, style, or ballet.

I find the girls I met last week and perch on a century-old

wooden pew. Pines sway behind the tall, narrow windows. This little white chapel is timeless. No matter how many years pass or what trends come and go, it will always be beautiful. Like a forest, a sunrise, or a perfectly executed arabesque. Like the creator we worship here.

I wish I could concentrate on that worship right now, fully safe as I'm surrounded by God's people singing to him, but my spidey sense warns of danger behind me. Avoiding Levi has become increasingly difficult, and I've even changed a couple of my routes around campus to avoid crossing paths. Seeing him here is the worst. He looks genuine, but I've learned the hard way not to trust appearances. Aiden called himself a Christian too, and I know how that turned out. I hate that I'm tempted to believe Levi is different, as if I haven't learned that lesson well enough by now. Every week, I sit on the opposite side of the chapel from him, a few rows ahead so he stays out of sight, but it never helps. I can still feel his presence behind me. I'm grateful when we split for prayer. I breathe easier tucked into a circle of girls. I'm safer this way.

The girls in my prayer group wave goodbye. A few people remain on the front side of the chapel, wrapping up. Levi is still inside, leaning against the back wall as he talks with a friend. His confidence is on full display as he flicks a Tic Tac box open and shut, open and shut.

Whatever, pal. Just ten more steps and I'll be out the door.

Trust in me with all your heart,
and do not lean on your own understanding.

My brow wrinkles.

Okay...

Levi pockets the Tic Tac box in his perfectly tailored jeans. I love fashion, not that I can afford much of anything. Mom and I used to search for treasures at thrift stores and on secondhand sites before I moved a thousand miles away. I recognize quality—the stitching, the color, the texture. Money doesn't buy style, but this guy clearly has both.

He meets my eyes as he calls a "Later, man" to his friend. He pushes off the wall and heads my direction. "Good prayer time?"

I hesitate, but this is the way out. I plow forward, donning my best disinterested face for good measure. "Yep."

"I'm Levi." He holds out a hand. The distrust in his eyes doesn't match his confident body language.

"Kit." I give an almost-wave, still on a mission toward the door.

He lowers his hand gracefully, transitioning to a blindingly charming smile. I might have winced. His smile reaches his eyes, creases forming at the edges. My heart reacts just like that catalyst in chem lab last week. Is it the smile or the proximity? I don't even know. This is different from before—he's a completely different guy—but my body doesn't know the difference.

"Mind giving me some advice?" he asks, before I can escape.

I glance at the door as my legs lock into place.

Trust you and don't lean on my own understanding? So don't run for my life from this conversation?

God must have told me that for a reason. We're in a public place. I guess I can afford a quick minute.

"There's this pretty girl on campus," he says. "We don't even know each other, but it's like she's avoiding me. Yesterday she did a full 180 when she saw me." His eyebrows raise in amused accusation.

Less obvious avoidance next time—noted.

"Should I take it as a compliment?" he asks. Another charming smile.

My stomach drops. Stay calm. Feign indifference. He'll move along when it's clear I won't stroke his ego. If I take the last two steps to the door, will he follow me?

"Maybe we got off on the wrong foot," he says.

I scoff. "My foot is fine." What am I saying? I shake my head. "Rumor has it you don't talk to girls much anyway." Too good to be true.

He studies me for a beat. Then quietly, "Maybe I had a bad experience."

I falter in a flash of compassion. "Oh. Maybe I did too."

His eyes drill into mine, then soften.

A guitar case thumps closed at the front, and I snap out of his gaze. Students chatter through the door. Some send us a second look.

Time to leave. "Well, good luck." Good luck? I hesitate with an irrational need to redeem my dumb remark.

His expression is caught somewhere between awe and amusement.

"Take Luck. Care for it. You too. All the Brian Regan phrases. Bye!" I slide my foot toward the door and end up in a weird chassé.

Outside, I rip out my phone. Normally I FaceTime Mom from my room on Sunday nights, but tonight I need a distraction as I walk.

She answers in seconds, effortlessly poised as she curls up on a patio chair. "Hi, sweetie! How was Praise and Prayer tonight?"

"Good." My pulse races, and I take a breath to steady my voice. Mom knows me too well.

"Talk to anyone interesting?"

"Um. Levi?" I pan around. The last thing I need is for him to overhear me saying his name.

She raises her brows in her elegant way. "That's a name I haven't heard. Does he live on Flooders?"

"Yep. How are Mav and Grey?"

She dives into updates about my wily brothers, but neither of us is fully distracted. She must be biting her tongue off to keep from asking more—she knows I shut down when her curiosity turns demanding.

I can't shake the feeling I'm going to see Levi again soon. My so-called disinterest only seemed to egg him on.

Two days later, I'm cutting through the scattered trees with Sophie and Mia, heading from lunch to our next classes. Saga is tucked in the far southeast corner of our tiny campus, about a ten-minute walk from Calc III.

Ayumi isn't with us—lunch is her "respite from people." Living on campus drains her quiet, introverted heart, and she's still figuring out how to avoid constant exhaustion.

One of my hands is full of books, and the other clutches a cookie I intended to save for later. It probably won't last another five minutes. The Cookie Monster is my spirit animal.

And then the most glorious—no, disconcerting—sight. Levi is darting across the field toward us, *Baywatch*-style. Or is the slow motion just in my head? It's startling—he seems too suave to ever be in a hurry. Mia and Sophie look to me for an explanation. I shrug them off.

Mia stops for his arrival, and we instinctively follow suit.

Levi reaches us with a muted rattle, breathing normally. "Nice morning." His green-gold eyes lock onto mine with a question. Move over, defibrillator—this guy can give a shock to the heart without so much as a "clear."

"Yeah, finally a breeze." Sophie plays it cool.

"No *Hitch* moves required ..." Mia says.

I clutch my books in front of me like a shield. "Going for a jog?" I can't have this guy thinking I'm impressed with him. I'm not.

The corners of Levi's mouth quirk, clearly amused by being called out. I'm surprised he takes it in stride. I figured he'd be too haughty to accept teasing. He introduces himself to Mia and Sophie who politely pretend to learn his name for the first time.

"How's your foot?" he asks me. "Still ... fine?"

I cover my barely restrained laugh with the cookie. "Foot's okay."

"I'm relieved to hear that."

I clear my throat. Pull it together! He's charming—that is precisely why I need to maintain my distance. Remember, he's just here for some attention. He doesn't know anything about me. I will not play into these perilous games again. I will not be the curious one in a horror movie. I hate horror movies.

Sophie shoots me a sidelong glance, like *What is happening?*

"Nice to meet you two. Kit." Levi gives a self-satisfied nod, popping a Tic Tac as he strides away. Always dressed to a T, he certainly didn't intend to jog in his spotless white sneakers and chino shorts. I want to think it's adorable, but of course I don't.

What is this? I hate that I can't control my own thoughts.

I can't trust a guy like him. I need to protect myself.

I am your refuge and strength.

I alone am your rock and your salvation.

I stop in the grass, lost in thought, until Sophie tugs my arm. She's already used to this.

CHAPTER FIVE

THERE'S LEVI AGAIN, casually leaning near the auditorium doors before chapel. His foot is propped behind him like the other night, this time on the red brick wall, in his obnoxious state of effortless style and confidence. I bet his senior portraits took two seconds. Swap the Tic Tacs for cologne, and boom—fragrance ad. Open, shut.

When he spots me, he brightens, but his thumb on the Tic Tac box moves rapidly. "Hey, Kit."

Forget the moody ad. That smile will be my undoing.

"James Dean wants his pose back," I blurt, forging ahead. Did I really just tease him again?

Before I reach the doors, he slides from his post and sneaks in a question, voice tight. "Coffee? After chapel?"

My feet stop defiantly. I compulsively gawk at him, like a zebra who stops to chat with Scar. His reputation as a confirmed bachelor contradicts that invitation. Is my information wrong? Is he making an exception? I compose myself and step aside to let the other students pass through the doors. He isn't doing this in front of an audience. No warrior stance, only hesitation. Nothing predatory, nothing I know to look for. Still, one of my hands wrings the other and a truckful of danger signs—think *Bruce Almighty*—bounces around in my mind.

Trust in me with all your heart,
and do not lean on your own understanding.
In all your ways, acknowledge me
and I will make your paths straight.

Not that verse again. I have plenty of ideas about how to make my paths straight, and none of them include that guy.

I sigh.

Okay … I hear you. But why is this verse only popping to mind around him?

"In need of more advice?" I reply to Levi. It's not a yes. I can't wrap my head around a yes.

He laughs, showing off his offensively handsome eye creases. "I could always use some good advice."

"Yo Jeeves," someone calls out.

"What's up, buddy. See you in there."

I feel a stab at my lip when I bite it too hard.

"I just want to get to know you better. Maybe hear some more one-liners." He looks innocent, hopeful.

No. Absolutely not. But the trust verse … Is that related here?

Am I supposed to say yes? This seems crazy.

"Okay," I manage.

He opens the door quickly, ushering me through before I change my mind. "Common Grounds, here on campus. See you soon."

Help me. This doesn't feel like keeping myself safe.

After chapel, my hands twist in knots in the Common Grounds line as I debate—stay or bolt? I cannot be a Bella Swan type who falls for the vampire that finds her scent delicious. For the love. There has to be a Team Jacob way out of this, right? His friend Austin seems sweet. I could nip this in the bud? I rub my temples. No. Zero boys. And I'm certainly not about to hit on some guy so I won't accidentally date his friend.

So why am I here, repeating the same mistakes I made with Aiden? He'd been the guy every girl wanted—baseball player, charming to parents and teachers, with a face like KJ Apa. Fit and muscular, with a crooked smile. I'd liked him since middle school —everyone did. By junior year, I was practically glued to my table at lunch just to catch a glimpse of him heading to gym. Pathetic, yes, but I thought that was as close as I'd ever get. So imagine when he strode up to that lunch table, gave me a lingering high five—apparently, that's a thing—and asked me out in front of everyone.

God was too important to me to date a non-Christian, but Aiden passed my test—he was a regular at youth group. Sure, he was cocky, flippant, and treated girls like they were disposable, but... it was Aiden. And he wanted me. Invisible Kit. I ignored every red flag and went out with him again and again, even though he knew nothing about me. I played into the attraction-only dating game I've come to hate.

And now there's Levi—charming and confident and attractive to a fault. Here I am, doing it all over again, as if I didn't learn this lesson painfully enough. A shadowy dread hangs in my mind, threatening, and then swoops down to cut a pit in my stomach.

What am I doing? Help.

I am your refuge and strength.

Levi slides into line with me, interrupting my dark thoughts. "What's your coffee order? Be prepared for me to jump to conclusions accordingly." His expression falls from half smile to furrowed brow when he sees my face.

"I, uh—iced mocha."

He shoves his hands into his pockets, taking on my serious vibe. "Any other details?"

"Small. With whipped cream." Is he going to think it's a date if I let him pay for me? Too late now, I guess.

"Got it. Would you find us a spot to sit?" He gestures gracefully toward the quickly filling cafe. The underside of his arm is smooth, strong, and corded with veins. Yes, I noticed. I'm not blind.

I find a good spot by a window. Table and chairs, not a couch. Plenty of people around.

I take a shaky breath. He's not going to touch me. We're in a crowded, public place. This is fine. The dark tendrils of fear swirl in rebellion. I map out my exit strategy, just in case. On the way over an alarm went off at the library—another student prank— and I nearly jumped out of my skin. At least Common Grounds is on the first floor of the student center. An easy escape.

CHAPTER SIX

I STUDY Levi as he takes his place at the table, drinks in hand. Somehow he manages a perfect mix of high-class polish and down-to-earth charm. I thank him for my coffee with a hand on top and bottom to avoid brushing his skin.

"What did you want to discuss?" I set my mouth in a not-flirty line. No more teasing. It clearly sent the wrong signals.

Great. He's amused again. "You, ideally. You have me curious." Brown paper crinkles under his fingers as he holds up a cookie. "Sweet tooth?"

I eye it with desire. "You did jump to conclusions, I see." Once my eyes reach his, they can't move away. Gold inner rings radiate into green. Full of warmth and intelligence, but a tinge of unease. My gaze manages to jerk down but gets caught again. When will the weather cool off so he'll cover up those incredible arms? I squeeze my cup. This isn't going well.

It's just research, like in chem lab. Analyze and summarize

what I see ... Based on my observations, Levi is confident and attractive. Simple. No big deal. Ignorable. "You first," I say. "Tell me about your family."

His posture slumps. Odd. Maybe it was my tone.

"Is your question directed toward my family's heritage or characteristics of the individuals?" he asks.

I tilt my head. What's with the formal speech? It doesn't match his usual laid-back body language. This guy is Shrek with all the layers. Too bad he doesn't look like Shrek.

"Individuals," I say.

"My brother is traveling Europe. My father ..." Yikes, his jaw clenches so hard I can see the tendons stretch around his jawline. "Enjoys sailing. My mother plans a variety of social events."

Is that all I get?

He lets out a small sigh. "Their lives revolve around ... " He purses his lips and shifts his jaw. "Status, Yale, the right connections. None of that holds appeal for me anymore."

I uncross my arms and squint at him. He's a mystery already. My childhood bestie Avery had money. It caused so much strain in her family. Unreasonable expectations, insatiable wants. Even back then I knew that growing up with less was a gift. For happy parents, she would have traded her bin full of L.O.L. Surprise dolls—and then the designer shoes—in a heartbeat.

"Have I answered the question to your satisfaction?" He raises teasing brows, snapping me back to the conversation.

More questions where that came from, buddy. "Mind if I ask why you don't want to be an Ivy League boy? Most people would kill to go to Yale."

"I prefer to make my own choices."

I bite my lips together lest I drool on this café table and give away how much I love that response. He sounds like a rebel *with* a cause. Because of his family? "Are you going home for fall break? To visit them?"

"I am going back. My granny is unwell."

Aw.

I edge forward and wait for more. Getting info out of this guy requires the patience of a spy.

"My mother will be away, and whether I'll see my father remains uncertain." His jaw snaps back into a vice. As he shifts in his seat, my fingers loosen around my cup. It's a guilty relief to see him like this. He always drips with poise and self-assurance.

"You're nervous?" I blurt. Filter, come back, I miss you.

With a smirk, he leans back and spreads a leg across the other. "He's not the only one who makes me nervous."

Wait. Me? "Sorry." I should lay off the questions. He's even more private than I'd guessed.

"Do you have siblings?" he asks.

I'm happy to share about my brothers and their antics. Recently they wrapped a giant slinky around two light posts across our small street, waiting for cars to come. Even our fun-loving dad was aghast at what a disaster it would have been if a car had come before he had.

Levi laughs openly, in stark contrast to all of his quiet prior reactions. Guys like him don't laugh at a girl's story. They always want to the be the funny one. A table of girls eye him like a prime cut of steak and get comfortable at the table next to ours. He doesn't so much as a flicker a glance. "And your parents? Were you raised by detectives?" he teases.

"Very funny. My parents are ... disgusting." I'm not getting the message across well. "I mean, they're great unless I have friends over."

"Embarrassing?"

"They just love each other so much that it's a lot. PDA, flirting, the whole enchilada."

Levi swallows hard. Did I say something insensitive?

"Please go on," he says.

"My mom is fiery in all the ways. She loves Jesus with everything she has. She's bold and fearless and ... regal somehow."

"Sounds like what I've seen from you."

I hide behind a sip of coffee. I've always wanted to be more like her. How could he know that? But compliments aren't safe. Not when they lead to expectations.

"Do you look like her too?"

I should have expected this. "No." I attempt a bored voice. "I take after my dad."

His gaze roams around my face, and I squirm in my seat.

"He has the deep blue eyes? The expressive face? The dimples?" A year ago I would have been a bowl of mush if a guy like Levi talked to me like this. Now I know that how I look is a liability and not an asset.

I trace the writing on the cup. They actually spelled my name right.

"What's he like?" he asks. "Your dad."

"He's a goofball, a big teddy bear. He spends Tuesday of every week in a rough neighborhood, playing pickleball with people and caulking their bathtubs." I half laugh. That wasn't a good way to describe all the things he does down there.

Levi leans back in his seat. "That's amazing." A pause. "I guarantee they're missing you. Your house is short a character."

Too charming. Time for a new subject. "What's with the Tic Tacs?"

He shrugs. "A small act of rebellion." When I edge forward, his smile tilts. "My parents wouldn't approve. And my mother hates that I fidget."

I'm drawn back to the few times I've eaten in a fancy restaurant or when I joined Avery's family at the orchestra and those high-end art galleries in the mountains. Was his whole life like that? "Status and connections, you said? You must have had a lot of behaving to do."

His eyes soften. "You could say that." He moves his jaw around again, as if he's weighing whether to say something. "Some of the Flooders are going to IHOP tonight. Would you join us? You could bring some friends along?"

My heart flip-flops. Why isn't he getting the memo? I've done my best to give not-interested vibes. I rub my forehead. But I felt like I was supposed to agree to this coffee meetup for some reason. And IHOP is a group thing. I should be making friends, not avoiding them because of one guy. Plus, watching Mr. Fancy Pants dig into IHOP pancakes like a commoner could be hilarious. I smile to myself—Yikes, he'll misunderstand that. "Okay," I nearly whisper.

"May I have your number? I'll text you details."

Before I know it, I'm cradling a brand-new iPhone in a Flooders orange case. "I used to go on daddy-daughter dates there as a kid. I'd always get a funny face pancake." Great, I'm babbling. And oversharing. I eye him as I return the phone, the proximity of his hand warming me in a way I don't appreciate. "Friends," I say.

"Alright." Those eyes remain on mine as he stretches his leg to pocket his phone.

"Oops. I forgot we have plans on the floor tonight. Old Disney movies. Maybe another time." Unable to pull my gaze from his, I stand up blind, coffee in one hand and quick wave from the other.

Shoot, a chair leg trips me. I somehow keep from spilling the coffee as I right myself, arms wide, facing away to avoid Levi's reaction. A scoff from the table over. Managing to avoid collision twice, I reach the exit. Ahh, the cookie. I beeline back to the table.

His eyes shine with awe and amusement as he holds it up. "Simone Biles wants her landing back."

I barely contain a laugh, thank him, and rush out.

CHAPTER SEVEN

TWO DAYS later I discover a foreign object on my desk—a brownie encased in clear wrapping and a pristine bow. I kick off my flats and grab for the thrilling present. Inside the attached envelope is a note on thick white card stock with an embossed border and monogram. My thumb brushes over the indent of "LCW" at the bottom. Of course it's Levi's. His style even extends to paper products. I rub my forehead, trying to read the boy cursive objectively.

Kit,
Movie night on Flooders tonight at 8.
Hope to see you there, friend. Bring anyone along.
—Levi

I bite my lip. It's Sunday, but Praise and Prayer is canceled for Labor Day weekend. Open Dorms hours on weekends are the only allowance for students to hang out on floors with the opposite sex. Rules to spare at this conservative Christian school. I haven't been to Flooders yet. Open Dorms on Sundays are only till ten, so we'd have a reason to bail right after the movie.

I make the mistake of showing the note to Sophie, who half-drags Mia and me out of our building at quarter to eight. Doubt drags at my feet as we cross the field. I should turn back. What am I doing walking to the lions' den? My feet stop mid-field as my mind spins, but Sophie tugs me forward, deciding for me.

Stepping onto the third floor of Albert Hall, I'm hit with the smell of burnt popcorn and faintly sweaty boy. The A/C is cranked up, and goosebumps line my arms. Someone's singing an unrecognizable song. Another guy joins in, passionately off key. We're spotted and greeted in seconds.

"Levi invited us," Sophie says, as if they're bouncers with a list.

Mia snorts.

One of the Flooders chuckles, like *Yeah, sure.* The other introduces himself, a smile growing.

I forget his name already because ... this hallway. Someone yells "fore!" before hitting a bean bag down the hall with a golf club. Another guy catches it with a baseball mitt and no shirt. One wanders toward us with his hand in a bag of chips. I could swear I saw someone riding a unicycle at the far end of the hall. I crack a smile, despite myself. My brothers would love this place.

"Where does movie night happen around here?" Mia asks.

Flooders 1 and 2 lead us through the chaotic cinderblock hallway, past the "Light Lounge" and into the "Dark Lounge," a jet-black room with a giant orange Flooders logo. Third-hand couches rest on homemade lofts providing stadium seating. A projector on the black ceiling shines the Netflix menu onto a screen on the front wall.

"Jeeves!" Flooder 1 bellows down the hallway.

I jump.

"You have visitors!"

I follow along as my friends chat with a group of freshmen Sophie knows. I only recognize Leo, the guy who rides an electric scooter everywhere on our postage stamp of a campus. Barely anyone my own age is in my classes because I earned so much college credit in high school. It's making for a weird start to freshman year.

Austin appears and beelines to us. We've been in class together for a month but we've barely spoken. That makes him friend material like nothing else could.

"Great spot for movie night," I say to him.

"Thanks. It kinda gives 'nightclub in the daytime,' huh?"

I forgot he has a Texan accent.

"Yeah," I say. "Meets vintage store."

He chuckles. "You mean garage sale."

Levi strolls in. I summon superhuman strength to focus on Austin.

"...we play FIFA in here too, and Madden. It's Kit, right?"

Confirm my name. Look friendly.

"Austin." Helpful that he doesn't try to shake my hand.

Levi joins us. "You made it."

Austin turns to Levi with an unreadable expression worth a thousand words in best-friend language. After two pats on Levi's back, Austin combs through short, dark curls and turns to Sophie and Mia.

"I was bribed," I say to Levi. Warmth spreads through my chest at his resulting grin. I glance away, keeping my guard up.

"Open to bribery. Good to know."

He points to a couch, and my skin chills. Fear tightens in my chest. My pulse thunders in my ears, as memories flicker.

"Here, you three can have the good seats," he says.

Oh. Oh, good. I let out my breath.

He squints at me. I deserve that. I'm being so weird.

Levi lowers next to a guy whose lanky frame is already spread onto an adjacent couch. He's holding a remote, and red hair pokes out of his ratty baseball cap. "Fixin' to start, y'all." His focus turns to me, and my split-second first impression of country bumpkin was way off. His peaceful eyes betray a contentedness and a certain wisdom, more than he should have from his short life. He is king of Zen, like Baloo from *Jungle Book*.

Levi's body language says that Austin and Mr. Zen are his close friends.

"Tucker," he introduces himself with a raised hand. "But e'rbody calls me Haymitch."

That's his floor name? I've read and reread *The Hunger Games* trilogy. I wonder why he was named that.

"Kit," I say.

Weird that Dangerous Guy has such sweet friends. Aiden's were just like him.

The Flooders lounge is like a living room full of my brothers' crew, and I miss Mav and Grey more than ever. The guys "participate" in the movie by shouting things at the screen and teasing each other. They even include me in their banter, pass their snacks around to share. This is the way to watch a movie.

Levi asks to walk me back to my building after.

I look to my friends for an excuse, but Sophie shoos me forward. Seriously? I need bouncers, not wingwomen. Is he being polite since he invited me? Or is this a "loop walk" that girls keep mentioning? His gentle half smile draws me along, one rebellious foot after the other, until I'm following him down the stairs.

He opens the stairwell door, and a wave of heat smacks me. Even at night, Texas is a furnace. Crickets chirp in the dark as I struggle to make out my building across the field. I rub my eyes, exhaustion tugging at me. Dark images from my nightmares flicker in my mind.

Dropping my hands, I startle. Oh right. Levi's here, glancing at me with amusement.

"Your floor is really fun." My words slur as I stifle a yawn.

"The feeling is clearly mutual."

A bug corpse the size of a golf ball makes a nasty crunch under my sandaled foot. Gross.

"What's with the dead bugs everywhere? Are those the ones that made all that noise a couple weeks ago?"

He confirms with a chuckle. "Cicadas. Texas is a weird place, but the view doesn't get old." He points to the cloudless sky.

I'm never out this late. Not anymore. I'd forgotten how beautiful the night sky can be, even here where the stars fight through the haze. My arm brushes something solid, and I instinctively yank back—just a gold wristwatch.

"It was my grandfather's." Levi holds it up. Embedded diamonds mark the hours on its green face. "He left it to me when he died."

"Oh. I'm sorry." I motion to his wrist. "I love it—it's timeless. I've never seen diamonds on a man's watch before." My eyes linger too long. Why is someone with a watch worth more than a car hanging out with the Flooders? And why is he interested in me? My pulse quickens, lightheadedness creeping in. Was I right about him all along?

When I finally look up, he's giving me some serious side-eye, his thumb drumming against his fingers. That's a reaction. But he says nothing as we near my building.

"Thank you for inviting us," I say, trying to ease the awkwardness. "And for the brownie. And your, um, beautiful note."

He nods once, as fancy and guarded as James Bond. Is that nod an East Coast thing or a Levi thing? What does it mean?

"Good night."

"Good night, Kit."

CHAPTER EIGHT

SOPHIE AND MIA make friends wherever they go. When some Flooders invite us back to Albert Hall, they head over while I finish up my homework. Ayumi passes, again. By the time I'm done, the games are probably wrapping up, but I make my way to the lobby as a gesture of friendliness.

Mia eggs someone on, pointing at his hand of cards. Austin and Sophie laugh at the end of the table. Austin sends me a head-tilt and fishes his phone out of his pocket. The group finishes whatever card game they're playing, and I carry over a chair to observe. A few minutes later, Levi saunters out of the stairwell but stops short when he spots me. His eyes narrow. He must be sick of girls following him around. I squirm in my seat, hide my hands beneath my legs.

No—I was invited here. By name. I straighten and frown from afar. *You don't own the lobby, your highness.*

From across the room, he swivels his head toward Austin.

They share a silent mini conversation, like Shawn and Gus would on *Psych*. Levi lets out a sigh and walks over. That muted rattle follows him everywhere.

I should stay, but the implication that I don't belong here just makes me long for my math books. I return my chair. "See you guys later."

"Time for a walk?" Levi says to the group, but his heavy hazel gaze doesn't drift an inch from mine.

My friends drag me along as everyone follows him outside. How did he do that?

Smug, he lets the others pass so he can walk with me at the back of the group.

I shake my head at him.

"Nice to see you again," he says.

I send him a look. "Is it?"

His lips quirk. "How'd you hold up against Samwise? He's notoriously hard to beat."

"I was too late to play, but Mia wiped the floor with everyone."

"Impressive."

"Always. So, why'd you get weird?" My filter malfunctions around this guy, and the condition is not improving with familiarity.

His slow pace gives us a buffer from the others. He faces forward and takes a breath. "People are too interested in the money I grew up with."

Oh. I'd assumed the trust fund everyone knows he has would be something he's proud of. "It's odd that everyone seems to want all of that."

He eyes me skeptically.

"I just mean, what a burden to try to spend all that money wisely. I wouldn't want to have to answer to God for that respon-sibility." I wince. Too much.

His countenance has changed in an instant. "Very wise. Money is a mark against me?" he teases.

I shrug apologetically. It's not his fault. He has no idea how many other marks he has against him.

He pulls out the Tic Tac box. Open, shut. "Do you like art?"

Random question, but I bob my head. "I love sculptures. It's remarkable that someone can use a hammer and a rock and end up with something graceful, almost alive."

He listens with rapt attention.

"I would love to see the *David* in Florence someday. Or any of Michelangelo's sculptures. I've only seen photos, of course, but there's so much feeling. Have you seen them? Have you traveled a lot?" I clamp my teeth together. No more rambling.

He hesitates. "I haven't been to Florence since I was a kid. I'm not sure if I ever saw the David. I mostly just begged our nanny for more gelato." He's avoiding eye contact? "But I've seen the *Moses* in Rome and the *Pieta* in Vatican City. My classical school had us do a trip for art history our junior year." He hides his hands in his pockets. "How's that for obnoxious?"

I frown and shake my head. He seemed so cocky, but he's insecure about this? "We grew up differently, but that doesn't make you obnoxious."

His tension eases. He seems ... sweet. Vulnerable.

"Did you ..." My voice fades out when I see his hypnotic gaze trained on mine, holding a question. The intensity there rattles my nerves, but the kindness settles them. My mouth curves up.

He motions for me to stop there on the sidewalk. I swivel my head to see others milling about on campus. This should be okay. Our group walks on, and I can't say I'm sorry to see them go.

"There's an art museum here in Pinecrest. It's not exactly the Accademia," he jokes, "but it might be worth an hour or two. Any interest in checking it out with me?"

Check it out with him? Every instinct says run, but something about the way he asks—gentle, almost hopeful ...

"You can renew my interest in sculptures since exams sucked it out of me." He cracks a smile, and I turn to goo.

His knuckles brush my arm, warm and gentle—

I jerk away.

Fear crashes over me, thick and suffocating, like tar sticking to my skin. His eyes soften with apology, but my breath comes in sharp, ragged gasps. I never should have let this happen.

How could I even consider a date? It doesn't matter if he seems vulnerable and endearing—I can't trust my judgment anymore. I've only spoken to him a handful of times. A date is completely out of the question. And if that weren't enough, the familiar terror continues to grow inside me like a rising tide, terror like I haven't felt since I was in the same city as Aiden.

"Friends, remember?" I say, my voice wobbling. Dread tightens in my stomach. The fear I've fought to bury rises fast and hard as nausea crashes in. Should I run?

I thought I was safe here. I thought this was going to be a thing of the past.

"Alright," he says. "Friends."

I try to focus on dragging my feet in the direction of my building. Levi responded with kindness. He respected my no. This is fine. I'm fine. So why do I feel like I'm on the edge of a cliff? His kindness is as unsettling as his charm.

Why do I keep praying for relief from my anxiety if it's the only thing keeping me from making the same mistakes? The black tendrils of fear push in harder. Oh no, oh no—I squeeze my eyes shut against the flashes of memory coming.

Rain. Tripping. The smell of waste and sticky floor. Curling into a ball as I drowned in red flags I ignored.

I blink, returning to reality, stomach clenched and churning and heart beating like mad.

I stare at my frozen feet and will the tears away. My heart rate is already calming. Compared to the ones at home, this was a lot better. But I needed my past to stay there. It was supposed to stay in Colorado.

More of this? I thought this place was an answer to prayer. Please take it away.

We're nearly back to my building. Without an explanation, I resume a fast pace, willing the side door to arrive sooner.

Levi follows silently. I check his expression from the corner of my eye. He's squinting at me as if trying to solve a riddle. *You and me both, pal.* Maybe he'll think I'm crazy and keep his distance.

"Good night." I badge in as if it requires all my concentration.

"Good night, friend." No sarcasm, just concern.

He opens the heavy door for me, and I step into the jarring, fluorescent stairwell. Moving away from him pulls against his magnetic forcefield. I shake my head and navigate the halls to my room and begin my bedtime routine, thinking and praying. I'm scared. Anxious. But also enamored. Fascinated. Infuriatingly, irrationally hopeful. But it doesn't matter anymore. I'm sure I scared him off.

Part of me begs to tell someone about my invasive memories, to lay my secret fears bare, but I know better than that. I will not make that mistake again. Mom kept throwing the "counselor" word at me right at first—everything online said the same—but I made it clear it's not for me. I can't bear to admit aloud the bizarre and terrifying patterns of my brain to anyone else.

I thought all of this was going to end when I came here. I thought … well, I thought wrong.

Sophie and Mia return to the suite, happy chattering growing quieter. Ayumi's asleep in our room behind me. I turn toward them, floss between my teeth, as they round the corner from the lounge.

"Well, well. How was the romantic moonlit walk?" Mia waggles her eyebrows.

I force a fragile smile around my floss. They saunter into their room, apparently not expecting a response.

I trash my floss and flop onto the mess of blankets on Sophie's bed, trying to focus on my friends. "Well? Albert Hall two nights in a row. Any Flooders stand out to you, Sophs?"

Her bright eyes answer in the affirmative. "Lots of juicy ones on that floor. We'll see."

I turn to Mia.

"That mess is not for me. When are you gonna see the crown prince again?"

I shrug. As Dad would say, I need that like a cat needs a snorkel. Or like a pilot needs a blindfold. Or like Olaf needs a suntan.

CHAPTER NINE

"BONE-IN WINGS ARE BUY ONE, get one."

As if Sophie needs a restaurant deal to plan an outing—we already know her better than that. I appreciate it though. Money is tight, and I mean a child's piggy bank could hold my life's savings in quarters. My parents taught me to stretch a dollar, so I can partake responsibly. I'll order the minimum and a water. Five bucks plus tip. I love all things spicy, so this is worth it.

"I'm down." I grab a jacket from the closet. What am I thinking? I hang it back.

"Yeah, it's barely September," Ayumi says, a San Antonio native. "You won't be needing that for a few months still."

Sheesh, Texas. "No wings?" I ask.

"I'm happy here. Thanks."

She's missing out on the full college experience, skipping almost every invitation we send her way. To each her own, I guess.

Sophie's still in the doorway, bouncing more than usual. "Mia and the others are meeting us at the parking lot. Ready?"

I wonder which other girls are coming along, but Sophie leads the way across the field to the Albert Hall parking lot rather than to our own. There's Mia, but she's standing with a group of guys. Oh, and Levi. There hasn't even been a full day for my weird freakout to blow over. And he keeps glancing at me as we approach. I pretend I don't notice.

Does he pay for a stylist with his fancy trust fund or does he just ooze with fashion sense like he does confidence and charm? Pretend I don't notice.

Chino pants and a T-shirt never looked so sophisticated. Like Harvey Specter on a day off. Pretend I don't notice!

I have to get a grip. I've been dodging my own thoughts for the past twenty-four hours, but if I can't trust myself to make good decisions, I'll wade through the sludge again. Even if it pulls me under.

Haymitch snaps me back to reality with a slap on Levi's arm. "Jeeves can fit eight in his rollin' mansion."

A Range Rover, huh? Not sure I've ever seen one of these up close. Odd that he doesn't want to talk about money but drives that thing.

In this pack of rowdy boys, not one calls shotgun. Some steal a glance at me. The group splits between Calvin's dented sedan and Levi's SUV. Sophie and Mia crawl into the third row of the Range Rover with Austin.

Oh. I've been unknowingly paralyzed while I thought it over. Why can't I think and walk at the same time? Just in time, I barge into the remaining bucket seat in the middle row before Haymitch can.

I grimace at him in apology. "I call the back seat, middle, with my feet on the hump!" Hopefully they know Brian Regan or now I seem even crazier. I'm not even in the right seat for that quote.

Haymitch chuckles. "Whatever suits ya." Feeling his way to

the next door, he slides to the front passenger seat and sends Levi a look.

Arm on the center console, Levi twists back toward me.

I don't think it's the Brian Regan quote that's amusing him. The lights are on in the car, and all I see is dancing hazel. I can't pretend not to notice, but I close my mouth and shrug, like his devastating handsomeness ain't no thang. On the bright side, he doesn't seem to think I was weird beyond excuse last night. Wait, but that's not good.

He points his head at the wide-open door beside me, but Haymitch is already unbuckled and closing it.

"Oh, you don't want your door ripped off? Whatever suits ya," I imitate.

Levi presses his lips together to hold back the laugh visible in his eyes. He switches the Jon Foreman to NEEDTOBREATHE. Good vibe change, good taste. Add them to the growing list of reasons this guy is obnoxiously likable. Too bad I'll be enforcing a cavern of distance between us. No bridges allowed, no rappelling, no hot air balloons. No transit of any kind across said cavern.

This SUV is indeed a rolling mansion. I turn in my soft and springy leather seat and come up with things to talk about with the guy sitting next to me. Flooder 2. Ethan? I was a coward to choose small talk over that front seat. I don't hear much of their conversation, but Levi and Haymitch seem like they've been friends a long time.

At the restaurant, Austin asks for the best-lit spot the hostess can manage—odd—and she guides us to a long table. Like the perpetual fourth grader I am, I veer to stay on the other side of the group from Levi. I don't appreciate the internal tug-of-war his presence incites. And now I'm thinking about that night again. Squash it down.

Holding Levi's shoulder as he navigates across the room, Haymitch's eyes are glazed and unfocused. He can't see? Trailing behind Mia and Sophie, I'm relieved I can sit at the end of the table butting up to the wall. Fewer people to talk to at once. I've always been a small group kind of person. Shoot, I should have waited. Levi maneuvers to sit across from me. Haymitch reaches to find the chair in front of him. He blinks and pans around as if his vision will return to him any moment. Levi levels his gaze at me and cracks a charming smile. He's doing a terrible job keeping up with his bachelor-for-life reputation, and I fight the instinct to feel honored. Concern and caution are more warranted, so I aim for those instead.

Austin whispers in Ethan's ear and trades with him to sit across from Sophie and next to Haymitch.

Sophie sings along to every word as "What My World Spins Around" plays in the background.

"You know my music, City Girl?" Austin asks her, pulling in his chair.

Sophie rears back in faux offense. Her happy eyes give her away.

"I would've pegged you for a Swiftie," he says.

"What do you mean *your* music?" she asks.

"Country music is small town music. Didn't you say you're from LA?"

"Uh-oh," I murmur to Mia. This will be entertaining.

"Right?" Mia agrees.

"I'm from Pasadena. It's LA county, not Los Angeles. And Jordan Davis just went on an international tour." She raises her brows at him. "He played in Stockholm and Copenhagen, but his music is only for small towns?"

Austin pushes his rolled sleeves to his elbows and bends over in mischief, resting his wide, hairy forearms on the table. "Good for him. It's still small-town music. You even know what the first line of this song means?"

Haymitch elbows Levi like this isn't Austin's usual.

"Let's see," Sophie says. "Cast, water, line, so ... fishing?"

"Ding ding." Haymitch lounges in his seat and adjusts his backward baseball cap.

Sophie tips her shoulder, proud. "Pretty good for a 'city girl,' huh? Besides, you don't have to live in a small town to go fishing."

"Okay, little lady," Austin says. "What's a back-forty view?"

She looks to Mia and me. "Can I phone a friend?"

"No idea," I say. "Sorry, Sophs."

Levi meets my eyes, but I glance away.

"Girl, I don't have one clue," Mia says. "Miami is south, not The South."

"Don't say it, Haymitch." Austin half smiles.

"What?" Mia asks.

Haymitch gestures to zip his lips. His vision must be back because his eyes focus again.

Levi chuckles. "'Don't mess with Texas' is more command than slogan."

"Haymitch doesn't think Texas is The South either," Austin says.

"You feel left out?" Sophie teases Austin. "Wish people wouldn't make assumptions based on where you're from?"

A pleased smirk grows on his face. "One point Sophie."

"I would have thought this was The South," I say. "The people in Pinecrest are so friendly and hospitable."

"'Preciate that." Austin says.

"And all the fried chicken spots," Mia says.

"And all the twang." Sophie sends the challenge straight across the table.

He sends her a flirty glance. "Does it remind you of my music?"

Mia points her head toward the two of them and leans to me. "Are we on board with this?"

"I mean, he *seems* safe." I keep my voice low.

"Safe, sure, but he's not bothering her?"

"Huh? She looks happy."

"The safest," Levi says quietly.

I swivel to him. He could hear us?

He sends me a reassuring nod. *You, on the other hand ...*

Haymitch interrupts my thoughts. "How 'bout you, Jeeves? You been here two years. What's your take on Texas?"

"I think the barbecue here is the best I've ever had."

"Preach," Austin says.

"The brisket is some'n else," Haymitch agrees. "Wish I could introduce you to 'Bama White Sauce though."

"Let's make it happen." Levi says.

"Christmas break? Maybe we can drag Samwise away from his family for a couple o' days."

"If you can convince Janie," Austin says.

"Janie?" Sophie asks.

"My baby sister."

"He don't like tellin' his sister no," Haymitch says to us.

"Aw," Sophie says to Austin. "You're a softie."

"She's, what, seventeen now?" Haymitch asks.

"Nearly. She's still a baby." Austin sends a look to Haymitch, who raises his hands in innocence.

"Janie won't like it," Levi says to us, "but convincing her might be within our power."

"You could sell a megaphone to a mime, Jeeves," Austin says.

Haymitch sputters a laugh.

"We've hung out with her at The Farm many times," Levi explains.

"It's not actually a farm," Austin says to us.

"It'll always be The Farm," Levi says.

Every time he speaks, his smooth voice is a magnet pulling me back, forcing my gaze to him. Each time, it's a zap of pleasure I can't afford. Sophie dives in headfirst, but I can't. Not after Aiden. No matter how kind or gentle Levi seems, I have to make better choices this time. Desperate for a distraction, I turn to Mia. "How are your sisters?"

Maybe she can anchor me back to solid ground.

CHAPTER TEN

WHEN OUR WINGS ARRIVE, Levi's gaze lingers on his fork as everyone else dives in with their hands. Some of my restrained laugh sneaks out, and his attention snaps to me. I wiggle sauce-covered fingers in his direction, eyes wide like it will horrify him, and then remember Project Ignore the Obscenely Attractive Guy in Front of Me. I lower my head before I see his reaction.

He maintains his polish, even joining us to eat wings like a caveman, and dabs the sauce off his nose when his bite errs. I mostly avoid detection when I peek across to enjoy his alienness.

On my way to the restroom, I weave between tables.

"Hey, Kit?" Levi's voice. He brushes my arm—light, innocent, but black claws of fear spring into my chest. I yank my arm away, heart hammering. The hum of the restaurant turns to a roar as a wave of panic crashes over me. My hands shake. My throat tightens. My eyes blur.

"Oh. I'm sorry I scared you."

I dash to the bathroom. He didn't mean anything by it and doesn't need to see my tears. I tuck into a stall and lock the world out, pressing against the door, fighting for control. I thought I could escape the memories, but they've followed me all the way here.

I was spared. God protected me. I haven't seen Aiden in months. What is wrong with me?

I hate this, God. I hate feeling crazy.

I fight the self-pity, the anger. I don't deserve it. I force it down, down. I wash my hands and face. With a shaky breath, I paste on a happy face that looks almost believable in the mirror.

Levi watches me as I rejoin the table. *Are you alright?* he mouths.

I lower my voice so that only he can hear. "I can be jumpy."

He nods once, apologetic.

Wow, he handled that well. I want to hug him for his kindness and understanding, which is absurd since his touch is what made me go bonkers. I settle for a little smile that he reciprocates.

"You have an impressive spice tolerance." Two fingers gesture elegantly at my empty hot wings basket. His hushed voice draws me closer.

"I draw the line here." I point at the sign on the table with the sauces in order of heat. Dad adds hot sauce to practically everything he eats. Compared to him, I'm a wimp.

Mia leaves me to nearly whisper with Levi as they carry on in conversation. Odd that she's concerned about the happily bickering guy but not the quiet, charming one. I'll have to look out for myself.

"I get teary-eyed about here." He points three sauces down.

"I wouldn't mind seeing that," I say. Oops, too comfortable.

"You enjoy making guys cry?" His mouth shows barely a whisper of the emotion his eyes betray, as if life has taught him to button up, but his inner thoughts have to come out somewhere. Right now they're all playfulness, but no creases. Yet. I wonder if I could make him laugh. I beat that thought down with a mental stick.

"Seems like the only time guys let themselves cry is after some sports game. Is that you?"

"The sport I cared most about in high school was swimming. My face was already wet, so no one will ever know." Laughter leaks out silently. Entrancing.

I'm dizzy from the dissonance in my head. He's just a guy, right? Just a strong, funny guy with eyes that speak volumes.

"Flooders win all the intramurals, so no opportunity for tears there," he says.

That's more what I was expecting from him. I roll my eyes with exaggeration. Okay fine, I am impressed. I'm a big fan of his athletic endeavors, but he can't know that.

Those creases grow pronounced at the corners of his eyes. Ah, there they are. "Want to know a secret?"

I edge forward. I'm back to a fourth grader—this time her crush is talking to her at recess. I'm such a sucker for authenticity and openness. Maybe because I know how wrong life goes without it. Maybe because I've gotten so bad at it recently.

"The movie *E.T.* still makes me cry." He's as sweet and cute as a gummy bear.

"You'd have to be soulless not to feel something for the little alien. In the tent with the scary scientists? I love that movie. Such a classic."

"Do you like when movies make you cry?"

"Some of my favorites make me boo-hoo cry."

"Tell me."

Mia's nearly shouting with enthusiasm next to me, but he appears to have no concern, attention trained on me alone. His gaze is steady, but something there hints that he's hiding some-thing—like there's more beneath the surface that he's deliberately keeping locked away. My happy meter is dangerously close to giddy, but I can't help but wonder what I'm not seeing.

"Mm, *The Fault in Our Stars, The Notebook, Five Feet Apart,*

A Walk to Remember. But I'm not always in the mood to be a mess." I haven't wanted to see those movies in months. Real life has been too emotional and confusing already.

"I haven't seen any of those."

"Maybe watch them from a pool."

A laugh escapes his mouth, but not a budge from his intense gaze on mine. I try not to grin or pass out.

The server hands out our bills. As planned, it's $4.80 plus tip. I can handle that.

"New Money," Sophie calls to me from down the table, pointing up to the song playing.

I played this in the suite earlier. Sharing music favorites is one of many perks of living with friends.

"Doesn't it make you feel something?" she asks Austin.

"Walker Hayes is good at that," Austin says.

An inscrutable look from Levi. There's a lot going on in that well-groomed head of his. In other news, his wavy hair is swept back from his forehead just right.

"That's why I love country music," Sophie says. "It's all stories. They might take place somewhere foreign to me, but the feelings are universal."

Austin sends her a cute smile. "Fair enough. I can share."

Out of character, she falls silent.

"I'd better give you my number so I can translate when needed." He points at her phone and pulls two fingers in, like *Hand that over.* "I'd hate for you to be confused about the lyrics to your favorite songs."

She scoffs but unlocks and passes her phone without hesitation.

On the way back, I abscond to the front of the pack so I can claim a seat in the back row. I learned my lesson about lollygagging. Sophie joins me and busts out the Ben Rector song "Range Rover." I half-laugh, half-shush her and sing along just quietly enough that Levi can't hear. I'm learning Sophie's love language is playing along with her fun nonsense. I guess that one didn't make it into Gary Chapman's book.

Back at the suite, Sophie shuts down my questions, but my own mind races with unwanted dialogue. I settle into bed, but my brain won't follow. The filing clerk in my mind frantically waves short- and long-term memories at me. What kind of lunatic am I, bantering with the suave, charming guy after my experience last spring? Especially now that it's clear my flashbacks aren't going anywhere.

Levi's ability to cut past the fear and pull me in closer is terrifying. I thought I could build walls high enough to keep out the danger, but he keeps slipping through the cracks. I wish I could talk to Mom, to someone, to untangle this mess in my head. I wish I could puzzle out what's safe and what's not. My inability to trust my own decision-making is crippling.

"AND THAT WAS the last of my not-boyfriends." Sophie dips a chip into the queso, far from embarrassed. "Kit's turn for an awkward story!"

We're snuggled in our suite lounge again, surrounded by a mountain of snacks Sophie bought today. The sofa and chairs in here are as uncomfortable as ever, so we're camped out on throw pillows. I love college. Our suite is like a perpetual sleepover.

"Okay, I have one." I pull my legs crossed and lean on my clumped-up blanket. "It was sophomore year—"

"Wait I forget," Sophie interrupts. "When did you suddenly get weirdly pretty?"

"That was summer before senior year," Mia says. "But don't ask about anything after that or she'll clam up and wreck our truth-telling." She raises brows at me.

She's not wrong. I refuse to go down the path of horrible-ex-boyfriend awfulness. And I won't talk about Levi—the reason I won't date him is exactly what I won't talk about. Then there's the mess with the girls from last year and the way they suddenly invited me to their parties and nail appointments once I was with Aiden. They accepted me and hated me all at once. And while they showed interest, my lifelong friends slowly distanced themselves. I didn't know how to handle any of it, and I wish so badly it had never happened. Now, I can't shake the nagging fear that Sophie might turn out the same way, so I keep it all to myself. Last year left me paranoid in so many ways.

"Anyway," I say, "I was feeling really woozy, so I left class to get something out of the vending machine in the cafeteria. It was one of the lunch times, so tons of people were around. But before I could get a snack, I passed out in front of the vending machine —out cold."

They giggle and imitate my dramatic visual of going unconscious.

"No idea how long I was there, but I came to and not a soul had noticed that I was lying there on the filthy carpet."

"What? Heartless," Mia says.

"Maybe. But probably they just didn't notice me. I told you I was invisible."

Ayumi half smiles like she gets it.

"Yeah, but I thought you meant, like, quiet," Sophie says. "Not that people literally don't see you when you need medical intervention!"

I shrug. That's the level of invisible I was facing. Even still, life as Visible Kit was so much worse.

"Well you came together nicely," Mia says.

"*Tad Hamilton,*" Sophie and I shout.

"Tie." Ayumi gives my arm a reassuring squeeze.

While Sophie and Mia half yell next to us, I whisper to Ayumi, "Want to share a story, or should I change the subject?"

She holds up two fingers—change the subject.

Levi

"Cards at MSC tonight?" Austin asks across the room.

"Yes." No need to consider. I know she'll be there if he plans it. I need to write the last lines of a paper, but I twist around to meet his teasing eyes.

He lies longwise on his sofa on the other side of mine and reaches across the ancient carpet to grab a tennis ball that had rolled under his desk. "Tomorrow we're going to McDonald's. And then camping. On the ground. With no shower. In for that too?"

He's taunting me, but the sad truth is I would be. I wouldn't miss a chance to be near her, even in those conditions. It's pathetic, really.

The first time I ever saw Kit she was taking caring of a stranger—at considerable cost to herself. It was an instant crush situation like I've never experienced before. But then I never would have talked to her again if Austin hadn't called me downstairs under false pretenses last week. I was prepared to write her off because of a single remark. I rake my hand through my hair. I have issues.

She no longer bolts at the sight of me, but I still have to earn her attention. I'm not mad about it though. I'm loving every minute. If anything, it's hard to be subtle. I can't keep my eyes off her when she walks into a room. I'm pitifully disappointed when she leaves. Like a sap. Hence Austin's reaction—he's never seen me like this. I've never seen me like this.

I have no idea whether Austin's sudden affinity for planning events off our floor is him going after Sophie or playing wingman for me. Those two have been planning fiends since we went out for wings. I've gotten to see Kit almost every night since. If it is a wingman thing, it's borderline heroic. It wouldn't be the first time Austin impersonated Superman.

Thank you for him. What a killer friend you sent me.

"She's getting cozier with you." He throws and catches the ball, just high enough not to hit his bed lofted above.

"If only."

He knows she won't even sit on the same couch as me. No hugs, no shoulder bumps, no touching whatsoever. But she's like that with every male on campus, so it's clearly not personal. I understand firm boundaries. I like her all the more for having convictions. And I respect that she's willing to be different, to hold the line when others think it's strange. Unfortunately, that makes me more attracted to her, which makes me want to touch her. It's not a great cycle, but it's all part of the beautiful package that is Kit Talbot.

"You know what I mean," Austin says. "She's all, 'Ooh, Levi, tell me more.'" Hands and ball under his chin, he blinks at me with the biggest eyes he can muster.

I do know. I feel a stupid grin on my face, but it's just Austin. I don't have to fake it with him.

Sometimes Kit goes slack-jawed and tongue-tied when her gaze hangs on mine. I may as well have won a trophy. My friends are the best, and Mia and Sophie are cool too, but it's a struggle to pay attention to the others when she's around. I just want to fixate on her and keep those beautiful dimples on her face all night. I want to see all her hilarious facial expressions and hear her jokes and opinions and stories. I'm insatiable in the Kit department. She's constantly getting quiet or asking someone a question, wanting to pass on the limelight. It's kind and selfless, but she always does it too soon. Sophie's all too quick to pick up the attention Kit lays down.

"Are you ever going to talk to me about Sophie?" I ask.

"Ahh ..."

This is so unlike him. He hasn't told me anything, and he's usually downright chatty about the girls he notices. Half the time he wants advice. He must be hesitant. Or concerned.

If Sophie's a big deal to him, I can certainly relate to concern.

It's easier to maintain our inertia. He dates nearly anybody and never for long, while I avoid girls like the plague. It's been working fine for us, and I'm terrified to step out of that. I certainly have my reasons. Panic wells up just thinking about them. This time is different though. I can trust her. She holds my money against me, for goodness' sake. Leave it to Kit.

I peer at Austin, waiting for more. Kit does this to me, and I blabber on about things I'd never otherwise share. Then again, it's probably more the big blue eyes staring at me as she waits. Like a whirlpool I sink in.

"She's cool. We're just friends."

Right. Not today then. "Alright, Samwise."

No more ridiculous dazing about Kit. I need to prepare for my student council meeting. It's a circus, but I can't quit. On the bright side, our vice president lives on Club, and I'll be listening for any hint of their floor camping trip. My floor has been plotting a prank for the ages, and timing is everything. This time, Club's resident advisor will find his car hoisted onto Bennet Hall's roof, a throwback to a legendary prank Flooders pulled off back in the 1960s. It'll be a cool nod to our floor's status as the oldest and most storied at Mayberry. We've got several senior engineers on board this year, including Haymitch, whose experience in construction is clutch. Dude's as competent as they come, handling pulley logistics and building like it's second nature, all while managing with a major vision disability.

I've also been tasked with finding a secret prep spot on campus to make sure our building efforts stay under the radar. That will mean persuading an administrator or two to let us use the space, ensuring they're neither entangled in the prank nor left feeling tricked when it comes to fruition. It's risky, but the guys are right—I'm probably the only one who can handle the politics.

I pull up my council notes on my laptop, refocusing on the task at hand. Soon the group will take interest for next year. Since I'm secretary, they'll expect that I'll want to be president senior year. I lean back in my chair and let out a long breath. I could probably manage winning the election, but it would require so much work. Winning Kit over is worth every ounce of effort, but student body president? It's not even something I want. For that matter, secretary isn't either. I don't know why I do these things. I need to pray it over.

CHAPTER TWELVE

SOPHIE, Mia, and I head west to the "lab building" after lunch. Every building on campus has a formal name, but students just call them by their purpose. At least Saga gets a nickname—otherwise, it'd just be "food building." Dorms stick to their official names. You know, more tradition.

I'm already sweating, and my hair sticks to my neck. I peel it away. It's the middle of September, Texas. Get your act together.

Oh.

Spotted—do you hear Kristen Bell's *Gossip Girl* voice?—Levi Whitaker striding with purpose from Albert Hall. Stay tuned for more sightings, Upper East Siders. XOXO. Gray chino shorts, white linen button-down, and that leather backpack ... Levi could've walked off a sailboat—or out of a *Gossip Girl* Hamptons episode. The backpack, with its simple flap and buckle design, adds an understated elegance to his look. Nothing he wears is flashy or trend-driven, just clean, classic. Well, except for those black-and-orange Flooders socks he sneaks under his pants. I clamp my mouth shut to keep Mia and Sophie from noticing him, so my greedy little eyes can take in Off-Limits Guy without ridicule.

Ever since we went out for wings, Sophie has invited Austin and his buddies to join us most nights. Or maybe we're joining them. It's hard to say since I just show up where Sophie tells me to. Sometimes we take a walk outside, look for stars in the often-cloudy East Texas sky, or meet at the Memorial Student Center, called MSC—one of the more straightforward nicknames—for a show or card game. On weekends we usually hang out on their floor in their lounges. Bless Sophie and her planning. We'd all be lost—or certainly less entertained—without her. She and Austin constantly scheme together, happily bickering.

Lucky—scary?—for me, Levi nearly always joins Austin. Their legendary bromance is even cuter up close. Each silently ensures the other gets what he needs and then teases and smacks his buddy's arm to keep it all under wraps. Yet another reason to find Levi supremely likable. Apparently I tally up the reasons he's dangerous as well as the reasons to like him. If only my brain had a mute button.

Whenever he's close my mind goes to war. Part of me insists I can finagle some way to make things work with him, but the rest of me revolts, insisting the risk is far too great.

Levi's fancy watch glints in the fierce sunlight. He still dodges the topic of his wealth like Neo dodges slow-mo bullets, but his unparalleled sophistication and self-assuredness give him away. The guy's a natural leader, a human magnet.

Even on a mission to class, Levi's swagger says the future doesn't faze him. How is he so steady? I try to trust that God has my back, but doesn't Levi ever worry? He seems driven by different motivations. His eyes flit about in observation and calcu-lation, as if he sees things I don't. Sometimes he gets up to speak with someone or refuses to do something and I can't imagine why.

He can be impatient, entitled, even arrogant when his intelligence is challenged, but when I try to compare him to Aiden, it doesn't stick. They're nothing alike. I hear Levi doesn't participate in some of the floor antics, like dog piles or wrestling, which makes me want to see him as pretentious, but stories float around about his former rap battles and prank wars that disprove the theory.

Doesn't matter though. I can't afford to get too close. He's triggered my two worst freak-outs since I've been here. Not exactly date material. No, I have to take care of myself. So I drool from afar like all the other girls on this campus. He'll lose interest in me soon, and hopefully I won't have to watch him flirt with whichever girl—

"Kit, snap out of it," Mia says two steps ahead.

I scramble to catch up.

At least they don't know the bear trap my brain got stuck in. My habit of introspection is saving me from some major teasing.

"*Tíguere*," Mia calls to Levi. "Go learn something."

We're just one building away now. Maybe she was waiting for the right moment to acknowledge his presence. More likely, she's just not as creepy as I am, accidentally searching for him all the time.

Levi turns, a smile widening. He steps toward us, then glances at the door. With a nod in greeting, he walks in.

"That nod. He's like an alien. I need to do some research." Oh no. That was my outside voice.

Sophie and Mia cackle at my expense. I cover my face.

"What do you have in mind?" Sophie asks. "*Gossip Girl* would make good research, right?" Like she read my mind. She pulls open the door to the lab building, her voice echoing in the empty lobby. "The old one, though, because Nate."

The damage is done. I try to accept that this research is happening as a group.

"Eh, too trashy," Mia says

She's not wrong. I've been trying to do a better job keeping the questionable shows and movies at bay.

"*Outer Banks*? Wait, all the Kook guys are bad." Sophie frowns, maybe taking it personally.

"*Gilmore Girls*?" Mia asks.

I prefer the high school seasons, but I keep that to myself.

"The late seasons with Logan. He's kind of like Le-vi," Sophie says.

There's a similar promise of adventure in his eyes, plus the blond hair. The money, the charm, the confidence, of course. Levi is so much kinder, more reliable, more compassionate. I shake the thoughts from my head.

Sophie purses her lips. "She's not convinced. Tristan is like the bad-boy version, kind of."

I shudder. Tristan is far too much like Aiden.

"Team Dean, Jess, or Logan?" Mia asks me.

"Jess all the way." My easy reply apparently surprises them. "What? He's smart and mysterious, and who else carries around a book in their back pocket?" Good thing I haven't seen Levi with a book in his pocket—that might just do me in.

"I can't believe it." Mia chuckles. "I had you down for a Dean girl. High School Dean, obviously."

I shrug. No, thanks.

"I'm with you, Kit," Mia says. "He takes a while to get his act together, but I was always rooting for him."

"Which team, Sophs?" I ask.

"I hope it's not weird since I just said he's like Levi. I'm Team Logan so hard." Sophie laughs.

Okay, it's a little weird, but way less weird than how my stomach just dropped imagining her going after Levi.

"How he calls her 'Ace'? I'm so into it," she says. "And he holds onto his friends forever. Ooh, and the Life and Death Brigade is so my jam."

"You would fit right in jumping off that platform with an

umbrella and a formal dress." I avoid the first comment like the land mine it is.

Sophie claps.

"Since we're not in alignment about which season"—Mia steers us back to the mission at hand—"we could always go straight for *Downton Abbey*."

The image of Levi at that enormous British estate sends us into a giggling fit. Just dress him in the tailored suit he no doubt owns—I would very much like to see him in it—and he would fit right in, especially with that formal voice of his. I don't think my friends have heard that though.

"Oh," Sophie says, "we have to do tonight, 'cause tomorrow I have to study for that insane bio test on Friday."

Mia and I blink at her. "You're going to study all night?"

"I mean, besides my run, yeah. I do study sometimes."

"Uh huh ..."

"Okay, fine. 'I am about to do something very bold in this job that I've never done before ... try.'"

I clap Sophie style. "Aw! A Jim Halpert quote! I wish Ayumi was here."

Sophie's grin drops. "Okay, fess up, Kit. Why are you still playing hard to get with Levi?"

"You did stare at him the entire way over here," Mia says.

I reel back. "I—I'm not—"

Sophie waves me off like I'm a personal affront, heading to chem lab. "See you guys at dinner."

CHAPTER THIRTEEN

"NO COOKIE TODAY?" Levi asks.

He's been asking to walk me back to my building sometimes, which I try not to overthink. But, you know, I do. *Downton Abbey* will start in the lounge in a bit, so we won't be hanging out tonight. These occasional walks back are the only time I get him to myself. Keeping my cool is my full-time job for every one of the five minutes. Don't freak out. Don't act like a weirdo. Don't gawk. Don't randomly quit walking.

"They only had oatmeal raisin left." I wrinkle my nose.

He chuckles. "No equal opportunity?"

"Not for cookies. Plus, Saga's lost their magic after I had this incredible brownie a few weeks ago."

"Oh, yeah?"

"I think that was the best brownie I've ever had."

"Good to know." He sends me a sidelong glance. "What are you up to tomorrow night?"

"Nothing with Sophie, but I always have work to catch up on. She keeps me busier than I should consent to." I love my schoolwork and need my sleep, so my recent habit of staying up late practically every night is a hundred percent to see him.

Pride flickers in his eyes—I'm busted.

"Could I distract you from your work and take you on a date?"

My heart rate takes off like it's trying to win the hundred-meter dash. Sadly, I don't know how much of it is because I'm happy to be asked—so happy—or because my brain is warning my body of danger.

How could I even make a date work?

Alone with him? Really shouldn't. Riding in his car? No way. One touch from him already sent me spiraling—twice. Why does he have to be so devastatingly attractive? He's making my confusing life even more complicated.

My shoulders drop in disappointment. How do I even begin to explain? I shake my head in reply and try not to spiral. *Seriously mixed messages. Sorry, pal.* I could probably walk somewhere or do something on campus, but I shouldn't suggest that. It would be too much to admit to my strangely stringent requirements. And I don't want to give him the impression that dating him is an option. Would. If. I. Could.

"We could study?" he says. "Very friend-like. At Common Grounds?" He sends the most adorable questioning face—soft and hopeful and not pushy at all. Also, he basically read my mind, which maybe should freak me out but instead gives me all the warm fuzzies.

"Okay." And by that I mean *Absolutely yes, I'm dying for a date-adjacent activity with you.*

This should be fine—it's harmless enough. But I need to stop smiling so much. Crinkles form at his eyes and do nothing to slow my heart rate. No need for aerobic exercise. Talking to Levi is all I need to maintain optimal heart health.

"Is six alright? We play at eight."

Words are unwise at this juncture, so I bob my head in response. I start a risk mitigation plan—Pay attention to how I feel. Have an excuse ready if I need to bolt. Travel light. Sit far enough away to avoid accidental touches. No skirt or dress, in case I go fetal.

It's complicated being me, but this is worth the risk. It's so worth it.

Flats on, I clutch my laptop, planning to do my easiest homework at Common Grounds. I can't expect to have much focus with Levi sitting nearby. Not sure if my computer will short-circuit from his magnetism, but there's a great chance my brain will—a pity because he's super smart, and I want to show him I can keep up.

One step out of my room, I freeze in front of the mirror over the sink. Like Jasmine covering up to go out into Agrabah, I've longed to hide under a hood and tunic every day and be invisible again. Safe again. I've felt nothing but bitterness toward that reflection for months. I blame it for the pain and fear I've had to bear. The desire to like what I see there is warm but itchy. Like a wool sweater.

I wedge the laptop into the corner of the countertop and brush my hair guiltily, as if I'm betraying myself. I vowed I was finished jumping through the hoops I did last year—looking my best to play popularity games for girls who would compliment me and then tear me to pieces when I turned my back. Why did I try to please them? I won't again. I don't anymore. I allow myself the luxury of wearing clothes I love, but I don't fiddle with my hair or do my makeup anymore. I don't want to impress girls who will hold it against me, and I don't want to impress guys who will get the wrong idea. I straighten the button-down tucked into my shorts, avoiding my own gaze. Digging out the mascara from my bag under the sink feels like crossing a line, but I swipe it on anyway.

The devil on my shoulder says it's super normal to want to look good for a not-date with a guy who leaves an electric charge in his wake. It says I'm not being weird—I'm finally being reasonable. But the angel insists Levi's interest is only skin deep, in how he can benefit. Or maybe the angel and devil are switched. The confusing girl in my reflection bites her lip.

Am I being stupid again? I really don't need some guy to be content. I only need you.

I don't think I hear anything back.

Well, this is a friend thing. Friendships are good. I'm doing it. I drop the mascara back in in the bag and draw in a courageous breath.

At Common Grounds the back of Levi's head is easy to find. He's working on his laptop in an armchair, leather backpack on the coffee table. His careless blond waves defy his put-together ensemble as always.

He cranes around and brightens. How bizarre that I'm the girl meeting up with the elusive Levi. Like I'm going on a date with Tad Hamilton. Everyone says he doesn't do this kind of thing. If I could only get to the bottom of why he's making an exception. No—I'm easy breezy. This is just a friend thing. Just some studying and coffee with a friend made of lean muscle and sunbeams for hair, radiating confidence and intelligence like it's his full-time job to make every girl on planet Earth swoon. Friends, yep.

Leg crossed wide, he holds up an iced mocha with whipped cream like a prince on his throne. He remembered my drink and arrived early to have it ready for me? Such a gentleman. A princely gentleman.

I take my place in the armchair next to his and accept my coffee, avoiding his fingers.

"I got you decaf since it's nearly your bedtime. Was that right?"

I chuckle. "Basically. Thank you."

A guy in a red floor shirt with cracked black letters swaggers across the room. "What it do, Jeeves?" He does a double take when he sees Levi's with me. *I know. Weird, right?*

"Hey, bro," Levi says. "Is A2 ready to get crushed tonight?"

"Puh. Must be dreamin'." He sends me a dude head-tilt.

I raise my hand in a wave, but he's already past us. "New year, new Jeeves," he murmurs.

"That's Dontrell Wayne," Levi says. "Best receiver on campus. He could've played college ball, maybe pro."

"Why didn't he?"

Admiration fills Levi's eyes. "He wants a different kind of life."

"You have your work cut out for you tonight," I tease.

"I do. Will you be there to cheer me on?"

"Maybe." Okay, definitely. "What are you working on?" I motion to his screen.

"Writing a paper for Jesus class."

I grin at the nickname. Austin told me they're taking "Life and Teachings of Christ" together. "Sounds like a worthwhile endeavor."

"Very."

"Do you bring your Jesus backpack to Jesus class?"

It takes him a beat. "Oh, Jesus in *The Chosen*?" His wall of reserved facial expressions cracks behind a laugh.

"Maybe it was subliminal messaging that made you buy it," I joke.

"Absolutely. I want to be exactly like Jesus."

Exactly like Jesus? I lose all self-control and sink into his eyes like quicksand.

"If only Jesus gave out extra credit for impersonating him," he says.

"Are you willing to wear a tunic around campus?" I swipe a hand around his current impeccable outfit. "Doesn't seem like your usual vibe."

His voice lowers. "If I thought he cared it would be worth it. Anything for him, you know?"

"Completely."

He really loves you, huh?

"Will you be whizzing through some math homework?" he asks.

I blink. Homework. Math homework. "Yes." Oh, it was a compliment. I tuck my hair behind my ear and formulate some words. "Calc III plots."

"Good times." Mischief appears in his eyes.

"Uh-oh. The Cheshire Cat wants his smile back."

"Well, I have a confession to make. I brought Chick-fil-A."

That explains the comforting smell wafting around. I bend toward him. I haven't had a Chick-fil-A sandwich since I visited Mav at work last summer.

He dons a faux-serious expression. "It's not a date. We're just in a coffee shop."

I roll my eyes for effect, trying not to grin, and set my things down on the coffee table.

He reaches for the bag stashed in his backpack.

Crash. A metal chair falls on the tile across the room. An awful slam echoes.

Black. Toxic clouds fill my body with unreality, with terror. That night in April yanks me back.

Barefoot. Slipping. Mud sticking to my legs. Rain. Sweat. Oil in the air. Asphalt jabbing at my feet. Faster. Bile rising. Gas station lights—can I make it? My dress tears. A door slams. Tripping. Scrambling. Faster. He's right behind me.

When I return to reality, I'm in a ball on my armchair. I can't choke down the torrent of tears about to fall. I try to breathe, to calm down. I can't. My chest tightens until I might break apart. I have to hide. I have to get out of here. Now.

"I'm sorry." The tears will escape any second. I jerk my phone and laptop to my chest and speed walk around my chair to avoid

Levi. He stands, alarmed. I relinquish my attempt at normalcy and run through Common Grounds, all the way to my room. I hear Sophie, but I shove my door closed behind me. Ayumi startles at her desk but doesn't say a word when I hide under my duvet like a kid afraid of monsters.

How can I be this fragile? Why can't I fix this? Losing my ever-loving mind over a single noise? It's absurd, awful, unlivable.

I knew this was a risk. I knew better than to think I could handle it. Time alone with Levi? Of course it was too good to be true. And now I have proof that I'm as broken as ever.

Why? Why can't I just be normal? Please fix me. I don't want to be broken anymore. I don't want this to be my life.

For those who love me, all things work together for good.
But how can this be good?

Fifteen minutes later, Levi texts. I wipe away the mascara—shortest-lived makeup ever.

> Are you alright? Can I do something to help?

> Yes. No, thanks.

> I left your coffee and Chick-fil-A on the bench by the door in case you want them.

He did?

My thumbs hover over my phone. What do I even say?

> That's so sweet, thank you.

> I'm really sorry.

Dread and humiliation coil in my chest and cling to my ribs. I brace myself for the inevitable questions.

> No need to apologize, Kit. I'm glad you're okay.

What? I stare, reading the words until they blur. This gentle, understanding response bonds me to him more than any date could have. I shake my head, overwhelmed.

CHAPTER FOURTEEN

I BRUSH dirt off my jeans and knot my hair as I glance at the deepening blue sky. Ayumi's snack table is a work of art, bright treats popping even in the fading light. Levi and Haymitch finish speaker setup. I check my phone—no news from Mia is good news—and kick a tuft of grass. Crunchy, but dry at least.

Austin holds straightened hands toward the focused projector as if telling it to stay put. "I'm gonna get a sofa over here for the birthday girl."

"A sofa, huh?" Lucky Sophie. Adventures all day, and now a royal seat?

"Where do you want it?" he asks.

"She'll love that. Front and center is good. The sooner the better, though, before people start setting up their blankets where they won't be able to see around her throne."

"Cool."

"Haymitch, want me to take over?" I ask. "It's getting dark out here."

"I can still see a lil' some'n. And I got my cane if I need it." He points to his backpack.

"Okay. Thank you both. I appreciate your help so much."

My heart flutters at Levi's charming smile. I roll my shoulders. Back to work.

A breeze blows wisps of hair back to my face and ripples across the patchwork of bedsheets hanging down the side of the building.

Ding. It's Mia.

> We're back

I wring my hands. Every time I think Sophie and I are good, she throws me with another reaction I can't interpret. I just want her to know I'm in her corner.

I pocket my phone and head for the parking lot, toward the slams of Sophie's Jeep doors.

"Birthday girl," I call. "We have a surprise for you."

"She's a real one." Mia points at me. "Planned all of this to the smallest detail. I'm gonna round everyone up."

"Thanks, Mia!" I say.

"You got it, boss." Mia blows us a kiss and strides toward Griffin Hall.

Sophie hooks an arm around mine while we walk. "Spill. This is so exciting!"

I allow myself a grin. "Almost there."

At the field, Sophie gapes at the sheets ahead, at the projector behind. Levi calls to Haymitch and they wave.

"No. Way. Kit!" Sophie jumps and claps and squeals.

"Lots of people made this happen." I gesture to Ayumi straightening her snacks, to Austin on his way across the field with Ethan and a sofa in tow.

Sophie's eyes flit from Austin to me, a shadow crossing her face, but she resets with a laugh. "Projected movies and piles of snacks," she sings, twirling like Maria in *The Sound of Music*.

"Yep. Only your favorite things. I have three choices of movies ready, but anything you want."

"Ooh, let's hear them."

"Well, *La La Land*, *Back to the Future*, and *Father of the Bride* all have scenes in Pasadena," I offer.

Giant hug. "Any of them. All of them. Thanks, Kit. Best birthday ever." But when she steps away, she swallows, darting glassy eyes away, and flits to Ayumi.

My shoulders droop. Nothing's ever simple with Sophie. I doubt I'll ever know what I did wrong.

———

Sophie prances into my room the next day. "Another one like clockwork," she sing-songs, handing me a beautifully wrapped fruit tart taped to a Levi envelope.

"Oh good, it's you this time." I drop my head back.

"Do you get major eye rolls from the others sent in here?"

"More like glare stares."

She cackles as she plops my desk chair to twirl in circles. "Can't blame them. I can't believe he gets other girls to bring you his presents."

"Right? Why doesn't he just text me to come get them?"

"Maybe to prove he can convince any girl on campus? Or to be sure they all know he picks you? It's kind of adorable in his Sir Levi way."

This is the third day this week that a gourmet dessert has made its way to my room, always accompanied by a charming handwritten note. I keep every note in my desk drawer. Maybe that makes me a creep, but I can't make myself throw them away. These beautiful white notecards, thick and smooth, covered in his precious boy cursive, must know they're not trash. Like the opposite of Forky jumping into the trash can, they would probably wake up *Toy Story*-style and climb back onto my desk, sensing their worth. In the desk drawer they must live.

I rip the plastic off and take a bite. "This is incredible, as always. Try it."

"Ooh, yes, please." She jumps up and the chair spins. "So how does it feel to be the chosen one?"

It's terrifying. Absurd. And tragically temporary, because a guy like Levi won't wait forever. He doesn't have to.

I shrug.

She stares me down with sudden and vicious disdain. "You could at least be happy about it. The guy hasn't asked a single girl out in two years. He picks you to lavish expensive desserts on, and you're like 'Not impressed. Try harder.'"

"It's not like that."

"Then what is it like, Kit?" She says my name like it's a curse word.

My gut churns with hurt, but no way am I going to tell her the whole story. Even if she does hate me in this moment. "I don't want to talk about me." I clear my hoarse throat. "Where did Austin take you for your birthday yesterday?"

She lets a breath out and looks anywhere but me. "To a creek. On an adventure."

"That sounds like a Sophie-dream situation. Why do you look so bummed?"

She shakes her head and walks out.

College is a weird place. In a few weeks I've already become fully engrossed in these people's lives. Sharing meals and nights and weekends together, living in the same tiny space, I already know my suite girls better than I knew my friends back home. But I do not understand this from Sophie. She and I hold back. I started it, so it's my fault.

And Levi—I have to keep him at arm's length. It's the only way I can cope with my life the way it is now, to keep the darkness in my mind confined to the edges. But his patient attention and smiling eyes don't abate. After our ill-fated study disaster, he hasn't asked me out again, but his sweets-sending certainly isn't nothing. I rejected his real dates, and I wouldn't dream of touching him. Short of avoiding him entirely, I don't know what else I'd do. I'm on a runaway train, and a fiery crash is inevitable.

CHAPTER FIFTEEN

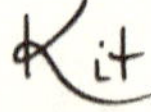

"HEY, Kit, c-could I take you to dinner this weekend?"

Matt? He's the quiet, unassuming guy from Calc III. Shy but sweet. His vibe is the complete opposite of Levi's or Aiden's—nothing intimidating, no effortless charm. His shirt hangs loosely on his skinny frame, and his hair is neatly in place. There's nothing flashy about him, but he seems gentle, with a kind face.

I've been fighting myself over Levi for weeks now. Proximity to him is exhilarating to the point of exhaustion. After weeks of sharing a friend group, my attraction to him, my confusion, the complication only grows. My mind jumbles when I gaze into those eyes, and my heart pounds when he smiles.

Matt and I are jostled by the stampede of students bursting out of the building after chapel. He ushers me to the side like I'm Simba. I covertly slink away from not-Mufasa's hand.

If I could just be content with someone like Matt—simple, comfortable, someone who doesn't leave my brain in complete disarray—maybe I could finally breathe. I stood that close to him, met him in the eyes, and not a cell in my body took notice. Maybe ... I could actually ride in his car like a normal person, not freak when he tries to hold my hand. My brother can drive me hundreds of miles no problem, but I can't so much as sit on a sofa with Levi?

Quiet comfort. Maybe that's what I need. Plenty of adults are satisfied in relationships without fireworks. I can't be so naive to assume I'm going to end up as thrilled and love-struck as my parents. I'm broken. Content and satisfied might be the most I can hope for.

Should I?

When we're far enough from the student wildebeests, Matt hesitantly turns to me. My stomach twists in knots to think of losing the relationship I'd always assumed could be mine someday, but I don't have time for that right now. An opportunity has presented itself, and this could be the escape I've been praying—

But Matt sighs at something behind me, like his plan is foiled.

"You couldn't seriously ..." Levi's voice, low and authoritative, reaches me before I even see him. His warmth radiates, close enough to touch—inviting but risky. My shoulders raise with pleasure as I fight the reckless impulse to step back into his arms.

"... be considering going out with that guy."

My shoulders plummet. *Excuse me?* I want to whip my head around and give him a piece of my mind, but he doesn't deserve the gratification of an immediate response. A quick study of Matt's face tells me he couldn't have heard Levi's disparaging comment. The guys must be looking eye to eye now, over my head. Matt continues like a statue in front of me, courageously attempting to hold Levi's gaze. Matt has some guts—I'll give him that. I've seen the face that goes with Levi's imperial voice, and it's enough to make lesser men quiver.

I keep my back to Levi and try to record all of Matt's good features. Brave, unassuming, comfortable. "Thank you for asking, Matt. Can we talk after class tomorrow?"

He confirms and awkwardly glances once more at Levi. Raising his hand in a wave, he takes himself away.

"At least give me some real competition." Levi slides up next to me and sneers at the retreating Matt.

"Your trust fund is showing," I bite back, sharp and cold.

He swings around until that look of condescension is leveled at me, but then his face softens.

I glare at him. "He could have heard you. He isn't like you, but he deserves just as much dignity."

Levi shifts his jaw.

"See you around, Levi."

I press a hand to my forehead as I walk away. He was way out of line, even if he's frustrated about my mixed signals. But ... this is my out. I've been caught in this exhausting loop—Like-Him, Can't-Like-Him—for too long. Now I have data. I can use this to end the cycle, to protect myself, to escape the sinking feeling of liking him so much and knowing I can't have him to myself.

⸙

Not a full day has passed since my resolution, but here's Levi, raising a finger, asking for a moment in a gentlemanlike manner. How did he know where to find me? Oh, Austin's in this class. He sneaks a peek at us as he disappears into the math building. I acknowledge Levi but don't speak, proceeding ahead. Remember —he showed himself to be condescending, rude, and pretentious. I do not need to give him another chance. I can't afford to give him another chance. I hold tightly to my books and to my grudge. I need them to keep him pushed back into obscurity.

Levi falls into step with me. "I was wrong. I apologized to Matt."

I snap to him.

"I asked around and showed up at his room."

I hide my shock behind a wall. "Did he think you were going to beat him up?"

He grimaces. "Maybe at first. Kit, I'm sorry. I really appreciate that you called me out ..."

With a few sentences, he's bludgeoned my resolve as if with a club.

"I was jealous, but I have no right to be. And I certainly shouldn't have acted like that. Will you forgive me?"

Cold dread settles in my gut. Oh, this is bad. His thorough and genuine plea for forgiveness is enough to dissipate my anger and then some.

He gazes at me with humility, lips twisting in anguish. I rub my head, trying to compute. A character flaw could help me change direction, but a mistake followed by regret, repentance, making amends? That's ... marriage material.

I move my books between us, as if it will keep him away. I can't afford to forgive him. I know what will happen if I do.

When I come to a standstill, he stops with me.

I impulsively test his sincerity. "You're used to getting what you want"—I dig in the knife—"who you want." That will be enough to bring out his true nature. I brace and silently beg for an angry response.

To my astonishment, he gazes at me like he's impressed, even enamored. "I guess I am."

Our train wreck of a coffee date was proof that I can't actually date him. So this? I can't have this. How do I get out of it? Falling for a guy I can't even be alone with is begging for heartache. But his slip up and earnest apology is beautiful proof of his kindness, his goodness, his gentleness.

No. I can't. No more of this.

Be kind to one another, tenderhearted,
forgiving one another, as God in Christ forgave you.

No, please. You know how it is. This isn't going to go well. I can't. Look at him. I can't.

Be kind to one another, tenderhearted,
forgiving one another, as God in Christ forgave you.

What a disaster, but I can't disobey. I could forgive Levi but refuse to hang out with him—or our group—again. But I won't. I know I won't. My friends are his friends now. He's everywhere. And he's ... him.

Fine. Okay. You're going to take care of this? I can't. I can't not like this guy. I can't keep this from going off the rails.

I smother my anxious sigh. "Yes, I forgive you."

Humility and relief shine from his eyes. He opens the door for me to proceed into the math building. "You say what needs to be said. I really like that about you." That soft voice is delicious—rumbly, like a special secret. I'm slow to translate the meaning because I'm distracted by the tone.

And he's gone.

My heart beats too fast and my fingers tingle. I'm jittery as I maneuver through the hallway. Matt will be getting a no after class. I couldn't distract myself with another guy to save my life. Or my heart.

CHAPTER SIXTEEN

"MIA COULD HELP TOO, but pick me!" I say to Ayumi, standing up after Thursday's game. "Calc One was my favorite class ever." I twist out the stiffness in my back from sitting on the sideline.

"Yes, pick Kit," Mia says. "I wouldn't exactly have heart eyes talking about limits and derivatives."

I gather the blanket we shared—muddy from recent rain—and wad it into a clump.

My arms freeze when I spot Levi sauntering toward us.

No big deal. Just a bold, insightful, thrilling guy who I can't actually date.

Mia kicks my butt from behind. "Speaking of heart eyes."

Ayumi takes the blanket wad from my arms.

"To MSC. I want chicken," Sophie says. "Bye, Kit!" she sing-songs.

Margot Robbie alerted us to some impressive Barbies out

there. Physicist Barbie, Diplomat Barbie, Supreme Court Justice Barbie. Ryan Gosling might have been "just Ken," but Levi has collectible looks too. This one is Dreamy Athlete Levi. Brimming achievement and flushed cheeks. And slightly sweaty hair that gives a magnificent texture to his waves, better than any mousse could manage. Not touching said hair is a battle between the logic of my frontal lobe and the instincts from my limbic system. Yes, I'm a nerd. Back to Levi—his biceps, which I've been watching catch and intercept for an hour, gloriously peek out of his shirt and tempt me to gape at them. This Levi always comes accessorized with an orange Flooders shirt, running shorts, and a black water bottle.

Who started the tradition of the sister floor coming to every game? Come along, they say, and watch the guys we know act like Olympians and flash their proud smiles and slap each other's butts. They're all just our casual friends, and nothing is strange about staring at them like this for an hour every single week! I haven't missed a game.

Levi arrives in front of me. "Hey, friend. Can I walk you back?"

I am the epitome of cool with my "Okay, sure."

He likes to call me "friend." If only we could be more Chandler and Monica and less Joey and Phoebe.

We set off, navigating through the pine trees that fill the space between the engineering building and the gym, rather than straight north across campus like the rest of the group. The yelling and chanting at the pond behind us makes for a distinctively Mayberry soundtrack. A dude floor is inciting some kind of mayhem. Levi probably knows who's getting tossed in, but his intense focus beams toward me. Open, shut goes the lid of his water bottle. "Thanks for coming to our game."

"It was fun. Your crazy catch at the end was amazing." Well it was, okay?

Levi beams.

"So, you managed to make a friend of Matt? He told me you stuck around after apologizing and played Madden on his floor."

A hint of his gentle, humble smile.

Only he could turn a mistake into a win. He's impossible.

"He's a cool guy," he says. "Good taste."

My smile slants.

"So, I'm not trying to overstep boundaries, but ... You were ready to go out with Matt, but you shoot me down every time. Mind if I ask why?"

The way his face softens—unguarded, vulnerable—makes my heart skip. I want to honor that openness. What kind of explanation would he understand? My feet grind to a halt. "I told Matt no because ... Levi, you ... you're ..." I'm out of words. He said I'm expressive. Maybe if I look at him openly he'll be able to magically read my mind?

I silently talk to him in my head, as if he's Edward Cullen. *Listen, I'm stuck. You've seen me do weird things, but I can't explain them. And I won't do anything that risks those weird things happening again. I'm sorry I'm so dysfunctional. But you're so dreamy and sweet and smart that you're ruining rom-coms for me. Even Lara Jean and Peter are no fun to watch anymore.*

What am I doing? I'm officially off my rocker.

Levi's gaze is deep and exposing. The connection drags me under—and closer. Doesn't eye contact release chemicals of some kind in the brain? I break away to clear my head.

"Take the time you need," he says.

Well, that didn't work. My feet carry me along again, north toward the bell tower. "So, uh, how are your classes going?"

"Not giving me too much trouble."

I raise teasing brows. "You're in upper-level software engineering classes. They're not giving you 'too much trouble?'"

He edges an elbow toward me, short of an actual nudge. "And how are your junior-level math classes going, my favorite freshman?"

I bite back a smile. "How'd you pick your major?" Maybe he'll spill a rare personal detail.

"Oh, I—" His eyes turn playful. "I'd better get to the point. You're going to hold out for the real answer, aren't you?"

My grin breaks through.

"It's petty, but I veered far from pre-law, econ, or business like my parents would want." He steps up onto a bench by the bell tower. "All I knew is that I wanted a challenge." He hops down and up another bench, *Sound of Music*-style. "I'm enjoying this though. I particularly like my software architecture class this semester. I think that might be the specialty I work on for my practicum next year."

Jackpot. Personal details.

"Do you have a project you're working on right now?" I ask.

He moves the water bottle to his left hand and holds out his right to help me down off the final bench. Just chivalrous habit, I assume, because he drops it immediately and watches me jump down. Aiming toward Griffin Hall, he describes his work building a distributed system. I'm Winnie the Pooh staring at a pot of honey. He treats me like I'm brilliant, assuming I know more than I do and that I can follow complex thoughts with ease. Everyone says that class is brutally difficult, and he's over here talking about fault tolerance like it's pre-algebra. Crazy Smart Levi and Dreamy Athlete Levi just combined in a moment of—

Oops.

He raises his brow over an amused smile, like he's reading my face. *Stop calling me out like that, Levi.* I shake my head to clear it before he can read any more of my thoughts.

"Cool," I say, like I'm fresh out of brain cells. Gotta redeem myself. "How exciting that you might have found what you're going to do for a living. It's overwhelming that I have to have that figured out in a year or two."

"It can be scary to trust that God will get us to the right spot. I haven't figured out when to stop and listen more and when to try something, trusting he'll guide me."

All the wonderful Levis are converging into one conversation. I can barely maintain composure.

"Maybe it's one and then the other?" I say, my voice quieter than I intend. "The stopping and listening comes naturally to me, but the go-and-try part ... it's a lot. I don't want to disappoint God. I love him so much."

His tender look steals the last bit of air from my lungs. Without a word, he turns away from my approaching building, quietly extending our walk.

CHAPTER SEVENTEEN

"CAN I ASK YOU SOMETHING?" I ask.

Levi chuckles. "You don't normally ask permission." He motions for me to go ahead.

"Why do you get weird when people act like you don't understand what they're saying? You're clearly extremely intelligent. Why the insecurity?"

He gapes.

"Sorry, I—"

"What do you mean I get weird?"

"You kind of … fuss at them." I hesitate, tucking my hair behind my ear. "With a face. A 'don't mess with me' face."

He lets out a breath. "For my father, our academic success was not optional. He wanted us to get into Yale by merit, to hold our own in his intellectual circles, like it was proof that our family was perfect, flawless." He shakes his head. "Maybe I'm still touchy about it. I sure liked your compliment though," he jokes. Quieter, "You really are one of a kind, Kit."

So much humility and authenticity. "Sorry, that was invasive. You're not mad?"

He pivots to effortlessly walk backward. "No, and I'll prove it. Ask me another personal question." His cheek twitches, like he's bracing himself.

I laugh. "Fred Astaire wants his moves back."

"Veronica Mars wants her interrogation skills back."

"V Mars! My brothers and I love her." I suppress the impulse to push him as he walks in front of me. "Okay, since you offered ... are you still all cagey with your friends? Your other friends, I mean."

His eyes flicker with guilt and amusement. "Usually. I prefer to think of it as being a good listener."

"You are an excellent listener."

The sidewalk veers and I point him the right direction. He doesn't miss a step.

"Any more questions for me? It's only fair." If I didn't know better, I'd think I was flirting with Off-Limits Guy. But my grin falls as I spot the door to Common Grounds—the one I went barreling through at our disastrous study date. A sharp reminder of the lunacy of this thing with him.

I turn back to his smile radiating into eye creases. Forget the door.

"I do have a question," he says. "Why don't you like hearing that you're beautiful?"

My mouth drops open, then snaps shut. I avoid his gaze—tricky when he's right in front of me—but his honesty makes me want to be brave. "It's sort of a recent thing. I was extra regular-looking until senior year, and now ... well, now I look different, and it hasn't been a good thing."

"It's not a good thing to be alarmingly gorgeous?"

I want that compliment to feel like one, but it sits in my stomach like a rock. "No. It's probably different as a dude—" I glance up, and he smirks. Great. "But for me, no. Girls haven't been very nice about it. And the attention..." Especially the bad kind. "I'd go back to regular Kit in a heartbeat."

We arrive at my building, and he pauses by the bench. "It would be impossible not to notice you're breathtaking, but that's not why I want to know you better. It's certainly not the only reason at least."

I don't know if I believe him. Or if it even matters.

"You're special, Kit, like no one else. The time I get talking to you—it's never enough."

Smart-Athlete-Vulnerable-Jesus-loving Levi is saying that to me? No, no, no. This is exactly what I was afraid of.

Help!

Levi

The bench taunts that she's going to run inside any second and let the heavy door slam behind her. Wide, scared eyes stare back at me, and my smile drops. I told her too much about how I feel about her—entirely too soon. Amateur move.

I pull my hand from my pocket and take a step closer. How do I soothe her nerves?

"Thanks, well, good chat, good game, byeee!" She dashes to the door to badge in and fixates on the pad on the wall, practically begging it to beep and unlock the door. She waves her ID in front, moving too much for it to register.

I shake my head, soaking in the extra five seconds with her.

Even as she tilts forward, waiting so impatiently to escape my presence, her gorgeous brown hair falls around her shoulders, catching the light of the building. She's biting her lip again. Those perfect hips sway as she moves her weight from leg to leg. I wish I could wrap an arm around her back and hold her hand to sway with her right there, no music required.

There the door goes, and she disappears through it.

A beautiful girl who doesn't like being beautiful. She's fascinating. And funny and real and kind and brilliant. She loves Jesus so authentically, so wholly. I'm trying to play it cool, take it slow, be patient as she comes around to the idea of dating me. To think just three days ago I almost blew it.

Thank you for a second chance. Make me like you, Jesus.

"What are you doing, *Tiguere?*" Mia's voice.

I resist the urge to snap my head around. Caught staring at the door like an idiot.

"Oh, hey." My best imitation of nonchalance. "See you two tomorrow." I start across the field.

Sophie starts singing "You Got It Bad."

Touché.

CHAPTER EIGHTEEN

PLASTIC TRAYS IN HAND, my girls and I sit down to dinner on Friday. This spaghetti isn't bad, but Mom's is better. The pull home is strong, even though I love it here. I'm counting down the days until fall break. Sophie launches into a monologue about G1's future flag football practices, undeterred by Saga's dull roar. She played club volleyball in high school, so it makes sense she's ready for some competition again. Across the room, our boys materialize in the cafeteria line, and a pack of A2-ers makes a ruckus at their table, standing to bro out in the cutest group hug.

"I asked Zoe what she thought about getting one of the Flooders to coach us this year," Sophie says. "She loved the idea. So I talked Austin into taking the job."

My head snaps up. *Oh, did you?*

"You know he played varsity running back in high school. His team won State. In Texas, no less. And the Flooders have won nearly all their games since he started playing quarterback."

She's so cute going on about Austin, though she's never admitted her obvious thing for him. Not that I deserve the truth —especially in this department.

"We will have such"—her speech slows—"a leg up ..."

I turn to follow her darting gaze. Another group of Flooders just walked into Saga. Just Leo and some other freshmen. Who is she looking at? She glances down the table and back at the door.

"... on the other ..."

I edge forward and interrupt in a whisper. "Which one?"

Sophie jumps. Her eyes drill into mine. "It doesn't matter. He blows me off when I try to talk to him. Not everyone can be Perfect Little Kit."

I flinch.

What do I do? Please, not a repeat.

Ayumi gapes.

"Hey!" Mia says. "What is your deal?"

Sophie stands. "Whatever. I'll see you guys later."

Mia shakes her head. "No idea. We'll get to the bottom of it."

Our weekly phone dates after Praise and Prayer aren't cutting it for me. I need to talk to Mom. I call on the way back from dinner, strategically avoiding FaceTime.

"Kit girl. I was just praying for you. How are you? Have you been ... mentally healthy?"

Not that subject. "Kind of the same. I'm fine though." Good thing she can't see my face.

"Have you found anyone you can talk—"

Nope, nope, nope. "Hey, Mom? Sophie's mad at me about something."

After a beat, "Do you know what about?"

I'm afraid it's the same thing as last year—jealousy. But I can't say that. What if I'm wrong? "She snapped at me out of the blue."

"Oh, honey, I'm sorry. College is weird. You bond so fast that you have bigger fights sooner."

Checks out.

"I ended up spending time with mostly guys my first year

because the girls were so ... dramatic," she says. "They wouldn't use their words."

Mom's standard phrase for lack of communication. I miss her.

"I'm sure you had little patience for that," I say.

"Mm-hm." I can almost see Mom's eyelids fluttering on the other side of the call.

Just be honest. It's Mom. "I'm ... nervous that last year is going to happen all over again. The awful friend stuff."

"I hope not, sweetie. But God provides in every way. If these aren't the friends God has for you, he'll bring along others. You can trust him."

Right. I can trust you with this.

"The quick bonding happens with boys too, by the way," she says. "I'd say more so."

"I can see that." Two nights ago Levi told me I'm special, that the time he has talking to me is never enough. Swoon, double swoon. But also, not good. I wish I could talk to Mom about it. Not telling a living soul has me bursting, but no one understands what I face. Anyone would just tell me to push through or give him up. So why bother asking?

"Oh?" She feigns innocence. "Have you been getting to know Levi better?"

"Yes."

"Does he love the Lord?"

She doesn't ask whether he goes to church or calls himself a Christian. Aiden taught me that those mean nothing on their own.

"He really does. He's a good guy, Mom, but we're just friends."

"I see." From her voice I can tell she actually does.

"Sophie, wait. Is there something I can do to … be a better friend to you?" *Drop the silent treatment, lady!* I can't have her bitterness hanging over me like a dark cloud. I have enough of those, thank you very much.

Sophie's barely said a thing to me for two days, so I've been waiting in the lounge to catch her since Praise and Prayer. It's Sunday night and past time to use my words. I'll be pushy if I need to so we can start next week fresh. Mia probably knows something, but I should do my own dirty work. Gossip is the worst.

Stopping in the doorway of the suite, Sophie turns to me exasperated—ugh, rude again—but comes to plop down on the lounge sofa with pursed lips.

I feel for Sophie. Being ignored by a guy you like feels awful. I've got a lifetime o' knowledge—*She's the Man!*—being invisible. I didn't get asked to a single dance before my senior year of high school. In fact, in sixth grade, I had a giant crush on this boy, Luke Buyers. I stood in the dark, echoey gym as the first slow song started at the Valentine's dance—"Thinking Out Loud" by Ed Sheeran. My friends paired off with their guys, and Luke walked straight toward me. I was so nervous I did a frantic 180, ran to the bathroom, and hid. Monday morning, I found out he hadn't been walking toward me at all—he was headed for my friend behind me. That was fun.

Anyway, I know what it's like, far better than Sophie probably does. And I didn't do anything to deserve her wrath.

She tilts her head back. "You know … Leo?" She catches some hair to twirl but drops it. "I just thought maybe I could … turn his head. He's cute and funny and … and I'm nobody to him."

Wait, the freshman who is quirky and—let's be honest—awkward? I know how guys are, so I would have thought he'd trade a limb for attention from vibrant and gorgeous Sophie. Tall, toned, and feminine. A soft dusting of freckles, contagious smile, and bouncing blond hair. In contrast, I remember when Leo chose to take a bite out of a cicada for his Extended Orientation task. I try not to shudder. I mean, he's kind and gentle, but Leo and not Austin? I guess I was light years off on that one.

"You're just—" Sophie gives a frustrated sigh. "You're so pretty and ... sweet. It gets to be a lot."

I squeeze my closed laptop. How dare she. I had far more than enough of this last year. I'm not even that sweet. I guess I keep my remarks to myself most of the time, but that's definitely not "a lot."

She picks at her nail polish and doesn't notice the smoke coming from my ears. "I'm sorry I was rude to you the other day. You don't deserve it. It just kills me that—" She stops. "Well I totally failed trying to talk to some guy—multiple times—and you don't even care that Sir Levi himself suddenly stopped his bachelor life to chase after you."

My grip softens. Levi's behavior makes no sense, and mine must seem equally bizarre. "It's definitely me who's doing all the sudden stopping."

That earns a chuckle. "I shouldn't take it out on you. I'm sorry. It's just a bummer, you know?"

"Such a bummer." What is going on in Leo's head? He'd be crazy not to like Sophie. My mind is turning, scheming. "Would it be totally over the line if I asked Leo about you?"

She purses her lips again and replies with a wave of her hand. "Whatever. Ask him, ask any of them." The other Flooders? "I don't expect it will make any difference."

If it's Leo she wants, it's Leo she'll have.

"Where are you headed?" I use my friendliest voice, too high-pitched. I hate myself a little for sucking up to her to avoid further conflict.

Sophie checks the time and glides toward the door, posture more relaxed. "Taco Bell with some people from bio." Her voice holds no snarky undertone. Seems promising. "Safe to say you're going to bed?"

"Yeah. Have fun."

"See ya."

Back to normal. I let out a breath.

Thank you for that.

I'm always here.

God's presence with me is more palpable than usual, and I sit with him for a minute before pulling out my phone. Nine p.m. isn't too late to text Levi, but he almost never texts me. I have to scroll way down to find him in my messages, and then my thumb hesitates over his name.

> Hey. Have you seen Hitch?

Bloop. Sent.

The gratification of an almost instant *ding* back.

> Hey, friend.
>
> I have.
>
> ?

> Could you help me with something?

> Anything.

I shake my head, enamored and annoyed. How can a one-word text message make my heart beat faster?

He has a class thirty minutes after chapel, so this will be short. I can be brave for Sophie.

> Coffee after chapel tomorrow?

> Absolutely.

I love that he isn't playing it cool with a "sure" or a "see you then." A grin spreads across my face until a chill runs down my spine. What are the odds another chair will fall?

This isn't for me. I can do this for Sophie.

CHAPTER NINETEEN

AFTER CHAPEL, I speed over to Common Grounds.

Excellent. I'm first in line, so I have my pick of seats. I order an iced mocha, thankful I have coffee punches from my meal plan so I don't have to shell out cash. I would order for Levi, but I was so nervous about him the other times we were here that I have no idea what he chose for himself. It's weird that I can learn so much about him and still not know his coffee order. I pick a spot on the farthest end with carpet—maybe a loud noise would be muffled here.

Please, can this time be different? Peaceful?

Levi strides in, glances at the long line recently formed, and heads straight for me.

"Hey, friend." He slides his Jesus backpack to the coffee table, retrieves his Tic Tacs, and sits. His elbows rest on the armrests and his leg crosses widely in confident Levi fashion. Open, shut. Yep, he's Mayberry's Tad Hamilton. Minus all the bad parts.

"Hey, Levi. I wanted to order for you, but I don't know what you get."

The cutest expression comes to his face.

"Why are you smirking?" I accuse.

"You're going to laugh at me."

I raise my brows.

"I usually get an Earl Grey Tea."

Sure enough, I tilt my head back and laugh. "Is it exhausting being so sophisticated all the time?"

He takes my teasing as a compliment, crinkles appearing. Open, shut goes the Tic Tac box. My skin tingles.

Time to focus. I glance around Common Grounds. No one I know, but I talk quietly anyway. "Okay, talk to me about Leo."

"Leo," Levi repeats, following my lead on volume. The grin drops off as he assesses me. His leg comes uncrossed, and he readjusts in his seat.

I wait with pen in hand, unsure why this is so far from what he expected. He said he'd seen *Hitch*.

"That scooter, of course. Silly humor. Quiet demeanor, except on the floor. Genuine faith."

That's important if I'm going through with this. I wait for more, although Levi's stilted speech gives me pause, and "demeanor" sounds almost formal.

"I believe he played golf in high school. Affinity for junk food."

I half snort. Compared to what Levi prefers, nearly everything is junk food. He eats impossibly healthy, with the exception of his Tic Tac habit. I've seen his imperial face more than once when Saga has nothing up to his standards, though I'll grant that he doesn't complain aloud.

"He leaves Twizzlers strewn about," he says, as if he knows my inner thoughts.

"Ah." The way Levi says "strewn about" is adorable. My pen scribbles purple notes into my notebook for later strategizing, but my mind is squarely on Levi.

"He has a penchant for puns." He keeps readjusting like he can't get comfortable. He's hiding something—something sad? I want to cheer him up, especially while he spends his break helping me. An urge rises to bring out the smile that's nearly always in his eyes. Maybe just a little flirting, without actually interrupting his train of thought. I'm no good at this. Really, zero practice, so I'll just imitate what I've seen others do.

I comb through my hair and ... clunkily catch on a tangle. Ugh, I give up with that and fling it all over one shoulder. A piece catches in my mouth, and I bat it away, like a toddler in her mom's heels prancing down a runway. This is not going well.

I tilt my head ... maybe a little too much, so I bring it back up a smidge. I must look like a malfunctioning robot. He scrutinizes me, not even laughing at my ridiculous behavior. Bleak. Head still almost tilted, I try just looking at him as if I like him. I mean, I do like him, obviously. I just constantly work to keep my face in line. It has a habit of embarrassing me.

To my horror, my "I like you" face results in his mouth drooping open the tiniest bit and his eyes falling sadder. Wow, I am terrible at this. He looks like I imagined Gale Hawthorne in *Hunger Games*—also the Liam Hemsworth version. When I tried to communicate silently that other time, it seemed to work so well.

"That's all that comes to mind," he says. "Have I answered the question to your satisfaction?" Reminiscent of our first coffee date—no, coffee meetup, or whatever that was—except his mood and delivery are so different now, sullen rather than playful.

"You did very well, thank you." He's so sweet to help me, and I don't know how to help him at all.

His sad eyes now hold something else, almost irritation? Why would that be?

"Is everything okay?" I ask.

"Yup."

Yup? So out of character. I shake my head. Back to the mission, I guess. "Has he said anything about Sophie?"

Levi's walled off expression relaxes to a wry smile. "Sophie."

I can't believe it. A few days ago we were all up in a tête-à-tête that totally freaked me out, and now he thinks I want some other guy? Leo, no less? Charming, confident Levi is far more vulnerable than I realized. I'm hit with a flutter and a pang. I guess I almost went out with Matt just last week. Pulling one of his looks, I raise my eyebrows and quirk my lips.

"Sophie. No, I don't believe I've heard him mention her."

He took my impression of his you-like-me face as insistence he go on? I sigh. Do girls practice these things in the mirror?

"You're going to play Hitch on Leo for Sophie?" he asks.

"Precisely." Now that he's back to normal, I check that I have all of the helpful details in my notebook.

When I glance up, awe and amusement glow in his eyes. How does he have entire monologues with his face? I can't seem to communicate a single thing with a look today.

"I need to get to class. Can I be of further assistance to you?" he teases.

"I'll let you know?" Will I get away with that response? I sure do. "Thanks, Levi."

Off he goes with a single nod and backpack in tow. I suck in a breath in an attempt to still my heart and consider the task at hand. Yeah, right. Levi, man among boys, is vulnerable to me, focused on me, invested in me. I should be floating to the sky, but instead the sky is falling.

CHAPTER TWENTY

Levi

I PRESS against the armrest of my trusty old couch to adjust my propped-up feet. I still feel like I'm getting away with something sitting like this while I work. My fingers are restless on the keyboard as I try to fix the code in front of me.

Sensing my distraction, Austin pounces, spinning around in his office chair to question me. "How's KitKat? Didn't you have coffee with her this morning?"

He calls her that to tease me, never to her face, though I'm sure she'd laugh and play along.

"She asked me, you know. It's progress."

"The pretty lady makes a move." He feigns intrigue. "Did she escalate to high fives?"

I shake my head at him, still in good humor. I get this a lot lately. I may as well have had a No Girls Allowed sign taped to my forehead for my entire time at Mayberry, so it's no secret to the other Flooders that I'm breaking down my impenetrable walls for her. The guys haven't tried anything with Kit, but brotherly ridicule at my apparent failure is enjoyed by all. They've seen girl after girl traipse through the floor to my room, and evidently it's hilarious that I've chosen the one who seems impossible.

Austin pulls on a signature plaid button-up for study group. "Still holding out hope?"

"There's something about her, man."

"She'll come around. She's just got the hard-to-get thing down to a science. Besides, you're still beating out the other guys who've tried. Two and a half coffee dates is nothing to scoff at with this one." He slaps me on the back.

Until I set him straight, Austin thought I was mostly interested in Kit because she's the biggest challenge. Not a chance—there's far too much to lose. Best case, I end up heartbroken or callous. Worst case, I fall in love with her and sacrifice my entire life's peace committing to someone who chose me for my money. I know, that escalated quickly, but I have a whole childhood to explain my terror of that outcome. It was enough to keep me away from girls for years after seeing Genevieve's true colors senior year. But something bizarre is happening. For the first time ever I'm willing to consider someone for real. Almost ... in a forever kind of way. Forever has been a new kind of f-word for me. I don't even think it. For so long I've seen every girl as a threat, someone who puts me at risk of a marriage like my parents'. And now, a future together isn't coming into focus with a girl I'm certain will return my affection, but with one I'm certain will decide based on the real me.

It's possible I've enrolled in a crash course on rejection, the public and humiliating sort. People at this small school like to gossip—ask me how I know—but I won't let that deter me. Kit's worth it because I'm so confident that I can trust her in every other way. I know that I know that she's the only one worth all the risks—the risk of being tricked like my father was, the risk of getting hurt again, the risk of public failure. I run a hand through my hair. This is a doozy of a crush, if I can even call it that.

"Anything I can do to help her along?" Austin asks.

"Thanks, buddy. I don't think so. I just need to figure out why she's holding off."

He nods. "I asked Sophie. I think she would've told me, but she says Kit's a vault."

Yep, a vault. "Your wingmanning is fire. If it weren't for you, I'd be limping along just trying to get her to show up at the same place and time as me."

"Got you covered, Jeeves."

As he collects his things, he hits the back of his hand against the palm of the other.

I've known him long enough to know that means he's nervous, probably about to ask a girl out. Still no Sophie. I'm usually better at guessing this kind of thing. I point to the Tic Tacs on my desk.

He grins. "Back atcha, man. Even a good wingman from here." He dumps a couple Tic Tacs into his palm and pops them in his mouth. "Later. See you at practice."

"Go route tonight?"

"Yes." He points at me, quarterback-style.

We've been perfecting that route. Football is my favorite intramural sport, and it's particularly rewarding this year with a certain new observer on the sidelines. Besides that, though, I want Austin to feel comfortable to pass more often when his knee is bugging him. He needs someone to look out for him more than most because he's sacrificial to a fault.

Haymitch whizzes down the hall on his bike, yelling to everyone in his drawl, "Practice at seven! Don't forget!" Never a dull moment on the floor.

I need to talk to Haymitch and Mateo. Now that I found a spot for our upcoming prank on Club, we should go over strategy and timing for building our pulley contraption in increments. We won't be able to carry 2x4s into the gym while people are walking around.

My gaze falls from the doorway to the cookie waiting on my

desk, covered in chocolate shots and wrapped to perfection by Miss Evelyn. The right message for the note has eluded me, so it's still sitting there, begging me to make a fool of myself. Two gifts a week sent to a girl who won't go on a single real date … I've never been so much like a stalker. But Sophie assures me Kit adores my little presents, so I continue. Kit bends toward me eagerly as her deep blue eyes smile into mine—she's not exactly waving me off.

My computer is sitting ignored on my lap. I won't be getting anywhere with this race condition until I have a clear mind, so I go to my desk. Time to write something and reset my focus. I tap the lid of my favorite fountain pen on the desk as I consider. Poetry? Not in my wheelhouse. "From Levi"? Boring. A compliment? Only if it has nothing to do with how she looks. Something funny? She likes movie quotes.

If I could only solve the riddle of Kit's hang-up about me, I could use these notes to answer the underlying question she holds. Is it my money? Do I seem pretentious since the Matt thing? Is it the bad experience she mentioned early on? Sometimes she looks scared for a minute. Nervous is an honor, but scared I hate. I want her to feel safe with me, valued, protected.

Those eyes betray that she's attracted to me—such a pleasure —but something else lives there too. The confusing anger is a thing of the past, but lately I see a hesitancy, almost like guilt.

And then I have her rare but harrowing reactions to consider. It must have been the loud noise that sent her into a panic and jetting out of our study date. My gut says she endured something terrible. Kit is private like me, so uncovering the truth may be a lengthy endeavor. Still, the mystery is a challenge I accept willingly. She's well worth the effort.

Leo appears in my doorway.

"Hiccup, what's up, man?"

He scratches the back of his neck. "Hey Jeeves, sorry to ask, but I need a favor. You hang out with Sophie, right?"

I want to laugh but maintain my composure. I would never break Kit's confidence. "I do."

"I think she might like me. I mean, that sounds stupid, right? She's so fun and cool and pretty. But she's been coming up to me and trying to talk to me and stuff. Dude, I just clam up every time. It's the worst. And now"—he drops his hands in defeat—"now I've completely stopped talking to her."

I motion for him to sit on my couch. Kit looped me into her shenanigans and said she might want further help, but what if Austin decides he wants a chance with Sophie? He's dating everyone but her, won't even admit to liking her. Plus, Austin is a legend. He could best this kid with a single smile if he decided to. I bounce my heel on the floor. I'll help Kit with this but unwind it if Austin changes his mind.

"I just need to send a quick text," I say.

I'm all too happy to have a valid reason to text Kit. I've been resisting the urge to text her so this doesn't become a text-only relationship. I suspect it would go deep fast and get weird between us in person. I'm in for the long game and can't afford that result, even if sometimes I have to wait for days to have a private conversation with her.

> Hey, friend. I have a lead on your Hitch situation. Mind if I cover this one?

I lock my phone and set it on the desk. It lights up, and I grab it like the last tray-passed salmon puff. Woah there. I'm a bit overeager.

> That's amazing, Levi, thank you. I trust you.

She trusts me. My desire to help is amazing. She uses commas in her texts.

I reluctantly release the phone and face Leo. "The right girl can make a guy act like an idiot."

"Yeah, exactly," he says with emphasis.

"I know the feeling, man. How can I help?"

He lets out an incredulous laugh. I appreciate his well-timed confidence boost. Kit's had the opposite effect on me.

"I dunno. You're Jeeves. I figured you'd know what to do."

"Are you looking for help being less nervous or winning her back now that you pushed her away?"

"Is that on the table?" Leo bends forward in anticipation. "Both. Dude, both."

I keep my face straight to maintain his dignity. I don't think anyone's ever come out and asked my strategy on these matters. I respect his initiative. "Alright. Being comfortable around girls is just a combination of practice and self-confidence. Practice talking—not flirting, talking and listening—to girls who aren't as intimidating, and then work up to the Sophies. And hit the gym every day, but don't let it go to your head." I wonder whether he knows his way around a weight room, but I won't ask. "They'll be fighting over you in no time."

Perhaps I'm over-selling it. Kit still makes me nervous after weeks. I find myself speaking like my father when she gets me particularly out of sorts. It never ceases to horrify me. And this morning I completely misread her nonverbals. She makes me feel like I'm sitting in the NFL's green room, waiting to get drafted. Leo isn't the only one wanting to win over a girl out of his league.

Lucky for this kid, Kit seems to think he has a fighting chance with Sophie, and she would know better than anyone. I certainly wouldn't have guessed as much. Why she'd want to match her friend up with anybody over Austin, I can't imagine, but I don't profess to understand Kit's decision-making. With time.

"Practice talking to other girls, work out more, and don't get cocky. I can do that. I don't need the fighting. I just want to get Sophie back to talking to me."

I understand completely. "As for winning her back, ease into it. Girls can be emotional about things, one extreme or the other. She might think you hate her or you're too good for her—"

He makes a disgusted face, and I choke down a laugh.

"—Or you have some other girl in mind. Start by looking over at her and smiling a little. After a couple days of that, maybe a wave or a passing comment."

He's watches me, enraptured.

"Take a breath and enjoy the chase. Hopefully she'll come around. But whatever you do, don't try to act like someone else. Just be the smoothest version of yourself."

Leo stands, and I follow suit. He shakes my hand hard, like he's leaving an important business meeting.

"No promises," I say. "Girls are unpredictable. But I have high hopes on this one."

"Thanks, man. God bless you. I owe you big."

I laugh. "He does every day. And no, you really don't."

He walks out showing far too much confidence in me.

I scroll through my quickly sent messages. I particularly enjoy my ironic nickname for Kit. I'll be her friend as long as she needs, though I'm growing impatient for her to come around. If my instincts are right, she's The—

No. Way too soon. If I'm not careful, I could be coming to Leo asking how to get myself out of a jam. The right girl really can make a guy act like an idiot.

I send one more message.

> Let me know if you see some improvement in the situation.

Another reason to talk to Kit is priceless.

I pull my journal out of the drawer and open to the last page of writing. My letters loop slowly. What am I trying to ask exactly?

She's here, on my sister floor no less, after those prayers last
     year. Could it mean what I think it means?

Nothing yet. I move a card and envelope out of the drawer. Back to my journal.

As I suspected, she loves you with her whole heart. But I wouldn't want to use you to get a girl. Can I tell her?

With a confirmation of sorts, I write on the card and then tap my phone. No answer to my text. Time to deliver this cookie before getting dressed for practice. I can't look at it a minute more or I'm going to wreck my own self-confidence.

Another week, another beautiful present on my desk. Can I really accept another of these with nothing to offer in return? I open the card with care, and the message stops me in my tracks.

Friend,
Your faith is beautiful.
—Levi

God? Did I meet the best possible guy at the worst possible time? You wouldn't do that, would you?

CHAPTER TWENTY-ONE

I BRUSH MY TEETH, praying for the courage to go to bed like I need to.

"Girl. IHOP." Sophie eyes my favorite threadbare pajama shorts and T-shirt. "You in?"

I spit and check the time: 9:04 p.m. "It's basically the middle of the night."

She waits for the correct reply.

"Yes. I'm in." Bedtime can wait. I'm relieved to put it off.

I pull on the jean skirt and top I'd worn earlier, slip my hair out of the knot on my head. A real outfit at this time of night is silly, but Levi will probably be there in his effortless sophistication.

"Levi will be there," Sophie sing-songs from the hall.

Bless you, wonderful planner, for hitting it off with Levi's best friend.

"Mamma Mia," Sophie calls. "Can you leave in five?"

"You got it." Mia glides down the hall and unloads her armful of books in their room. She must've been with other friends when she got Sophie's IHOP SOS. Now she's leaning against my doorframe, arms crossed, dark brows raised knowingly. Here comes the teasing. "Skirt on, hair brushed at nine p.m."

Yep. She gives me a hard time, but I know she just wants me to be braver. She has no idea why the Levi thing is so complicated.

"You're the most beautiful 'disinterested party' I've ever seen. Like Mr. Darcy." She pats me on the head.

I keep my mouth shut and wave goodbye to Ayumi. She's probably thrilled to get the room to herself so often.

At the restaurant, Haymitch and I form airplanes out of paper napkins and covertly test their airworthiness. I laugh in delight when mine manages a second in flight, only to bump our pendant light and fall to the table. A trip to IHOP is such a treat compared to our usual lazing around campus.

Levi and Mia discuss sports news, which I neither know nor care about. Sophie and Austin bicker about whether the server said his name was Jake or Blake. It was Blake, but I wouldn't interrupt their flirty sparring.

"Come to Mama." Sophie taps the picture of strawberry cheesecake pancakes.

"Mm. Great choice." I unstick my legs again from the vinyl seat. Pants next time at this place.

"You gonna order tonight?" she asks.

I shake my head.

"I'll share mine. No one needs that many pancakes at this time of day."

We both know Sophie's daily afternoon run leaves her hungry enough to down that whole plate.

"Either way." I cover a yawn. I'm just happy to be with my friends, even if I should be in bed. Maybe I'll have a nightmare-free night and still get some sleep.

"I'm gonna ask him for all the bacon and eggs they have," Austin says.

"Wait, wait," Sophie says around her laugh. "I'm worried what you just heard was, 'Give me a lot of bacon and eggs.'"

Austin's eyes shine. "What I said was, 'Give me all the bacon and eggs you have.' Do you understand?"

I'm not sure if I'm smiling at their chemistry or the Ron Swanson reference. These two confuse me.

A few minutes later, Levi leaves the table and ends up in a conversation with Blake. Mr. Charming can befriend anyone. Mia and Haymitch discuss their next poker tournament. They have several other mutual friends and often join the intense chips-only games.

"Austin," I say. "I hear you're going to coach the G1-ers in the ways of the football."

He reclines, elbows spread, hands behind his head. "You know it. I'm gonna make a champion team out of y'all and revel in the glory."

Everyone laughs. G1 has a terrible intramural record. I'm pretty sure they didn't win one football game last year.

"We have Sophie and Mia this year," I say. "There's actually a chance of that."

Mia swings bent arms in a premature celebratory dance, and Sophie gives me a high five.

"Don't sell yourself short," Austin says to me. "I have you down for kicker."

"How 'bout that." Haymitch chuckles, spinning his baseball cap forward.

Apparently my lack of athleticism is obvious to others as well. Elbow on the table, I place my chin on my hand and send Austin a puzzled look.

Levi returns to the table.

"My running back here wants you on the team." Austin nudges Sophie, who develops a glimmer.

"Come on, Kit," she says. "You can't miss out on the fun."

"Ever play soccer as a kid?" Haymitch asks.

I shake my head. Everyone is staring at me now. "I mean, I

kicked the ball around with my brothers sometimes. I didn't play sports."

"You certainly enjoy watching them live," Sophie says.

I send her a look and avoid Levi's reaction.

"*Pobrecita*," Mia says. "She was too busy reading five books a week and winning the mathletes competition."

I chuckle. She isn't too far off.

Levi's focus beams toward me. "Enlighten us. What was Tiny Kit like?"

I hide my hands beneath my legs. "About the same. I did read a lot. I loved ballet."

That sends half of the table into hysterics.

"You stop in the middle of the path every time you think too hard," Sophie says. "How did you manage ballet?"

"Sounds like how readin' poetry can help a stutter," Haymitch says.

Noah's dad says something like that in in *The Notebook*. I wonder if Haymitch has seen that scene. It's nice of him to stick up for me.

I shrug. "Dancing always cleared my head."

"I can see it," Levi says.

"Totally," Mia says. "I thought she was joking at first, but in a way it fits perfectly."

"When did you quit?" Levi asks.

"Two years ago."

He edges forward like he's going to press further, but luckily he holds back. I don't want to discuss this in front of everyone.

"Ideas on how I can translate that skill to the football field?" Austin asks.

"You'd better keep me at kicker," I say. "I'll see if I can find someone to teach me." I cringe. I walked right into that.

Everyone at the table turns to Levi. Haymitch tips his chair back to arc a napkin ball at him. Mia snorts. Austin raises brows at Levi, who smiles charmingly at me. Sophie hasn't made a teasing remark. She's studying Austin.

Quick, someone else in the spotlight. "Mia, what position are you playing?"

My change of subject is successful, and I can settle back in my seat. Levi sends me a wink, and my heart flutters. Lessons with him would be a blast. Might even be worth the horror of all those eyes on me every week, and that's saying something.

When the food arrives, Blake places a funny face pancake in front of me. I politely remind him that I didn't order anything, and he gives a far-fetched reply. There was an extra and I don't need to pay? I turn to Levi. He knows about that particular child-hood memory. He's half smiling but refuses to meet my gaze, cutting his Belgian waffle and strawberries with refinement. Sweet Levi. When he glances over later, I mouth *Thank you*. He pretends to have no idea what I'm talking about but those playful eyes say otherwise.

CHAPTER TWENTY-TWO

A FEW DAYS LATER, I find Sophie in the suite and tap her foot resting on the coffee table. "Hey, girl. Any change in the Leo situation?"

She lowers her phone with a Tigger-worthy sitting bounce. "Totally. Funny you should ask. He's been acting super weird, but like, in a good way."

This is Levi's work. Who could do better than Mr. Charming himself?

I sit cross-legged on the sofa. "Tell me more!"

"Okay so, we have a lot of our classes in the same building, and I pass him a bunch walking around. There was like a phase one, and for a couple days he would sorta-kinda smile at me, but it was more like this."

I laugh at her exaggerated grimace.

"After that, he waved at me for a few days. I was kinda mad at him still, but the waves were nice, so I started waving back a couple days into phase two."

It's weird that Sophie has been sitting on this information. "Your narration is amazing. Go on."

"Phase three was he would stop and say exactly one sentence. Like, 'It's a beautiful day, isn't it?' and 'Have a good class.' But he never waited long enough for me to say something back. He would just walk away super-fast, like he was nervous."

"Nervous is a great sign."

"Right? It's like he's trying to convince me, and he won't stop long enough to see I'm totally in already." Signature Sophie-clapping.

I mirror her. "I'm so excited!"

She hugs me. "Me too. Thanks for asking."

"What's going to be phase four?" I ask.

"Maybe he'll actually let me answer him!"

We giggle.

"You can witness it tonight, I bet, or sometime this week," she says.

It's Spirit Week at Mayberry, which means there are school-wide traditions for days. Car Cram is tonight. Apparently each floor tries to fit as many of their residents as possible into an old VW Bug. Other days we'll have root beer floats, a homemade-boat derby at the pond, roller skating—G1 and Flooders are dressing up 80s-style this year—and other fun nonsense. We'll be seeing even more of the Flooders this week than usual.

Sophie bursts into song. This time it's "Sunday Best" by Surfaces. I chime in and sing with her.

Before I think hard enough about it, I send off a text to Levi.

> You've achieved hero status.

A quick reply.

I have a bad feeling Hiccup earned that praise instead.

You must have coached him in the ways of charm. Sounds like he's become a Levi apprentice.

My hand flies to my head. I never would have said that in real life.

You think I'm charming?

Ryan Gosling wants his rizz back.

Leslie Knope wishes she could compliment like you.

Levi, you rainbow-infused space unicorn.

Kit, you clever land-mermaid. Your heart is even more perfect than your face.

Try not falling for a guy who misquotes *Parks & Rec* like that.

It's Thursday night, which means I'm at the Flooders game. Levi is all over the field, catching balls and blocking passes, while I sit on the sideline, trying and failing to be as cool as the root beer float I'm finishing off. It's impossible not to watch Dreamy Athlete Levi, but I'm working hard to keep my expression in check, lest the other girls remember to tease me mercilessly. "Kit's drooling again," Mia reported last week. Sophie always sings clever but mortifying songs. Even Ayumi smiles knowingly. I love my friends, but they pull me way out of my comfort zone—not sure I like it. As for the rest of the floor, so much gossip goes around about me. It doesn't help that I offer zero explanation for why I refuse to date the most sought-after bachelor at our little school, but I don't know why my thing with him is so interesting to everyone. There are plenty of other girls with a love interest who are actually doing something about it. I guess Levi and I are a strange pair. The prince and the pauper. The athlete and the nerd. The guy who wouldn't date anybody and the girl who won't date him.

"When that chem test beat ya up and stress ya, but ya see that Levi playin', it remind ya of ya blessings," Sophie raps.

I double over at that one. I love "Church Clap." One of Sophie's best lyric swaps.

The girls giggle as they try to recite the fast-paced verses and clap beneath their knees.

Clouds roll in, and the air crackles with foreboding. I shiver, despite the thick, warm air.

"Mamma Mia!" I call.

Arriving late, she sits with a flourish. I scooch to her, and she wraps an arm around me.

"What's good, my friend?"

"How are you?" I ask at the same time.

"Chillin' like a mango that hasn't fallen."

I spit out a laugh. "What?"

"My cousins taught me that one." She grins. "It's good, right?"

"It's amazing. Are you coming tonight?"

"I'll be there. Sorry it's been a while. I got kinda outta control there for a minute." She lowers her voice. "I met some guys. I kinda got a bad feeling though."

I clench a fold of the blanket beneath me. I know how stories like this end.

"Girl, relax. Nothing happened. I'm just saying I was hanging out with them a bunch and now I'm not."

"Oh." I breathe again. "I'm glad the Spirit guided you."

"Ya know, I hadn't given him credit. Thanks for that."

I hug her again. "So happy you're here. It's never the same without you."

She beams until her brow furrows. "You wanna tell me why you looked like you saw a ghost when I said, 'bad feeling'?"

Face forward, shake my head. Maybe she'll let it lie.

I didn't used to be like this. I used to ask my friends about everything, always wanting advice, someone to lean on.

"Yeah, I figured," Mia replies to my silence. "It doesn't have to be me, but you gotta talk to someone. Start working yourself up to it."

Do I wait for her to taper off with the pushy advice, or do I have the guts to tell her to cut it out? Maybe a subject change?

"*Es necesario.* Kit?"

Saved by the rain. The fat drops fall fast. I've been in East Texas long enough to know this will be a downpour.

"See ya" is all I say to my friends. They know I always bolt back to my room when it rains. Storms are a dangerous catalyst for me now. It's a felt loss. I've always loved the rain. I used to sit on our covered patio with Mom watching hail or lightning during summer storms. Now I just want to be alone, even more so with a chance of thunder.

The remaining girls accommodate the rain, apparently pleased for a diversion from the usual. The prepared ones expand their umbrellas. Sophie waves girls out of her way and yanks my blanket out from under them to hold it overhead. They giggle like kids in a homemade fort. We've seen before how our boys revert to childhood playing on the mushy field after a hard rain. I'm sorry to miss it. I drag myself and my empty cup away, not bothering to cover my head. Levi stretches out an arm and lifts a few fingers in gentlemanly salutation. I raise my hand in a soft wave.

Pleasant drips grow into splatters, until a distant rumble opens a pit in my stomach. I increase my pace. Guys slide down a hill, using Saga trays for sleds, but Mayberry silliness in action can't even make me laugh. I try to remember that it could be worse. It could have been so much worse.

CHAPTER TWENTY-THREE

A FEW DAYS LATER, I'm writing a paper for Bible class, tapping my foot to Forrest Frank, pajama shorts on. I'll never know how people do their work in constricting pants. I study the black and white prints of my family that hang above my bed as I consider what to write about covenants.

Ding. Ooh, a text from Levi is a rarity and always read immediately.

> Hey, friend.

> Can I drive you to the airport next week?

An image pops into my head—against my will, of course—of playing the airport game with Levi. When Mom sees PDA at the airport, she clasps her hands at her chest and lives their bittersweet moments vicariously, as if watching strangers hello and goodbye is better than a movie. She says couples can get away with way more

PDA at the airport, hence the name the airport game. So corny. I forcibly dispose of that daydream and answer the text that started this line of thought.

> Thanks, but my flight leaves from DFW.

Dallas is a two-hour drive away and far cheaper to fly from than the tiny airport nearby. I'm going to take a bus all the way to Dallas to save money—a lot of money—but all the bus stops mean the journey will cost me many hours. On the bright side, I'll probably get my homework done before I even get to the airport.

> I'm flying out too, remember?

> Send the details for both of your flights?

His insistence is sweet. He'd save me several hours, not to mention how much more comfortable his ride would be. Still, the odds of our flights being at the same time are next to none. He must be planning to change his flights to align with mine. And this late? It'll cost him. He's impossible ... and the offer is too good to pass up. But how could I manage this without sitting in his front seat? Sophie. She hasn't bought her flights yet, always so last minute, but I bet she can be convinced to come with us. Pretty sure she can use her mom's credit card for whatever she likes.

> Thank you. So generous of you.

> Can Sophie come too?

Nerves fill my gut. We've never covered the I-don't-ride-in-the-front-seat rule. Then again, he's a smart guy, and I actively avoid riding shotgun every time he drives our group somewhere.

> Of course. Tell her I expect a road trip playlist for the ages.

A hauntingly beautiful adaptation of "Someone Like You" floats in from next door. I can't bear to interrupt, so I wait until she putters out.

"Hey, Adele," I call.

And now Sophie's in my doorway, beaming.

"Can I just say I love living next door to you?"

She laughs.

"Also, Levi offered to drive us to Dallas next week. You still planning to go home?"

"Girl. Yes. Send me your flights, and I'll make sure mine work for your drive."

"One condition. You have to ride shotgun."

She bends toward me. "Have you lost it? You could sit there and stare at his face for two hours. Twice! No way am I going to let you sit in the back and play third wheel."

I know the loss. I have taken a strong liking to that face. "You ride shotgun both ways or you can't come."

She stares at me, incredulous, but doesn't press. "You're insane."

I nod, oddly comforted. She says it like a sad fact, not to taunt or tease. I'm so tired of pretending to be normal, so her directness is a balm, removing the need for my cracking facade.

She waves her hand. "Fine, but you're breaking it to Mr. Dreamboat. He'll think I'm trying to steal him from you or something. Acca-awkward."

I desperately hope she never tries. She's beautiful. And functional.

I pinch the bridge of my nose and consider the real hurdle. How do I explain to Levi why I never sit in a guy's front seat? Everything is so complicated and I'm exhausted. My head closes in on itself just imagining telling him the whole truth. It would be so much worse than with Tess—

I shake my head. No crying right now. Squash it down.

"I'll tell him," I finally concede. "He says he expects a road trip playlist for the ages."

"Ooh, yes. It's gonna be stellar. Just wait."

I'm sure it will be ... if she remembers to book her flights.

She spins away, humming.

I chuckle at her version of "Come Fly with Me." Sophie has a knack for pulling me out of my Eeyore moods. Always by accident, but I'll take it.

CHAPTER TWENTY-FOUR

PLEASE, *no nightmares tonight.*

I brush my teeth again, stalling. Maybe there's mouthwash. I fish under the sink. There. My teeth are spotless now. What's next? Clipping my nails? I close the drawer with a sigh. Enough. Wash my face, go to bed, and deal with it. If the nightmares come, they come. It's nothing I haven't endured before.

I hear Mia stride into the suite as I turn on the faucet. Her determined steps are a dead giveaway.

"*Mira*, we need to talk." From behind, her resolute gaze catches mine in the mirror.

Uhh. I pat my face dry with a towel and twist around. "Sure ... what's up?"

"You've been doing this thing that drives me nuts. I've been thinking, and it's sort of like an inferiority complex? It doesn't make any sense to me because you have a good head on your shoulders." She motions along as if it will help me interpret. "I mean, I know it's not a 'You Don't Know You're Beautiful' kind of problem." She drops her hands. "What's happening to me? Sophie has me talking in song titles. Anyway, you're one of the few girls I know who isn't insecure about how you look or who you are, which is just mature and awesome of you."

Okay, that's really nice, but this is clearly the sandwich method.

"So what's with all the deferring?" She lifts her hands. "You're all 'No, you pick the movie. No, you tell your story. No, you first in line. No, you choose the plan.' You do know nice and kind aren't the same thing, right? You let Sophie walk all over you. You won't take up space. And, obviously, the whole general Levi thing."

Get me the condiments. It's the sandwich method all right. "Whole general Levi thing?" I ask, and immediately regret my active listening.

"That guy is falling for you, and I know you're here for it. You wanted him day one, but you're still holding him off like the Secret Service. If you have a reason, I would get that, more than most, but I have a bad feeling you're deferring again. *Qué te pasa?* Are you assuming he's gonna move on? Are you letting some other girl snatch him up? Luckily, he's picked exactly one to take a liking to, so that doesn't seem like a huge risk, but seriously, Kit, cut it out!"

When will she quit yelling at me? I'm paralyzed with the towel in my hand. I must have stepped back, because my spine is flush against the countertop.

"Am I making you mad? I'm not trying to make you mad. I just want you to think clearly. I want all the good things for you."

What is this? What do I even say?

Be kind to one another, tenderhearted, forgiving one another, even as God in Christ forgave you.

Tenderhearted. Okay.

"Mia, I'm trying to listen. This is a lot."

"Here's the thing—I love you. You're sweeter than southern

sweet tea, and you're not even southern. I just want what's good for you. Do you get me?"

"Uh, thank you?"

"Stop watching your life pass you by and go do something, ok? Kick Levi to the curb or make a move. Just, something."

I'm not going to figure any of this out by standing here staring at her. I need to respond somehow, make this end. Maybe I can just look at it like an essay prompt. Analyze and summarize.

"So ... you want me to be more assertive and take opportunities as they come?"

"There it is!"

Something kind and relevant to wrap it up. "I'll think on that. Thanks for wanting to help me, Mia." I sound like a robot.

"I love you." With a hug, Mia rolls out.

I release my breath. I have no idea what to do with any of that, but at least it's over.

⁕

Mia's words follow me all week. Every time I defer. Every time I'm anxious to soothe someone's frustration. Every time I do whatever it takes to make someone happy—is that niceness rather than kindness? I had never considered before that those are different. My usual reactions are sickeningly sweet to my ears now. I hate every bit of Mia's insight. I have enough to think about without adding this bombshell to my reality. But also, I can't ignore it. I've never thought of myself as someone who grovels and tries so hard. I guess it's just subtle enough that I didn't know it was there. I'm pretty confident and, when I do speak up, I say what I mean, but I don't feel free to take up space, to change people's plans, to cost them too much effort.

I don't want to talk to God about this. Not this too. I still spend time with him in the mornings, still read my Bible, but I pray about anything else.

The night before I fly out for fall break, I perk up at a text from Levi.

Hey, friend. Up for a walk tonight?

Yes, yes! Be cool.

Sure. When?

Now?

"There's something I want to ask you about," he says a few minutes later.

Cue the dread. "Okay?" I squeak.

"Tell me more about ballet?"

My held breath tumbles out. That's an okay topic.

"You lit up when you mentioned it. Why did you quit?" His stride has purpose tonight, like I see him around campus, in contrast with his usual lazy saunter when we walk together. I jog a step to keep up, and he slows to my pace.

"My dance school fell apart after my sophomore year, and it didn't make sense to me at the time to find another one and reacclimate to their approach. And I really hate tryouts. And I knew I wouldn't be dancing after high school. Plus, it's really expensive, and my parents had already been paying for it for years." My arms hang heavy at my sides. Yes, I had reasons, but I regret it.

Levi frowns. "Did you dance at home? After you quit?"

"You keep saying 'quit.' It's not like swimming, where it's a feasible hobby forever. But yes, around the house, just messing around. I find myself dancing whenever I'm on a hardwood floor. But nothing formal. I haven't worn pointe or any dance shoes since." I shrug. "I got a job as a file clerk after that. I took hard classes. Life was busy and eventually I stopped overthinking it."

His fingers fidget and drum. Where are his Tic Tacs? "Would you dance again? If you had a chance?"

The answer surprises me even more than the question. "Definitely. But I don't know how that would ever happen." A loss registers in my gut. "What's going on in that head of yours?" I nearly push his arm but smother the impulse.

"Can you dance barefoot?"

"Technically yes, but I couldn't do pirouettes or *fouettés* well, and they're my favorite part."

He looks to me for explanation.

"Sorry, turns." Why am I apologizing? Mia would hate that. "I could manage in socks or sneakers. Why?"

His gaze dips to my sneakers. "What kind of shoes would you prefer to dance in?"

"Well, now that I'm out of that world, I wouldn't want to destroy my feet again with pointe. I like lyrical shoes. They're like the front half of a ballet slipper." I chew on my lip. "Are you trying to out-Veronica Mars me?"

He tilts his head playfully the direction we're walking. "Come with me—"

"Levi?" I stop to face him as dissonance blares in my head. It's rude to interrupt him. I'm messing up this mission he's on. But I can't manage whatever he has planned. I play with my fingers and try not to think about Mia.

"I don't know what you have in mind," I say, "but I'm not up for dancing right now. I'm sorry. I—I need a bit to wrap my head around it. And besides, I'm completely out of shape."

His look says *Yeah, right.*

"I'd pull something if I just went and tried to dance again." And I couldn't bear to let him watch me all clunky and out of practice. But more than that, wherever we were going was probably going to be enclosed and alone. I don't trust my mind to behave.

I rub my temple. The little lady pulling files in my brain is usually very accurate, but I wish she'd take a break sometimes—I don't need to remember every relevant memory every single time. I certainly don't need Mia's lecture bouncing around my head right now. I hate this. And I hate that I hate it. And I hate that Mia was right about me.

Hands in his pockets, Levi studies me gently.

Mia would have a fit—she'd say I'm missing another opportunity. But the file clerk in my mind keeps flashing memories of every time I've freaked out and humiliated myself in front of Levi. I'm not budging on this.

But Mia might also tell me to stop stressing about turning him down. That he can handle it, that I'm allowed to take up space. Still, my stress isn't going anywhere, and the file clerk flaunts a dozen examples of my overthinking.

Then again, Mia would probably say I shouldn't be trying to please her in this random debate in my head. At that, the clerk throws up her papers in frustration.

"Sorry," I finally say. How many sorrys move me from polite to groveling? "I hate to mess up your plan. You're so sweet to care about this." *Say it's okay.* I stare at his sneakers. *Don't be mad.* Or do. I don't know!

Two knuckles brush my jaw and I jolt backward. My heart hammers and my mind swims in inky black.

Levi flinches. "I'm sorry. I wasn't thinking."

All I can manage is a wan smile as I about-face toward to my building. I've ruined his thoughtful idea and affectionate touch. May as well cut my losses and end the walk too.

He follows along silently.

Remember that scene in *Hitch* where Eva Mendes wakes up on her couch? Hitch is picking up coffee, but she doesn't know and she lectures herself with numbered points into the pillow? As soon as I get to my room, that'll be me.

CHAPTER TWENTY-FIVE

SOPHIE IS as upbeat as her road trip playlist, harmonizing to "Leaving on a Jet Plane." Her song choices are amusingly literal. Meanwhile, I'm deteriorating into Carl from *Up*. What if I tricked Levi? What if he didn't realize I wouldn't sit in the front seat? What if he spent his money and changed his flights and didn't even have the result he aimed for? One of the rare times I stood my ground with Sophie was to insist she sit in the front with him. What is wrong with me?

I wonder if Levi is nervous about going home. Maybe his granny is worse. Maybe he's bracing for a run-in with his dad. And here I've been scheming and moping and self-involved. I want to ask, but he's so private. And Sophie's here. Because of me.

He looks perfectly content up there, tapping a thumb on the steering wheel to the beat. But something sinister whispers that I need to make up for his trouble, to pay him back ... like with

Aiden. I shudder. Shoes off and legs curled up under me, I slump in the seat behind Levi and watch a million trees fly by on I-20.

My grace is sufficient for you,
for my power is made perfect in weakness.

Well, I have plenty of weakness.

Sophie is calling me. I ease my mind back to my surroundings and see Levi checking on me through the rearview mirror, brows furrowed in concern. Sweet Levi. His reflection relaxes and grows tender.

It's even worse with him than with my friends, isn't it? I didn't ask him to wait around for me, but I don't discourage him either. I can't make his kindness or friendship or gifts worth his trouble. I can't make myself worth his trouble.

"It's just her zone-out thing," Sophie says. "Don't worry, she's not mad or anything."

Levi nods knowingly.

CHAPTER TWENTY-SIX

COLORADO SUNSHINE BLAZES through the window as banana bread crumbs fall from my mouth. Perched on my kitchen stool, I stuff the last bite in. Comfort captured in a moment. This dry mountain air on my skin, in my lungs. My toes in fuzzy socks point diagonally from my barstool, switching position absentmindedly in a seated *changement*. I blame Levi. My toes want to point and my legs extend since he asked me about ballet again.

My brothers are at school and have soccer till late tonight. I'll see them Saturday. I consider texting friends who stayed in town or are visiting for break, but brakes squeal in my mind at the thought.

What was that?

I step from the island and try a pirouette. Yep, it's like riding a bike, so to speak. A pirouette is far more natural to me than bike-riding. I try a double. Not great. It'll take some more practice. I use the fireplace across the room to spot and try again. And again. Deep plié. High *passé*. Press my shoulders down. Spot once, twice.

I slide in my fuzzy socks back to my bar stool. Even in my failing, dancing again feels like ... freedom. Freedom from my thoughts, my worries, the past, the future. I wonder if my ballet slippers are still around. Maybe in the basement? But my feet have grown since.

"You have a crazy month at work." My parents are in Dad's office, arguing like Hermione and Ron.

"Right, so it's good timing for you," Dad says.

A pause.

"What am I going to do with you?" Mom says.

"It's settled then." A grin in his voice. "Next Sunday for your day of solitude. Make me a list, and I'll cover your stuff that day."

"Thanks, darling. I'll put in a good word for you when I talk to Jesus."

Dad laughs.

Those two have something special, extraordinary even, something most married people don't seem to have. The spark is still in their eyes, the like with the love, after all this time. They end every day chatting and joking on the front porch or on a walk. They choose each other over all the lesser things, even my brothers and me. Neither of them gets it right all the time—believe me, I'd know—but what they have is exactly what I want some day. My chest tightens. If that's even on the table anymore.

I can't sit still, so I stand and try the turn again.

Mom glides into the kitchen and catches me. "Was that a double?" She rests her hip on the island.

She remembers. I used to practice constantly. I could usually land a triple once upon a time.

"Nearly."

"I love that you're dancing again."

I shrug. "Ready for our walk?"

"Ready."

I pocket my phone by habit but lay it back on the island.

Lately I have a stronger impulse than usual to check for messages, not that Levi sends me any. I had hoped he'd make an exception since we can't talk otherwise. He doesn't even have socials to stalk.

She notices with a Mom-smile and leads the way to the front door.

The crisp October breeze is a pleasure. Eighty degrees instead of a hundred is Texas's idea of fall weather. Here, I wake to frost, and the streets brim with color. The trademark aspen-yellow, bright red, deep purple. A few trees still have their vibrant green leaves. A rainbow of color.

"It's so beautiful, huh?" Mom says. "God timed your trip home perfectly to see this."

"He really did." The trees in the mountains must have already lost most of their leaves by now. I would have missed it all if I'd been a week later. "You're going to the mountains to pray next weekend?"

"You heard about that? That man ..." Mom calls him that when she's feeling particularly affectionate.

I roll my eyes, but a smile tugs at my lips. Cringey as ever, but I wish Levi could meet them. "Anything specific you plan to pray about?"

"My time mostly. I want to be openhanded with it. Things are so different now that you three are growing up." Her elbow nudges mine. "I could get a job, but it doesn't always feel like the best way I can contribute. It'll be so good to have space to listen. I need to know what Jesus wants from me."

Now that I go to a Christian school, I know more than ever to appreciate that Mom never uses churchy language. She just talks about Jesus like the friend he is.

We stroll in comfortable silence down the sidewalk, surrounded by fall's beauty. I wave to Judy across the street as she persuades Stella the basset hound down the sidewalk.

"What are your Mayberry friends doing for fall break?" Typical Mom.

"Nice of you to ease into it. You want to know about Levi?"

Mom purses her lips guiltily.

"He flew to Connecticut to see his granny. She's not doing well."

Her expression softens in compassion as she leads the way across the street.

"He's around a lot, hangs out with that group I've told you about. With Austin and Haymitch." I've told her about my activities during our weekly phone calls, but I avoid mentioning Levi, so this is coming as a confession.

Her face alights with excitement and maybe relief. She silently asks for more information, but I don't offer any.

"I see," she says. From her voice, I know she does.

"Can I ask you something?" I ask.

Her thankful look pangs my conscience.

"I can't stand the thought of seeing any of my friends while I'm home."

That wasn't really a question, but her head bobs. "Incomplete love. Your old friends stuck by you for years but let you down when you blossomed into this beautiful young woman. You are God's incredible creation, Kit, like a sunset or the night sky or wildflowers. Your beauty isn't about you—it's meant to point us to our creator. Anyway, your new friends last year did the same, really, just opposite. They accepted you for how you looked but were too self-consumed to ever care who you are. Incomplete, conditional love messes us up. It's not what God wants for us."

My thickening throat tells me she's probably dead on, as usual.

That's it, isn't it?

"How do your friends at school treat you?" Her voice gentles. "Do they love you unconditionally?"

"Ayumi yes, but she's not around that much. Sophie, I don't know. It's weird between us sometimes." Levi has been a true friend to me, even while I confuse him and reject his advances and refuse to explain my bizarre behavior. Is that unconditional friend-love or is it strategic? "Mia seems to. She word-vomited on me last week, but I think that was her way of taking care of me."

Mom watches.

"She said I make myself small, that I let Sophie walk all over me. But, last year ..." I nearly whisper. "I can't do that again."

Mom side-hugs me as we walk. "You think you make yourself small so your friends don't have a reason to bolt?"

I shrug and nod.

"God will provide, sweetie. You can trust him."

I can trust you. If these friends leave, you'll bring others. You did this year.

I can tell Mom's praying too. It's so good to be home.

I run my fingers along needly leaves as we pass a spruce tree. The pine needles on campus are too high to reach.

I would ask Mom's advice about getting him—both hims—out of my head, but she can't help with that. She wouldn't understand why I want to be freed from my feelings for Levi. She's been with Dad since they were younger than me. And Mom doesn't know anything about memories that haunt, about moving on from someone because it couldn't work. I need so much more help, but she couldn't possibly understand.

***

Cozied into the chair on my front patio, feet crossed on the ottoman, I finally admit it to myself—I've made zero progress since Mia cornered me at the sink last week. My walk with Levi and car ride weirdness prove that I'm still not taking up space, and the few times I speak up are only to avoid some worse fate. Mom helped me see I have reasons, but I wish I could be brave and fierce like Mia. I wish I could just go and do like Sophie. I wrap Mom's chunky white cardigan tighter against the chill of the morning.

I wanted to tackle this personal development thing on my own. I feel like I'm already spending up my prayers on my broken mind and my broken sleep and my confusing relationships with

Levi and Sophie. But spending up my prayers isn't actually a thing. And I can't live like this. I need help.

So ... even this "smaller" problem is too big for me. I can't even discern my own motives half the time, much less change them.

Trust in me with all your heart,
and do not lean on your own understanding.
In all your ways, acknowledge me
and I will make your paths straight.

Whole heart. Not my own understanding. I guess this is how you want it then, huh? You want me to come to you for everything. Well, here's yet another problem. I plop open hands onto my lap. You'd better take it too. I've got a long list I keep sending off to you, but it's not too long for you. It's most definitely too long for me. I'm too overwhelmed to even think about it.

I let the breath out of my cheeks and follow a squirrel's path as it jumps to the blue spruce near me.

So Mia's speech ...

I don't know what to pray, so I grab the journal and green pen I brought out with me. Time to write it out.

> Apparently I needed to hear that I don't take up space, but yuck. I hate seeing this in myself. I thought I was just being polite. Sometimes it is that, right? But you're showing me how I'm trying too hard to be

I click my pen as I think.
I write,

> Lovable. I don't want to be too much trouble. I just want to slide by unnoticed. To avoid losing friend after friend like last year. But I can't afford to be such a follower.

I stare at the curb along my street. I can almost see Aiden's gleaming blue Audi parked there.

Please help me see it right so I don't mess up my life again.
And so I can be a genuinely good friend, not just an overly
agreeable friend. Kind and not just nice.

**See what kind of love I have given to you,
that you should be called my children;
and so you are.**
That verse again. I chew on my lip.

I'm your child. You love me, and that's enough. Make me like
you. Change me so that any deferring I do comes from love
for people and not from protection of myself.

I slump down and lay my head on the top of the chair. I try to
make it stick.
*You love me already, and that's enough. Help me get it through
my head.*

CHAPTER TWENTY-SEVEN

ANOTHER NIGHTMARE, as if to remind me that flying back to Texas is no escape from my own mind. I calm my breathing and squint at the red numbers on my dorm room clock. 3:00 a.m. My fists clench into my blankets. I'll never get back to sleep.

Like so many mornings, my nightmare has me stuck in a loop.

I can't figure out how I let it happen. I sink again into the fogland of memories. I could get out of this one—I'm not yanked down like from a trigger—but I succumb, trying to make sense of it for the millionth time.

Cafeteria, high five, dates, pulling away, talking to Mom, promposal, dress.

I knew. But I didn't know. I saw. But I didn't see.

Why?

The nightmares aren't improving. The questions that nag at me aren't answered. My mind is no less disturbed than months ago. I'm losing hope I'll ever get better. Maybe I'll find time for a nap this afternoon and the world will feel like a better place.

Probably not.

What am I supposed to do?

God brings to mind an old song by John Mark McMillan. *"So Heaven meets Earth like a sloppy wet kiss, and my heart turns violently inside of my chest. I don't have time to maintain these regrets when I think about the way he loves us. Oh, how he loves us."* Tears fill behind my closed eyelids as I whisper-sing it to him.

Okay. I don't get it, but you have a plan.

—ℓℓℓ—

After classes I find a beautiful boxed cupcake on my desk. It must have been hiding in Levi's suitcase. Arms dangling, I plop onto the chair and blink at it. Levi is still sending presents in pursuit of an implausible relationship. I rip open the envelope underneath.

Friend,
You were missed.
—Levi

Friend-appropriate yet affectionate. I shake my head, warmly and wearily. He is impossible. Impossibly stubborn, impossibly sweet.

What do I do?

I rub my burning eyes. After I get my work done, I can take a nap. I crawl onto my bed to get started. Legs splayed wide, I lean on either one as I study. Soon I'll have my splits back.

Ayumi walks in. "Hey, Kit? I feel like I'm supposed to tell you something."

I straighten. "Okay, shoot."

"It's not our job to figure it all out. That's not how the world works. Our job is to lean into God's presence, to love him and obey him. That's it."

Is this the answer to my question?

Distinguishing the difference between caution and paranoia has always been tricky for me. Like when I check class reviews and end up cross-referencing every available course. Or when I set strong passwords and then create codes so complicated that I can't even remember them. Or when I try to learn from my dating mistakes and opt for swearing off boys forever ...

I trace the edge of my book. Ayumi's right. It's not my job to figure it all out, and that's a profound relief.

Lean in and obey. So, more listening to him. More waiting for God's ideas instead of jumping in with my own ways to protect myself. More trusting him on the strategizing front.

"I'll think on that," I say to Ayumi. "Thank you."

Help me wait for your plan. Help me listen. I can't do this on my own.

CHAPTER TWENTY-EIGHT

SOPHIE AND AUSTIN chose a walk for tonight. Energy buzzes around the six of us as we circle the loop on campus. I missed our crew. Plenty of couples are out here holding hands, but our exuberant group is never intimidated by the previously romantic vibe.

Haymitch rests a hand on Sophie's shoulder for help navigating. His baseball cap is turned backward to allow every bit of light down to his eyes. He's been trained to notice every movement and adjust his walk accordingly, but she still calls out warnings for him like "Step down!" and "Rock!" I hate that I've never offered to guide him. I almost did a couple times, but I'm too chicken to breach the touch barrier. My rules are keeping me afloat, even if they are extreme.

I cover an escaping yawn. I didn't get that nap, and I'm floating in a fog of sleep deprivation.

"I know you have your swag on, *Tiguere*, but try to keep up," Mia teases.

Austin glances over his shoulder with a knowing look.

Levi winks at me to explain his speed. Always so charming—he can't help himself.

"I got a nice surprise this morning," I say, more mysterious than I mean.

"Oh, did you?" he says.

Against my better judgment, I run with it. "Yes, gifts keep appearing in my room."

"Mm. Are those ... *welcome* surprises?"

"Oh, very. Well, they're delicious, I mean. Whoever procures—"

Amusement lights up his face at that word.

"—them has an excellent record. I admit, the notes in boy cursive are my favorite part."

His lips press together, but laughter leaks out silently. "Boy cursive?"

Oops. My internal phrase just became external. "Mm-hm."

"I know someone who went to a classical prep school. They only taught him cursive, poor guy. Never learned print. Now he's handicapped. Maybe he's the one"—he almost laughs—"procuring them?"

"Good detective skills, but it's certainly not a handicap," I say.

"No?"

He isn't the least bit insecure—I don't need to say anything else.

"No, it's ever so charming." I suppress the instinct to cover my face. Who am I, Cinderella?

"Lucky guy," he says.

I read about a study that showed tiredness has a similar effect on the frontal lobe as alcohol. They are definitely onto something.

"Have you thought any more about dancing?" he asks.

He's so selfless to remember the things I might be thinking about. I want to be more like that.

"I couldn't stop dancing at home. I kept finding myself stretching, doing piques from room to room. It's your fault," I tease. "You made me realize how much I miss it all."

Earlier today, Mom texted me a picture. As she flipped through old photos in motherly nostalgia, she came across one of my first year of dancing. My tiny arms stretch stiffly into an adorably atrocious arabesque. My chubby three-year-old cheeks are bright with deep dimples, my eyes barely visible because I'm smiling so hard.

Am I brave enough? I inch my phone out of my back pocket, open the picture, and hand it to him. The Levi laugh I expect will be too good to miss.

No laugh. Instead, delight engulfs his face. My heart skips.

"You're so happy," he murmurs.

As I return my phone—and vulnerability—to my pocket, commotion surrounds us. A1 blue and A2 red flit around campus.

"What are they doing?" I ask him.

"Albert Hall Capture the Flag. Flooders play winner next week."

He pushes the sleeves of his Henley to his elbows, uncovering the four-inch tattoo on his forearm I've somehow never asked about. He starts to say something, but I pick up his right arm with both hands to read it upside down. "HSMS." Something's wrong, but I can't put my finger on it. This arm is incredible. Strong and smooth and covered in veins. There's a box of Tic Tacs still—

Ah! I drop it like a hot potato and yank my hands to my chest. What was I thinking?! My knees lock, breath goes jagged. I brace for the worst—for the darkness to pounce, for the memories to claw at me.

But nothing happens. My heart pounds, but I'm still here. Somehow, I'm still here. And Levi stopped with me. Shuffling to catch up to the others, I shake out my hands and then squeeze them together. I peek at Levi's face—pleasure and amusement. He really has no idea what goes on in my head.

"And you shall love the Lord your God with all your heart and with all your soul and with all your mind and with all your strength," he says, pointing at the letters for heart, soul, mind, and strength. Those veins poking up through his skin and wrapping around his forearm—I just felt those with my own fingers. A restless ache washes over me. The way he chose to remember to keep first things first is amazing. He's amazing.

I want to pray, but I don't know what to say. I try to release my anxiety, my wants, my fears to God.

I'm always here.

"I love it," I finally say.

Those eyes. They're tinged gold-green even at dusk.

"Rock!" Sophie calls for Haymitch.

And then I trip over it.

Levi catches me, steady and brief. I want to relish the spreading tingle of his hand on my skin, but it's ruined by the claws of fear that lurch at the corners of my mind. Nauseous and woozy, but I'm not dragged under. Again. Why not? My breath shudders out.

Thank you.

I still don't get it, and I love patterns. That's probably why I've always liked math. While I was home and had some brain space, I sat down and charted my freakouts based on recent memories. Time was on the x-axis, severity of the trigger was y-axis, and severity of the reaction on the z-axis. I even plotted the 3D graph in MATLAB like an ultra-nerd. Blue for sound-based reactions and red for touch-based. I gleaned very little from my well-executed graph, and I couldn't even show anyone. Well, I could have shown Mom, but I didn't.

I proceed with the conversation in rebellion of the darkness still in my mind—and the helplessness to even understand it. "Any plans for another tattoo?"

Levi looks ahead, maybe to check whether anyone else could hear, maybe to consider whether to tell the truth.

Sophie is discussing her parents with Haymitch. At the front, Mia and Austin laugh about some story. Their fast pace separates them from the rest of us occasionally, and then they pause as we catch up.

"Just one." Levi hesitates again. "If I get married someday, I want a tattoo as my ring." His left hand stretches. Then, even quieter, "That isn't permanent enough, but it's the best I can do."

I gulp.

He raises his brows, a smile growing on his lips. I know that look, and he's not wrong.

I clear my throat, force out a "Good idea," and run toward Mia's curls ahead. She throws an arm over my shoulder with a ticked-up eyebrow but no questions. I cling to that simple, solid touch, wrapping my arm around her waist.

Austin slows to trade spots.

Sophie hums the somehow easily recognizable *Fresh Prince of Bel-Air* theme song behind me. She recently found "the *Baby Will Smith Show*," as she calls it, and we've been watching it in our suite sometimes. I shift side to side to Sophie's beat.

"Girl, you are finally lightening up." Mia shakes me. "Let's go!"

I send her a wry grin. Must be the delirium.

"Turn it up, Sophie!" Mia says.

Delighted, Sophie moves Haymitch's hand to Austin's shoulder and skips to the front with us, boys left in a line behind. She starts over and sings with gusto.

I find the courage to rap along with Sophie, even break out in silly hip-hop moves with my girls, all while working hard to ignore the assumption that Levi is watching from behind.

CHAPTER TWENTY-NINE

"SPILL. I'M SO BEHIND." I curl up next to Sophie on the lounge sofa. "We're always with other people, and I still haven't heard about phase four."

Classes are over for the day, and I can usually find her in here during the lull between classes and invitations to hang out. She's stayed hush-hush about the Leo thing, and I've been concerned she'd get the wrong idea over text.

"Phase four was actually talking. Like, an entire conversation before break. It was a big leap."

"And?"

"We talked about his shirt. It said 'Where There's a Will, Hey! There's a Whale.'"

That Sophie-sized grin lifts my shoulders to my ears. I'm thrilled for her.

"It's kind of an inside joke now. Oh, and for phase five I gave him my number."

"Sophs! He was going to get there! In like phase twenty-six!"
We giggle.

"I was ready to skip ahead."

"Did you text over break?"

"Totally. I let him text first usually. Unless I see a funny pun because I have to share those, obvs. He sends lots of whale emojis now. It's hilarious."

"Aww! This is amazing."

"I know, right? I thought you would be the only one to end up galloping off with your guy."

Except ... no galloping here. My memories are still angry protesters, screaming and raising picket signs, but my heart is running off without my consent. I study the pine trees out the window, trying to make sense of my thoughts. "God takes care of everything so much better than we could," I say.

"It's not like he cares about this thing with Leo," Sophie says.

That pulls me back. "Of course he does."

"You bring up God more than anyone else I know."

"Thank you," I say with feeling.

She snorts. "I didn't really mean it like a compliment as much as just a fact, but sure." She leans on her elbow. "Okay, but I do have a question though. Do you ever get like a strong feeling that you should say something?"

"Definitely."

"Is that just like your gut, or do you think it can be God telling you to say it?"

So cool. Give me the words.

"Sometimes I know it's God," I say.

"Because...?"

"It can be hard to tell. I think the key is to get to know him so well from his Word that you know if it's something he would say. Practice helps too. And I think we should always be cautious if we're going to attribute a feeling to him. But absolutely, he gives us words to encourage each other. And sometimes to confront."
Oh. Like Mia a couple weeks ago. And Ayumi.

"Okay well, this isn't really either, but I feel like I'm supposed to tell you that I talk to a counselor sometimes. Like on Zoom, 'cause she lives I don't even know where. She started as a Christian trauma counselor or something but I talk to her 'cause I struggle with depression off and on."

"Oh, Sophie, I had no idea."

"I know. Anywho, I'm doing fine right now. But I said it, so" —she directs her gaze upward—"there ya go!"

Something stirs in me, wants to ask questions, but Sophie is already bouncing off.

You want me to know that Sophie has a counselor?

The mind of a person plans her way, but I direct her steps.

CHAPTER THIRTY

SOPHIE BURROWS into the corner of our lounge chair. We still haven't figured out how to get cozy Flooders-style couches in here since the lounges come pre-furnished in this building.

I might need to escape to my room to focus enough to do my homework. I have to eke out every minute of study time I can, what with Sophie's rigorous social calendar.

Her happy scoff is a dead giveaway that she's texting Austin. How do I bring that up without making her defensive about Leo?

"Austin?" I ask, trying to sound casual.

"Yeah."

So much for that.

"Open Dorms tonight?" she asks.

"If they're up for that."

We just spent our sunny Saturday morning playing frisbee with the crew. In my case, it was far more of an attempt. I play along with what these obnoxiously athletic friends of mine want to do. After, we snuck our lunch out of Saga and hung out on the grass field too, so I doubt the guys will want to hang out again. Levi usually wants to get his floor time in, always intentional about his hours. Plus, those three guys have been up to something—they won't say what, but I'd guess an elaborate prank. I overheard something about Home Depot.

Ding. Oh goodie, it's Levi.

> Hey, friend. Avengers or Avatar?

I carry my things to my room as I reply.

> Avatar

It's so rare to get a text from him, so I drag it on longer. I'm reminded of a Mom-ism. Rather than "I couldn't help it," she says, "I didn't help it."

> Boat or plane?

> Boat

> Hot or cold?

What a thrill that he's playing my little game.

> Cold morning, hot fire.

> Fiction or nonfiction?

> Fiction, unless it's from you.

Ouch.

> Telepathy or teleportation?

> Teleportation

That would certainly simplify things. I could just zoom myself somewhere private when I feel the memories coming back.

Okay, time to work. I set my phone on the dresser, all the way across the room from my bed. Cozy shorts on, I crawl onto my bed, determined to knock out some studying.

But Sophie appears in the doorway. "Movie night on Flooders later. I guess Levi wants to watch *Avatar*."

I grin. Sweet Levi.

Sophie acts like that's the most normal response in the world. "Do we have any snacks around here?"

"Chips in the lounge. Might Leo be there?"

"He'd better be. And I'm actually going to sit on the same couch." She feigns shock.

I roll my shoulders, trying not to be offended. Or unbearably jealous.

"I'm just saying," she mumbles, and pivots away. I've never hinted to Sophie what goes on in my head. Or to Levi. I'm just in my own little world over here, trying to cope with my life. Yes, it's my own fault no one knows, but it's staying this way. I'm not spilling my guts again. Not after last time.

I eye my phone across the room and guiltily retrieve it.

Mountains or beach?

A certain girl from the mountains at my beach.

My heart flutters on overdrive. Levi at the beach. Levi at his beach. I want to know so much more about that, but I've boxed myself in with this little game. Also, Levi with no shirt, swimming in the waves. I have never seen this presumably glorious sight. If the walls of the campus pool could talk, they could give a sneak preview.

Light or dark for a walk?

A certain guy with light hair and a light in his eyes. Any walk with him.

I grimace at my brazenness. Fingers spread across my face as I type a question with the other thumb.

> Think about what's close or far off?

> I think about having you close. Sadly, not so far.

My stomach somersaults, and I toss my phone onto the bed like it's radioactive. How does that tiny rectangle have power over me? Even the screen begs me to be braver, to be more open, to put the truth out there. I wag a finger at it. No more, phone. You're staying over there.

I pull on my favorite secondhand Sevens for movie night and retie my navy wrap sweater. The girl I see in the mirror is steadily changing, different even than last week. Knowing Levi has stirred something deep inside me. A restless contentment. A soothing exhilaration. He's a thrill and a comfort. He makes me feel like it's okay to be me. It might even be okay to look like me. The reflection of my shaking head goes blurry as I yawn.

I didn't sleep much again last night. More nightmares. Staying awake during the movie might be hard, but I'll borrow a blanket and get cozy. Then again, Levi will be there unsettling me in the best way ... one couch over, like always. I haven't touched him since that unwise moment with his tattoo. My skin on his again sounds glorious. I wonder if his palms are calloused from his weight lifting. I wonder if his face feels scratchy at the end of the day. I wonder how warm and settling his hugs would be.

No. I have to stop thinking that way. It's not helping me cope with my reality. It's kindling a desperation to change something, a desire to forget about my constraints and live dangerously. But I need my constraints. They keep the pain at bay. The less memories of that night, the more doable my life is.

CHAPTER THIRTY-ONE

SOPHIE BABBLES as we cross the field. I try to listen. It's the only thing keeping my legs moving. I still get nervous on the way to Flooders. Walking down the hall with Levi is a whole thing. Think *To All the Boys* back pocket spin—without the back pocket part, of course. I can do this. It seems important to Levi for me to join him on his floor sometimes, and I'm not going to pass up more time with him.

We're early this time, so no one is waiting to greet us when we push out of the stairwell onto Flooders. Levi shares a room with Austin near the end of the long hallway, but I've never seen it. We always hang out in the common rooms when we're here. Dare I sneak a peek? Sophie stops in Leo's room, so I officially have an excuse. Maybe eight rooms line each side of the hallway with another stairwell at the other end. I duck when a football soars by, barely missing my head.

"Sorry, Kit!" someone calls. And the football has already vanished.

Two familiar Flooders pause their gaming strategy to part for me. I wave back and wish for the millionth time that I could be invisible again as I trek down this intimidating hallway. Then again, even back to my ordinary self, I couldn't blend in here in Testosterone Land. I'd need Harry Potter's invisibility cloak.

I overhear a conversation in a room I pass. "Guess he's still on the suicide mission. Maybe she'll shut him down in front of everyone."

That jerk had better be talking about someone else.

Finally, the other end of the hall. I peek in a door on the left. A lineman on Levi's football team wordlessly points me to the last room, and I step over with jitters. I hope it's okay that I'm showing up at his personal space unannounced.

Door wide open, Levi is stretched out longways on a couch in the hoodie jacket and running shorts he wore to play Frisbee earlier. His strong legs are showing off, bent and mostly bare. One foot taps in the silence, accommodating his need to fidget without Tic Tacs in his typing hands. He's laser focused and hasn't noticed me. I'm surprised to see his couch is as ancient as the others on the floor.

That hallway left me out of sorts, but the sight of Levi ignites a fire that thoroughly warms me. I don't belong out there, but somehow I know I belong in here.

Seeing him in his room in his comfy clothes feels like a breach of his privacy. It must be better to break his focus than to stand here creepily staring.

I hold onto the door frame and lean in without actually crossing the threshold. "Levi," I whisper.

An instant signature smile. Graceful as always, he swings his legs around, crosses the room, and sets down his laptop on the desk next to me.

With a laugh in his eyes, he whispers to follow suit. "Kit."

"Do you want to finish?" Shy, guilty, or hesitant, I don't even know. "I interrupted."

"A welcome interruption. Let me just save my work." He types a few buttons and closes the laptop. "Want to come in? I'll give you a tour."

I take a single step inside and point to the couch. "That's where you write your code"—and at the desk—"and this is where you write your boy cursive?"

He chuckles and nods.

It's so intimate to be in his room. Austin's side is apparently by the window. Trash that hasn't made it into the can litters the floor. Books and papers conceal the top of the desk. A quilt made of T-shirts is about to fall off the lofted bed over his own old sofa underneath.

Levi's bed is lofted, too, above the couch I found him on, with more organized blankets. His side of the room is neat but lived in and smells pleasant and familiar. I didn't think I'd been close enough to him to know what he smells like, but I've had whiffs of this before. Mint and fresh laundry with a boyish twist. I covertly steal another inhale.

Two giant monitors sit on his desk next to the door. His Rover keys attached to a Flooders-orange AirTag case sit in a wooden bowl at the corner. Very trusting. And so tidy. I wonder if he cleaned his own room before coming here.

Past him, his closet is open and organized. Surprisingly few items hang inside, all of supreme quality, of course, and not a brand logo in sight. Everything is new and curated and, knowing him, sustainably sourced. I've seen him wear almost every piece. It's like he moonlights as a minimalism influencer. Did he run away from home with the shirt on his back and order what he needed when he got here?

Levi scrutinizes his running shorts. I bet he feels the need to change clothes. He never wears athletic wear except for athletic activities. I keep my mouth shut. Standing outside his room while he changed would be awkward. Plus, these shorts are my favorite.

Apparently I'm off the hook because he holds an arm out to the hall. "To the Light Lounge? Dark Lounge is taken tonight."

I bite my lip when he leaves his phone on the desk, remembering the last texts I sent to it.

A searching look appears, like he's trying to read my mind and connect the dots. He leans on his desk and asks just above a whisper, "Are you ready to be honest with me?"

My gaze shoots away from his, then back, then away again. No, I can't tell him what or why. I tried that once, and I know how it would go. I couldn't bear his reaction. The one I got before was already ... But from him? No. Humiliation and horror at the mere prospect. Besides, to what end? It couldn't possibly help, only hurt.

The best I can manage is to hold his gaze and try to communicate without words. It helped once before. I bravely peer into the watchful hazel. I'm closer to him and must have inched forward. Or was that him? I try to explain, to say I'm sorry, to tell him how much I like him, admire him.

He moves his jaw around in his way. "Alright."

With a big breath he leads me into the hall. The Light Lounge is at the opposite end where I came from. Navigating the chaos at Levi's side is different than the last time I was on the floor. Some of the guys give off a weird vibe. Last time Levi was the top dog with obvious respect and rowdy approval, but now his reception is split. Some guys walk by slapping his shoulder with a "What's up, Jeeves," but a couple only give a halfhearted "Hey," and one even sneers at him.

I don't want to be vain, but this feels like my fault. What if they're knocking him down a peg because of my publicly known refusal to date him? Or because he spends so much of his time with our little friend group when he used to spend it all on the floor? I want to make a scene, kiss him so passionately right here in the hallway that their jaws drop to the floor. How I'd relish every second of it, whether anyone noticed or not.

But.

It's always "but" with me now. I squeeze my hands together. I'm not going to squash this down. Just address the reality. The risk—almost promise?—of having a flashback right here in the hallway outweighs the possible reward. Still, maybe a public whisper in his ear could do the trick. I can be brave for him. Drawing so much attention will be nerve wracking, but for him I'll do it.

Nearly to the lounge, I motion to Levi and face him squarely, blocking out the knowledge that we're visible to anyone down the entire hall. He grinds to a halt. I grab the zipper sides of his open jacket. Clothes! How have I never thought of this loophole before? Those green-gold eyes widen, sending a rush through my system. His feet move to point toward me as I pull myself up to my toes—parallel *elevé* ... no idea how I have the brain space to think of ballet at a time like this—and lean close to the side of his head. He's still moving, and my lips brush the bottom of his ear. My body reacts only positively. No fear threatens. Should I do it again? I'm barely tall enough to reach his ear, so I step closer to whisper in it.

I let my lips brush his ear as I speak, sending tingles from my lips to my spine. "You look so good in these shorts." Was that too much? Am I a hypocrite for complimenting how he looks? I'm barely functioning here. My mind heaves and creaks under the weight of my body's closeness to his. I come down from *elevé*. I'm still holding his jacket and never want to let it go. Can I drag him everywhere with me just like this? Especially if he'll make that delicious face as I do it.

His eyes are full of thrill, a tiny smile slowly broadening. The hallway is dead quiet, and I glance over to a dozen staring eyes—the original point of this exercise.

Levi's whisper in my ear jolts me back. "They're thinking I'm the luckiest guy." He slides a small step toward me, all affection and playfulness.

We'll touch if I so much as take a big breath.

I want his breath back in my ear, his cheek next to mine. I

blink too slowly, and I'm sorry to see I dropped his jacket along the way.

He squints, as if to figure me out, and his face falls. "You wanted to help?" he asks, too softly for anyone else to hear.

How did he read my face like that? It's disquieting.

I push hair behind my ear. Before I have a response, he reaches up and tenderly tucks my hair behind the other ear. My lips part in pleasure. I don't instinctively recoil. No fear is lurking. His fingers are soothing, warm, blissful. But why? Maybe because Aiden never touched me like that? I can see in his face when he snaps out of his apparent daze and realizes what he's done.

I beam at him shyly. Oh right, there's a group of dudes watching. I motion to the Light Lounge and he follows along, speechless.

Austin barrels out.

"Samwise?"

"Skipping the movie. Going to the gym." He jogs toward their room.

Did I do the right thing, God? I forgot to ask.

College Kit is surprising me.

CHAPTER THIRTY-TWO

WHEN I OPEN the suite door after classes on Monday, Sophie is standing in our lounge with her hands on her hips.

"Uh-oh," I say. "It's the scheming face."

"Okay, listen. We pull all four mattresses in here and make a sort of trampoline."

My head tilts back as I laugh.

"That's a yes!" Sophie starts pushing the furniture to the edges of the room. "And then we can pile on the blankets and pillows and watch a movie. Or more *Fresh Prince*."

"Ask Mia and Ayumi before you wreck their beds. Maybe we could do a book-turned-movie?" Books-turned-movies are my favorites. Sure, they're never quite right, but I like seeing my old book friends again.

Sophie beelines to her room and pushes her mattress on its side through the hall.

I do the same, except I compulsively fold my blankets first and set them on my desk chair. Ayumi is in here studying at her desk.

"Sophie has a harebrained idea to put our mattresses in the lounge and make a trampoline. You in?"

Ayumi says, "Whenever I'm about to do something, I think, 'Would an idiot do that?' And if they would, I do not do that thing."

My head tips back in laughter for the second time in two minutes. I love these girls.

She purses her lips, pleased I love her Dwight impression. "Sure. You can take it now, or I can bring it when I'm done with this."

An hour later Mia does a running cannon ball into the lounge, surprising squeals out of the rest of us. College life is weird and wonderful.

Things between Sophie and me are so much better. I get to live with sweet, hilarious friends. I've made improvement in my quest to take up more space. Still, I don't get it. Why is God answering all of these minor prayers instead of the emotional handicap I beg daily for healing from? Was the Levi-hallway thing an answer to prayer, or was it just me being reckless?

≈≈≈

I meet up with our crew at MSC for another movie night. Levi, knowing it's a favorite of mine, suggests Live-Action *Aladdin*. Austin and Haymitch tease him for it, but he takes it in stride. Apparently Austin's little sister has already made him watch it more than once.

I love watching my friends watch my favorite movies. Afterward, we move outside to make room for another group and end up laughing and messing around until late. When everyone starts heading off, Levi asks to walk me back. But with MSC only two minutes from Griffin Hall, I veer toward the auditorium instead. He doesn't mention it apart from a flicker in his eyes.

As we walk, a guy I don't know calls out, "Jeeves, my man." A frequent occurrence. Levi seems to know every dude on campus. "How'd you do on that test?" Friend Guy stares at me, apparently amused.

"Hey buddy. Glad it's over." If I know Levi, he aced it and won't dare say as much. He doesn't brag anyway, but he'd die if people knew he ruined the curve. "How'd you fare?" he asks.

"Had a good cry in my room after," Friend Guy says.

"Kit, this is Arjun. Or Jimmy."

"Floor name?" I ask.

"Short for James. James Bond," he says with flair.

Levi chuckles.

"They still won't tell me what it means so I'm going with that."

"Bond for sure," I say. "I'll be sure to spread the word."

"You've got a keeper here," he says to Levi. "Thanks, Kit."

Arjun starts to raise his hand—oh no, not a high five—but Levi holds out a fist bump, suave as ever. What a relief to avoid the awkward hand drop.

"See ya, dude." Levi guides me back to our path to nowhere.

I wave over my shoulder. "Nice to meet you, Arjun."

"Nice to meet you, Kit," he calls with a teasing voice.

"How's your family?" Levi asks. "Excited to visit them at Thanksgiving?"

"Well, no." I pull the sleeves of my oversized sweater over my hands. "I'm not going home. I'm ... nearly out of money."

"Oh." His head jerks back. "Kit, I'll—"

"No, Levi." I so wish I could accept that from him.

"Please? I want to." He playfully tugs on my sleeve. My fingers tingle in false anticipation, and I almost cave.

"Thank you, but we're not ... I can't ... It's your money, not mine."

"I—"

"Have you talked to your family lately?" I interrupt.

His mouth tilts. I took the redirect right out of his playbook. "Somewhat."

"Yeah?"

"I've been trying to call my parents once a week. Everett and I usually text about sports or the news or something." His hands burrow into his pockets. "It's hard to get through a conversation with my father."

The first time Levi ever mentioned his dad, his jaw was clenched tightly. He's still tense talking about him, but noticeably less so.

"It's always 'What connections have you made at that school? What is IHOP? What is your strategy behind that alliance?'"

He's saying it in a funny way, but no laugh comes to me. Not only is his relationship with his dad strained, but Levi's life is foreign now. He seemed like an alien for a reason. How much of an adjustment must this be for him? He probably grew up with a yacht at the dock and tuxes hanging in his closet.

"My mother didn't ... Let's say she had mixed motives for marrying him. They barely speak anymore. He knows why she sticks around and just coexists with her because it's in his best interest."

I want to ask what that means, but I hold my tongue.

"He and I still have a lot of ... a lot to work through, but I hate that for him. At least he won't leave, so there's still hope."

There's still hope. I forget how spoiled I am, how unusual it is for my parents to be so committed for so long. I don't know how to comfort him. I wish I could give him a hug. "I'm really sorry, Levi."

"When you said your parents were gross—or disgusting, right?" He hesitates. "I didn't know a couple could still be like that after twenty years."

"Like Walker Hayes and Laney."

He half laughs. "Stan much?"

"Maybe a little."

"How do they pull it off? Your parents."

I've been watching them my whole life. It's a lot of data to squish into a sentence or two. "For one, they talk about marriage differently than other people do."

"They don't trash talk the other?"

"Just the opposite. But I mean that they say the purpose of marriage is to honor God. That it's to make them better, not to make them happy."

"But they're the happiest couple around? That sounds like Jesus, doesn't it? He's always saying upside down things."

You are, huh?

"And?" he asks. "You said 'for one.'"

"Oh. Well, they talk every night. Not just chat but talk-talk. And they play. Seems like people forget how to play when they grow up."

"Play?"

"Like sneak attacks. And chase. And flirting. Play."

He nods, in his own thoughts, then shifts gears. "Have your brothers been up to more antics?"

"Always. Mav told me today that they stumbled upon a life-sized velociraptor on Facebook Marketplace. He and Grey are going to borrow a buddy's truck to strategically place it outside their friends' bedroom windows. One house each night for as long as they can get away with it."

He bends forward in a hearty laugh. "We need to get them to Flooders."

"Does your floor have something planned? Is that what you've been doing with Austin and Haymitch all covertly?"

"Our big prank is postponed for now. How are your parents?"

"Mm-hm." It's only fair that he can keep a secret. "My phone's been blowing up with the family text chain. My dad somehow just now discovered GIFs. He's quite enamored with the concept." I shake my head. "I miss him. I miss all of them so much. I should call more, but it's weird talking to my brothers and dad on FaceTime. I never had to until this year, and we're still not used to it."

Levi smiles sadly. "Are you sure I—"

"What about your brother? Everett? Is he still in Europe?"

"He's back for now, taking a break before law school next year. We used to be buddies, but"—he shrugs a shoulder—"since I left, we don't have much in common anymore. Oh look, we're here." Like the door has saved him.

I have my card out to badge in, but I pause by the door and twirl it in my hands like Allegra Cole. "Hey, Levi?"

"Hey, friend." Mm, that soft, lazy voice.

"Thanks for sharing with me about your family," I say. "I like it when you tell me things."

"Anything."

On that serious note, I call a "good night" and bolt inside. At least I don't fail to badge in for an eternity, like that one time. When I'm safely out of view, I stop and lean against the wall, pressing my hands onto my face.

What am I doing? Are you shaking your head at me?

CHAPTER THIRTY-THREE

AFTER HIS NEXT GAME, Levi leads me past the pond toward Saga. "So, my family has been on my mind since our last discussion." Is that his formal voice?

"Tell me more." I twist to him playfully.

He softens with affection. "I want to be ... more intentional about being Jesus's love to them. Do you have any advice?"

"Oh. I'm honored."

Is there something you want me to say?

Blessed are the pure in heart, for they will see me.

"This sounds kind of random, but one of the Beatitudes comes to mind. 'Blessed are the pure in heart, for they will see God.'"

He releases the air from his cheeks. "That's helpful. Thank you."

I tap the side of my leg, trying to wait. "Well?" I lift my shoulders and lean toward him, like I'm trying to get away with something.

A smile tugs at his cheek. "I think I'm hearing two things. First, that God wants my whole heart." He gestures to his tattoo. "And second ... I wish they would just be real with me. I'm going to do my best to do that for them."

Yes, God. Open their hearts. Help them be real with each other.

"I'm giving you some excellent practice," I say primly.

He chuckles with me and nudges my arm with his water bottle. "Thank you."

My insides ache with some unknown emotion. I wish yet again that I could hug him.

"The thing is ... my father used to rail on me constantly. He'd sit at his desk and make me stand there while he told me all the ways I was failing him. As if he would seem capable and stable if Everett and I were. I can tell Jesus is changing my heart slowly, helping me let go of the anger, but ..." His water bottle lid is going to break any second. "I'm afraid he thinks I started following Jesus, unenrolled at Yale, left Connecticut because of rebellion or spite. I'm afraid he won't be able to see that I had to figure stuff out, do things differently, because that life can destroy a person. Jesus said it's easier for a camel to go through the eye of a needle than for a rich man to embrace God's way, and I get it now. I want my father to find the hope that I have, the peace. He's so relentlessly paranoid about ... certain things. I just wonder if I can help him at all if he doesn't even understand my reasons."

His honesty is so precious to me. Tenderness swims in my chest along with a thousand indiscernible thoughts. I want to stop and answer the way God wants. I'm not sure I should say anything.

Please give me the right words. Keep me from saying anything that isn't from you.

"If you're afraid you're an obstacle to your dad meeting Jesus, I can really only imagine the opposite. But there's one thing you can do. You can keep praying for him and not stop. Set a reminder in your phone, every day, every few hours even. In my experience, God honors earnest, consistent prayers in faith." Do I still believe that? My gut clenches. "Sometimes I wish prayer were more of a magic trick, but it's never a cop-out. It's the best strategy we have."

A streetlamp's glow betrays Levi's wet eyes. We meander the rest of the way in comfortable, contemplative silence. When we arrive at my building, I whisper good night but stall by the bench, standing closer than friends do. I run my fingers down his open jacket, thumbs brushing the fleece underneath. His intense gaze catches on my mouth and my heart tries to crack my ribs. He snaps away.

Back in my room, my hypocrisy crashes over me. I will never fully reciprocate his vulnerability and openness, lay my own secrets bare. I can't. In yet another way, I'm not earning my keep in our relationship.

What do I do with all of this? What's the difference between necessary boundaries and withholding affection? What's the balance between taking up space and treating him fairly? I know he deserves so much better. I curl my legs up on my bed and rub my face.

I still don't get it. Please help.

In the dark of the early morning, I shuffle to the lounge with a blanket.

A psalm about fear.

I type his prompt into my AI app, which recommends Psalm 56. The more I read, the more I hunch over my phone. It's like it was written for me. There are no people hunting me down like David, not since that night I can't forget, but fear itself hunts me day and night. Two verses jump off the screen. "When I am afraid, I put my trust in you" and "You have kept count of my tossings; put my tears in your bottle. Are they not in your book?"

I slump down to rest my head on the top of the chair cushion. That's a big bottle, a long book. I squeeze my eyes shut.

I'm always here.

Please take this away.

I know you're always here, but I don't want to do this anymore.

I hate it. I'm exhausted. In all the ways. And the nightmares are awful. Please take them away. Take away the terrible memories, the fear of them coming back at any moment.

I beat my head on the cushion, past frustrated and inching toward anger.

It doesn't seem like a yes.

Fine. Then show me what to do next.

CHAPTER THIRTY-FOUR

ON SATURDAY NIGHT I whisper for Levi to walk me back earlier than usual. His eager nod shoots a thrill up my spine.

These late walks back with him are my favorite minutes of the week. I push aside the nagging feeling that I should stop, that I'm stringing him along.

Our steps match pace on the sidewalk. I squeeze my hands and peek over. Learning about his beautiful inside has made his outside even more irresistible. His eyebrows raise a fraction, and his lips twitch. He's getting better at reading me.

I need a subject to distract me from my jitters. "So, Jeeves, tell me—you didn't really have a butler, did you?"

He rolls his eyes. "I did not have a butler."

"Or I guess Wodehouse wrote Jeeves as a valet."

"No valets either. I put my own clothes on."

I tilt my head. "You are kind of like Valet Jeeves—clever and helpful. And you'd never allow Bertie to embarrass himself with a hideous waistcoat."

His cheeks twitch. "I've been told I should read Wodehouse. Have a book here you can lend me?"

"Nope. You definitely should though, and report back?"

"I'll see if I can get it done over Thanksgiving break."

I'm giddy. Book club with Levi. "So your floormates were totally off on your upbringing? Or just teasing you."

"No, they were mocking me for having a household staff, and I did. But I'd rather pretend I'm Ask Jeeves. Like I'm the source of all knowledge." He makes a ridiculous pompous face.

"Yeah, right," I tease.

"Alright, how about the source of all 'useful' knowledge?" he asks.

I raise my brows with humor and challenge.

His eyes laugh in return. He offers me a Tic Tac and shakes one into my hand.

"Do you ever regret your decision to come to random East Texas instead of fancy Yale and all that entails?"

"No. I miss the ocean, and The City sometimes, but the life I left wasn't … satisfying. I couldn't stay in Connecticut around all the same people. My family, my neighbors in Greenwich. They drop cash in frantic search of something better. Cars, parties, jet-setting, girls, whatever it is. It never works. They never feel better for long. I know my parents don't. Only Jesus changes things, changes the heart, satisfies. Still, transitioning has been … a process. I'm not cured of my upbringing because I came here."

You must have brought him a long way to be able to see the world he grew up in so objectively.

Be transformed by the renewal of your mind.

"Sometimes I want to just donate my share of the family fund to charity." He motions with his hand. "Get rid of the responsibility, as you called it. But I have this feeling there's something God has in mind for it." He shrugs. "For now the distributions are paying my tuition. My parents certainly wouldn't."

So many private words he's entrusting to me. And then it hits me. "Wait, just the income from your trust fund's investments covers tuition here every year?"

Levi glances at me, amused. More than that? My stomach turns. My experience with Avery's well-off family has absolutely no relation to that kind of wealth.

"Sorry I asked. And that I started on this subject. I know you don't like talking about this kind of thing."

He taps my arm with his Tic Tac box before depositing it in his pocket. "Don't be. Samwise knows, but he still thinks money makes everything easier. You're the only one who seems to understand."

I blink at him, at a loss.

"You understand that it's not a cure-all," he says. "That it can be a detriment, a danger. You're the only girl I've ever met who counts it all against me."

"Hey ..."

That pulls his gaze.

"You're not your money. You're Levi. It was a mark against dating you, not against you-you."

"Is it still?" So quiet.

I shake my head, but I can't afford to continue this line of thought.

"Discretion about money is still uncomfortable for me," he says, back to normal volume. "At home, people just know how much everyone has. It's no big secret."

"People here would probably get weird and jealous and ... conniving about that kind of thing."

He tips his head.

I hate that he's experienced that already. "I won't break your confidence."

"I know. I trust you, Kit."

He trusts me. "I'm so impressed with you," I blurt. "I've never met someone so unaffected by money. You're swimming in it, but you don't even seem to think about it. It has very little to do with who you are."

With vulnerability in his eyes, he gives a small smile. "I want to accept your compliment, but I'm afraid I can't. I think the mentality is just different, depending on how a person grows up." He gathers his words. "Middle-class families seem to spend a large portion of their lives preparing and maintaining the ability to make enough money. Does that seem right to you?"

School, college, jobs, promotions, saving for retirement. "That does seem like the status quo, although 'enough' varies a lot. Not for you?"

"No. Where I'm from, parents don't expect their children to compete for scholarships or to ladder climb in some career. I grew up assuming money would never be an issue. My parents raised me to focus on status, connections, maintaining the family image —" His jaw clenches.

I wince, imagining little Levi standing in front of that desk.

"That kind of thing. Living differently than that should really be my bar for impressive."

"I know you to be humble and authentic and kind, none of which fits well with what you just described." His spiel only reinforces my opinion of him. He's a wonderful person. He sees his faults. He wants to grow. It's so rare to find someone like that, and I know he's the kind of person I want to be with forever. If I were to chart my Levi crush, it would be an exponential function rather than linear. Every new thing I learn about him, every peek into his beautiful faith, every mark of his kindness and gentleness bumps me higher up the y-axis. Every day my fondness for him grows faster than the day before. Like Aladdin, I hear the genie buzzing in my ear—"Mayday! Mayday!"—but I swat it away. "Nice try negating my compliment though," I tease.

His brow moves up and down, like he doesn't know whether to be honored or concerned. "Thank you." He dips to toss a pinecone at me, and then another, sparking a full-on pinecone war. Gleefully, I pelt him with the pinecones near my feet as I scurry behind Arma Chapel. I gather an armful and spring them on him around the corner.

He laughs my favorite hearty laugh. "Behold the Pinecone Queen."

I curtsy, daring him to show me the formal bow that must be in there somewhere. No luck today.

Levi continues our walk. "I have a confession to make. I watched *Beauty and the Beast*. Austin was on some date, and I hid in my dark room streaming it alone on my couch." He chuckles at himself, and I can't help but join him.

"Why?"

"I was curious about your floor name."

I open my mouth, but no words come out.

He half smiles, sheepish.

"What did you think of the movie? It's good, right?"

"It was certainly informative. I learned that Belle is well read, loyal, intelligent, kind ... What else? Desired, slow to pass judgment, quick to refuse arrogant men." He shoots me a look. "Do you agree with my findings?"

I agree hesitantly.

"It's one of the best floor names I've heard, really. So much complexity is captured. My sole reservation is that Disney Belle is inferior to you in every way."

I nearly fall off the sidewalk into the street. His arm catches me effortlessly and guides me back. My arm tingles in pleasure, but vicious fear claws past the edges of my consciousness, robbing my joy and yanking me to a stop. No, no. Will I be pulled under?

Breathe.

I seem to be safe from a freakout at the moment. My shoulders fall in relief.

Thank you.

What were we talking about? Oh. "They just know I like to read."

He shakes his head in affectionate disagreement. Suddenly his happiness deflates. "Kit. Am I playing Gaston in your story?"

Gaston? As if Levi could ever be so hateful, so ignorant, so despised. I shake my head forcefully, stomach clenching.

"Can I be the Beast?" He steps close, otherwise uncharacteristically still.

I gulp. Is this a DTR or a character analysis? "Levi, you're ... a perfect hybrid, all mixed up and transformed by Jesus-magic. You're strong and impressive like Gaston, but you're vulnerable and want to grow like the Beast. The real Belle couldn't help but ..." I trail off. Saying this is making me face how strongly I feel, what a mess this is, how angry I am that I can't have what I want. I crane my neck away so he won't see the tears welling. There is no happily ever after to this story. I'm just buying time like a coward, a selfish coward. Restraining the tears requires all of my focus.

"Are you alright?" That soft, rumbly voice.

I half laugh that my tear hiding is helping nothing. He's always so attuned to my feelings.

I nod, daring my nose to grow at my lie. With a wobbly voice, I ask, "How many eggs can you eat?"

He bites back a laugh. "You are a constant delight. Thank you. For what you said." He inches a hand toward mine, but I turn to drag myself down the sidewalk. He follows silently along, but I won't face him. I can't handle whatever reaction he's having, no matter what it is.

I should warn him—tell him something, at least—before this gets worse. I owe it to him. My mind is unreliable, hateful enough to make a simple touch agonizing. I care about him too much to lead him on anymore. I muster up the courage to spit out the bottom line, what I haven't told him for months. "I can't make that ending happen. It's impossible."

"Why not? Kit, look at me. Why?"

I wrap my arms around my stomach, unable to bring myself to accommodate the request or the questions. Maybe with more time, I can develop the kind of selfless courage I need to tell him what happened, to tell him how broken I am.

Help me. Fix me. I hate that I'm confusing him. I don't want to hurt him.

When you are afraid, put your trust in me.

But how?

A Tic Tac box snaps shut.

CHAPTER THIRTY-FIVE

TONIGHT. Before I chicken out. After my talk with Levi last night, I know it's past time to tell someone something. It has to be here and now.

Levi and I still go to Praise and Prayer nearly every Sunday, but not together. I've made a habit of praying my way across campus, both there and back. It's sacred time for me—time I have to keep separate from the thoroughly distracting presence of Levi. He took the hint early on and sits far from me each week.

The group that gathers varies, but a core circle of girls is always there—girls I've come to trust. Strangers in a way since they're not in my classes or on my floor, but my anonymity here feels safe. It's probably messed up to lean on people I don't really know more than the ones I do. Add it to my growing list of flaws.

During prayer time, we split into small groups to share requests and pray for one another. God often brings a verse to mind for someone. I always leave feeling lighter, grateful. I need this time.

Tonight, cross-legged in our little corner of the chapel, I'm honest but vague. "Please pray for healing for my"—my voice breaks—"my mind."

I hate this. I hate the questions that might follow, the judgement, the assumptions. This is more than I've told anyone besides Mom and Tess. But I'm trying. It's a step.

Please bless my attempt, God.

The girls squeeze my shoulders, hold my hands, and pray earnestly as tears slip down my face.

One of them shares a verse placed on her heart: "The Lord is good to those whose hope is in him, to the one who seeks him; it is good to wait quietly for the salvation of the Lord."

Hugs follow, and soon I'm the last one in the corner. I rise and cross the chapel. So much is left unanswered, but I release a deep sigh as I push open the creaky door. Sharing something was progress. I did it.

Heal me. I'm desperate. Help me place my hope in you.

Levi

Kit's leaving Praise and Prayer with tears on her cheeks. The back of her gray sweater expands and contracts as she sighs. I know to give her space on Sunday nights, but it takes everything in me to glue myself to this pew. I need to comfort her, to fix it, whatever *it* is. The chapel door clicks shut behind her, one more way she's shutting me out.

I need some quiet before heading back to the floor. Everyone's finished praying, so it should only be a few more minutes before I have this place to myself. I spin my Tic Tac box and slump into the pew.

Finally, I'm alone.

Somewhere along the way, a thrilling chase became a race of desperation. I'm disgusted with myself. Never before have I followed a girl around like a lost puppy. Never before have I been shot down again and again. Never before have I needed to give up an ounce of my pride. I gave that pride to Kit, but I want it back. She lured me in so close with affectionate looks and unbelievable compliments and intimate talks ... and then blew it all up with some vague comment about impossibility.

I can't get comfortable. The air is still and growing colder. The rustle of falling Tic Tacs. The zipper of my leather jacket. The scratchy red pew cushion. And this cavernous room that Kit loves so much.

I should teach myself to forget her, to distract myself with someone else, to show Kit that I heard her "impossible" loud and clear. Ada? Victoria? Chloe? They aren't Kit, but they wouldn't shrink back like I'm poisonous. They wouldn't send mixed messages.

A squeak and scrape cut through my thoughts. Haymitch shoulders his way into the chilly chapel and folds his white cane—he must have walked here alone in the dark. He shuts the door with his heel, casting a long shadow as he moves around the pews, serene as ever. He's praying.

No.

Talking to Haymitch is the last thing I want to do right now. He's wise, profound, has a way of getting to the heart of things. I want none of it. Besides, I don't talk about this. Sure, he's my buddy, but it's like I told Kit—I listen. I don't share.

Did you send him, Jesus?

That's not the gut feeling I wanted.

Alright, fine ...

I pull myself up in the pew and prepare a voice far more congenial than I feel. "Haymitch, how are you, man?"

"Jeeves, buddy. I'm just fine. Can we talk?"

I grunt honestly. My mother would be appalled.

"If you're up for it, I think you'd better." Haymitch takes a seat in no hurry. "Kit's messin' ya up, huh? Been there, man."

Oh good, we can talk about him. "Tell me. The girl back home?"

The faint grimace on his face tells me there's a sad story there. "Another time, my friend. You have enough to think about at the moment."

I'm curious to get to the bottom of that and surprised I haven't heard more about it, but he's probably right. I lean on the pew, stretching my back.

"Wanna talk in my room?"

"No, thanks."

He knows I don't want an audience. "So, why you all bent outta shape?"

My mouth opens, but I close it back.

"We've been friends a long time now, Jeeves, and I'm better for it. You're a next-level kinda dude. Smart as all get out and fun to be around. But more than that, I always know I can count on you, that you'll have my back."

That's generous of him. Where is this going?

"It's time for me to do that for you. It's time to say it like it is, my friend."

CHAPTER THIRTY-SIX

Levi

"I'MA GO OUT on a limb and say this is a 'Kit's into you, but' situation," Haymitch says.

"Well, yes. What does it matter if she's into me if she won't—" I stop.

"Won't what? Kiss you?"

I run a hand through my hair. Do I have the guts?

If this is your idea, help me be honest.

"She won't do that either, not even close, but no, she won't give me a chance."

"What would a chance look like?"

"Honesty, for one. She has secrets she won't share—important secrets. I'm pretty sure they're the reason we can't progress."

"You seem to be progressin' just fine in the googly eyes and get-to-know-you departments." He eyes me. "You're 'bout as guarded as they come, Jeeves. Sure ya ain't callin' the kettle black?"

I edge forward. "That's the thing. I tell her anything she wants to know. That's not ... something I do. Like you said. But she won't do the same for me." I try to challenge lightly. "You hang out with her. There's a lot there."

"Fair enough."

"She won't go on a real date, won't so much as shake my hand, but she'll roam around campus with me all night with this look in her eyes. It's confusing, man. And then yesterday she told me that a future with me is impossible. Without a word of explanation." I shake my head. "No one has ever put me through any of this nonsense." I want to pull all of these words out of the air and hide them away again. I don't tell Austin half this much.

"Yeah, that ain't normal, Jeeves. Most e'rybody else has been rejected over and over by now. Rejection with lots of words, not enough words. Pretty sure it all kinda sucks equally, dude. You gotta be the only guy in the nearest three counties who's never been humiliated by a girl."

It cut deep that Genevieve was only with me for my family's influence and connections, but it wasn't humiliating. People were impressed that she was all over me, and then they said I was crazy for dumping her when her true colors showed. As if I'd stay with a trophy-wife type after growing up in my family.

Haymitch pulls me out of my reverie. "You think you met your match?"

I hesitate.

Fine, honesty.

As Kit said, she's been giving me a lot of practice.

"She's more than that, in whichever way you mean."

Haymitch's head bobs slowly, and the melancholy remains. I'm itching to drop this subject for that one, but he shut it down for today.

"How 'bout that. So keep fightin' for her. What d'ya have to lose?"

"Well, my pride—"

Haymitch makes an "ehhh" sound like the horn in a basketball game. "What else ya got?"

I'm trying. Help me.

"The guys on the floor are—" How to phrase it?

"They ain't followin' you around like ducklin's with their mother?"

I roll my shoulders. He's right, but I'd never cop to that analogy.

"Ehhh. Your confidence is dwindlin' big time, and they're pickin' up on it. Is that all from friends-with-flirtin'-but-not-benefits, or is there more?"

I smirk at that description. "Maybe there is." I sit up again, thinking it through. "Like I said, Kit and I really talk. She has a way of getting me to tell the truth, so she knows more about me than anyone ever has. And she's making—accidentally, usually—she's making me see my flaws in a big way."

Haymitch bends forward. "She really is good for you. Mind tellin' me what you mean by that?"

Where to begin? Since gaining my footing freshman year, I thought I didn't care about my reputation. Apparently that was a luxury of being on top. I used to be proud that I had given up my family's status and the ease it had always brought me. I thought I'd started from scratch, but no—I was trained up for social success and leadership since infancy. I'm well liked, well respected —or was—*because* of how I was raised, not despite it.

Kit has been shining light on all of my happy delusions. She told me I was humble and genuine. What a joke. She's accidentally wrecking everything I've built, starting with my false self-confidence.

I stare at my hands. "Talking with Kit has shown me I'm not the guy I thought I was. I'm not the guy I want to be. But that guy is so different that I'm not even sure how to get there."

"Okay. Keep in mind that right there is life with God. He's usin' Kit, but don't be tempted to treat her like the Holy Spirit. Go straight to the source."

A good reminder.

He's praying again. It's settling to know that he's following orders and not making this up himself.

Thank you for him. Give him words I can hear. I don't want to miss what you're saying.

"What's buggin' you the most on the floor?"

"The Kit comments, the teasing. It's not friendly anymore. Some of the guys … It's like they're making themselves feel better. Or is it still about the prank?"

In particular Mateo, or Gru as we call him, is still resentful that I've delayed our entire floor's prank for a girl. I can't blame the ones who are frustrated—I'd be annoyed too—but Mateo has taken it too far. I talked to the guys about this before I did it. They can trust me to make it up to them.

Haymitch tilts his head like he's keeping something to himself. "The guys know you'll make the prank happen next semester. Kit bought you some time with the suggestive whisper, huh?"

"She did. And that's one of the worst parts of this thing with her."

"How's that?"

I squirm on the pew. "I know we're buddies, but I can trust you, right? I don't like talking about … feelings."

"That for one is no big secret, my friend. Yes, you can trust me."

Okay, here goes.

"She's never done anything like that before. Getting so close to me, touching my clothes, making that face." Her lips on my ear. I suppress a shiver of pleasure. "Our texting had gotten flirty that day, but …" How to put it? "It wasn't when we were alone in my room—she stopped in the middle of the hallway. She hates attention. I'm pretty sure she did it to help me and not, you know, because she wanted to."

He grimaces. "Dude, yeah. That's the one time you want a girl to be selfish."

Interesting way to put it, but he gets it. "And worse, she felt the need to help because she was intuitive enough to see the weirdness on the floor. I didn't need her to know about that."

"The more she knows about you, the more she likes you, cares about you. That's progressin'. When she sees some'n she wouldn't pick, she'll have to decide if she can live with it. But it sounds like she don't hold this against you at all, that she likes you so much that she wanted to set the record straight. In that way, it's hard to beat."

She likes me so much that she wanted to set the record straight? Could that be true?

"You can't hide all the ugly and expect a good relationship."

I give him a look.

"I know, I know, you and Kit is a whole thing right now, but that's temporary."

Is it? I circle back to my earlier thoughts. "I don't know if I'm up for this, Haymitch."

"Count the cost. Bail now if ya ain't down for the brutal part. Reminds me of what Jesus said about buildin' a tower and all that."

Count the cost. I don't want to sacrifice my reputation, my place on the floor, my pride … not when there's less than no guarantee.

"The hard part keeps on, ya know. Say you marry her? Lots more o' that to come."

"I'm just … I don't have to put up with all of this."

"'Cause Kit's not your only option?"

I tip my head in acknowledgment.

"Victoria and whoever else?"

I tip my head again.

"You'd never so much as taken a girl to coffee since you showed up here. The reasons you had still apply, am I right?"

A sigh escapes without my permission, giving me away. He's right. I've continually thought Kit's the only girl I can trust completely, the only one worth the risk. But I'm not thinking of getting serious with those other girls. Nothing close.

"It's still an option, dude. You can go nuts and date all the girls. You'll break a lot o' hearts and have to live with that, might even learn to hate yourself for it, but it is an option. Those other girls may be easy—in all the ways, even, whew—"

I cringe. He does not mean that as a good thing.

"But they won't be like the one you picked outta the crowd, and you might just lose your chance at what you really want."

His words linger in the air, and I lean forward to rest my arms on my knees. I could never lead Kit to believe I've moved on because of the physical stuff. She's worth so much more than that. And, fine, a fling is a bad idea. But do I really go on like nothing has changed? I could pull back and give her a taste of her own medicine? Couldn't hurt my chances. There was no wiggle room in her "impossible."

No.

I might give up on Kit, but I won't hurt her.

I've tried everything I can think of. I can't convince her to give me a real chance. What do I do?

My head rolls back. "It's not my job to convince her, is it? If this is what God has for me, he'll do that part."

The floor stuff sucks too though. I hate it.

"My reputation isn't my job either. It's time to let it go, to be tenacious. That's who I want to be."

Haymitch relaxes against the pew like his work is done. "You got a lot o' guts, dude, uprootin' your life, startin' fresh. Speakin' o' brutal, 'member your first couple months at school when Storm and those guys put you on blast? They advertised the life you ran away from on the back o' your shirt, but you stuck with it. And you've been tenacious, as you say, this year too, givin' Kit three long months to mull it over. I know that feels like a real long time around here. Prolly felt like three years. So talk to Jesus. Find out if you're s'posed to use that savage will o' yours to keep waitin' this girl out."

Savage will. I crack a smile. "Thanks, man. I've been asking. I don't always know what he's trying to say."

"Same here. We get it eventually, I think, if we keep listenin'. I was just readin' in Jeremiah. He asked God some'n and it took ten days to hear his answer. Kinda shook me. Jeremiah was doin' his God-given job to listen and it still took forever. It ain't always a quick thing."

You want us to keep pressing in, keep listening. Sounds like you.

"There's some'n else," he says.

"Gru and them. Do I let them rip on me or push back?"

"I dunno, man. I think that's a Holy Spirit call."

Sounds right.

You want me to trust you. With Kit, my reputation, with every-thing. Heart, soul, mind, strength.

Alright, let's do this.

I clap my hands together. "Thanks, Haymitch. I did not want to have this talk, but God sent you to torture it out of me. I appreciate it."

He laughs. "You really are a next-level dude. I'm so lucky to know you." He slaps my arm and stands. "I'll take it all to the grave. Speakin' o' secrets, I take it you haven't shown her yet?"

"Not yet. I don't want that to be the reason she changes her mind." Then I'd always wonder if I was enough. No. This apple is falling far from the tree if it kills me. Still, I want every good thing for Kit, even if she rejects me, trashes my heart. I shake the thought away. No use imagining the worst. I'm in this.

"I get it. You gonna give it to her either way?"

"Absolutely." I'm glad he asked—I don't want him thinking his help was for nothing. "Where to now? I'll take you."

His cane is already unfolded. "Not this time. Thanks, buddy."

Thanks for dragging me along to what I need. You take good care of me.

I step out of the chapel into the cold air. It's stark black out here.

You got me through this. Tomorrow too, right?

CHAPTER THIRTY-SEVEN

Levi

BACK ON THE FLOOR, my resolve is tested immediately. Mateo, Ethan, and Noah are in the hallway.

"Jeeves," Mateo calls out, "when are you gonna let it rest with your embarrassing stalker project?"

My jaw snaps shut.

Can I say something?

I stare him down and walk past them.

"It's pathetic."

"Knock it off, Gru," I try.

Make me like you, Jesus. I don't want to put up with this punk, but it's your call.

"Just saying. You're such a pansy now, groveling over a tease."

I backtrack to Mateo and get in his face. My fists are clenched, and I hope he sees them. I'm ready to push him, even fight him, if he says something else about her. "You will not speak about Kit like that."

Mateo flinches, then forces a shaky laugh. "Fine, whatever, man. Relax."

I turn and go, endeavoring to keep my fists to myself. I'm so fed up with all the grief I'm getting, but I can be tenacious.

My room is empty. Austin must still be out with some girl. A new one every week—it's starting to worry me. I should convince him to open up, but who am I to pry? Kit says I'm cagey, like her.

I have the sudden urge to grab a book I read last summer, *Love Does* by Bob Goff. I thumb through the pages till I land on a portion I'd highlighted.

"But I've always wondered if, when we want to do something that we know is right and good, God places that desire deep in our hearts because He wants it for us and it honors Him. Maybe there are times when we think a door has been closed and, instead of misinterpreting the circumstances, God wants us to kick it down. Or perhaps just sit outside of it long enough until somebody tells us we can come in."

Yes. That's it. This is for me—I just know it.

Alright, I'll sit here outside the door. Even if it's death by a thousand cuts.

My girls and I settle in before chapel. Sophie's evocative rendition of "Perfectly Loved" fades out when a pack of late Flooders swagger up the aisle in search of seats. Their usual spot must be full.

Leo waves enthusiastically, toothy grin widening. He's getting more comfortable with Sophie. Austin sends us a dude head-tilt. When Levi spots me, he graces me with the most elegant of nods.

He seems off, but that makes sense. The Belle conversation was the last time we spoke alone. I tuck my hands under my legs and hold his gaze. Something in me begs to send my cowardice packing. I'm sick of overthinking. I hate pushing him away.

I draw in a calming breath—time to focus on Sophie. "Leo is so into you, Sophs."

"I'm just glad he isn't all weird anymore."

Sophie's thing with him is out in the open now, so I lean around Mia and continue. "How's it going with you two?"

Ayumi squirms next to me.

"I mean, good-ish." She shrugs a shoulder. "The good part is, he just, like, says what he's thinking. It's super refreshing. He said he just liked me too much and that's why he couldn't talk to me. It's cute, right? I hate the guessing games."

The guessing games. I know too much about sabotaging a relationship with those. I want to know more about the "ish" part, but chapel is about to start. Not the time.

"That's awesome to hear, Sophs." Mia side-hugs her. "Except now two of you are all gushy and boy crazy." She points a finger down her throat. "How about that nod, Kit? King Charles couldn't be more formal than that guy. Your little alien."

My grin drops. He isn't my alien to claim. He can't be. Unless something changes. Unless I change something.

Make me brave? Can I ask that?

⸻

Austin plunks down next to me in Calc III—it's not a test day. He never sits next to me during a test because I "write too fast." Whatever that means.

"Morning, Kit," he says, giving me another unreadable look. I wish Sophie were here to translate.

"Good morning." I'm about to say more when a girl from class walks over. Instead, I pull out my phone. He'll be busy until class starts.

"Austin?" she says.

"Yo."

"Do you ... have a pencil I can borrow?" A sophomore in an engineering math course, but she doesn't bring writing utensils to class? Doubtful.

Twelve unread messages this early in the morning. I'd bet my graphing calculator it's our family text chain. Mom's always been big on breakfast together before school. Even a thousand miles away, they sometimes text me while they eat, like I'm still part of the conversation. I just hope I haven't missed my chance to join in this time.

MAV

> Kit's turn. CHOOSE YOUR OWN ADVENTURE. You see two staircases. One rises into the sky. One descends into the ground. Which do you choose?

GREY

> Too easy. She's never gonna pick the path into the ground. Remember when she used to sneak into our room at night because she was scared of the dark?

MOM

> She did have that archaeology phase in fourth grade.

GREY

> So now it's a dinosaur dig site she could walk down into?

DAD

> *Bones and Booth GIF*

> *Stairway to Heaven GIF*

MAV

> She's not a big fan of heights either. That's why this is an ADVENTURE.

GREY

She's taking forever. Don't college students
know they can text in class too?

MOM

Ahem.

GREY

I wouldn't. No way. I have too much to learn.

MAV

It's 7:30 there. I can't imagine college students
signing up for a class that early in the
morning.

DAD

Jeopardy GIF

It's not the same without the music.

MOM

Love you, Kit girl. Good morning from your
favorite family!

Good morning! Stairs to the sky. The big blue
Colorado sky. You guys are nuts. I love you all.

GREY

Macadamia?

Almonds?

Pistachios?

Cashews????

A laugh sneaks out of my mouth. Mav is allergic to cashews
and calls them "poison."

Pencilless Girl looks between Austin and me. *Don't mind me.
I'm absolutely no hindrance to your Austin-date goals.*

MAV

Hey I'm the one asking the questions here.

Except Grey is texting this for me while I drive.
So that's confusing.

And we're def macadamia nuts. To call us
cashews would be the greatest insult.

Almonds. Still palatable in large quantities.

MAV

I think that's a compliment.

You get to the top of the staircase and see a
hot air balloon and a rocket ship. Also a ninja
starts up the stairs after you. What do you do?

A staircase doesn't seem like a safe place for
a rocket to take flight. I'll step into the hot air
balloon. And I invite the ninja to join me for a
pleasant journey.

GREY

You achieved the impossible. Mav is
speechless.

Picture of flummoxed Mav at the wheel

He says he needs to provide multiple choice
next time so you don't go rogue with the
kindness.

DAD

That's my girl. Bravely inviting ninjas to hang
with no fear. Sounds like Jesus.

Jesus GIF

MOM

So proud. See, Kit? You're the bravest of all
of us.

That afternoon I spot Levi headed to his car—Grey would correct me that an SUV isn't a car but a vehicle—and I wave as I pass by. I just finished dropping off a research book for my Bible paper at the library. I don't usually see him at this time.

With a cajoling tilt of the head and a sad smile, he calls, "Can I tempt you away from the studious afternoon ahead?" His pace continues, like he has no hope I'll agree.

But something in me clicks into place—or maybe out of place. I dash toward his parking spot, ignoring the screams of my better judgment. I have to get in the car before I change my mind. This is my chance to be who I want to be—to be Brave Kit. I'm doing it.

CHAPTER THIRTY-EIGHT

I IRREVERENTLY REVEL in the shock on his face as he opens the passenger door and I bound in. This is happening. Bewildered, he makes his way around to the driver seat and eyes me as he presses the button to start the car.

Guess that was a yes to the brave prayer? No idea what I'm doing. You're right here with me, right?

I'm still thrown off by the extravagance of a Range Rover. I ride in it whenever our group goes off campus, but I've certainly never been in the front—my rules don't allow this under any circumstances. The navigation system is huge and flashy, and opulent wood accents and leather line every surface. I turn to him, remembering that time in his room two weeks ago. I don't belong in this car, but somehow I know I belong here with him.

"I was going to trade it in for something more earth-friendly and ... economical," he says, "but it's one of the only things I still have from home."

Inside, he's just a kid far from home like the rest of us. This ostentatious tank makes so much more sense now.

"I get that."

His shoulders relax. What an honor that he cares what I think.

I kick off my flats—his seats are spotless, and I won't be the one to dirty them—tuck my left leg beneath me, and angle toward him. Today I'm adventurous. Free. I may as well be in a convertible with the wind in my hair. "Where are we going?" I ask.

"I have a treat to ... procure," he says, struggling to keep a straight face. "Just north of the center."

Still buying me gifts after our last conversation? I push the thought away. No overthinking. "How'd you get into swimming?" I ask, pointing at the indoor lap pool as we leave campus.

"I tried swim team in high school and loved it, trained hard wanting to make the Yale team. Now I'm hooked."

"You made the team, didn't you?"

He smirks and shrugs. "Yes. Not that it mattered."

"Is there anything you can't achieve?" I tease.

He shoots me a look.

I put my hair behind my shoulders and pretend not to notice. "Do you miss the competition side? Of swimming?"

"I do, but intramurals are fun. And swimming is still my favorite stress reliever. The rhythm and the sounds and the work." He navigates north through Pinecrest, a city made up of an affluent north side and an underprivileged south side. The buildings grow starkly more suburban as we drive.

"You're at the pool every morning?" I ask.

"I swim three times a week, but I'm there every day, even on weightlifting days. The pool is reliably empty if I show up early enough, so I bring my Bible and journal and sit on the plastic chairs." He half laughs. "The things I have to do for some time to myself."

"How early do you have to get there to have it to yourself?"

"Six thirty."

My lips part. So much discipline. For exercise, I'd be

impressed. For time alone with Jesus? I have goosebumps. "You'd better keep walking me back early so you can get enough sleep," I say coyly.

His lips quirk. "I'd better. Are you protecting a morning routine with your early bedtime? Or just staying one step ahead of the rest of us?"

"That's funny coming from my favorite over-achiever," I tease. "I just wake up early without meaning to, way before the others, so I have the lounge to myself for a while. We have a pretty view of the pine trees and sunrise, and I read my Bible in there with my coffee."

"Sounds perfect—except for the waking up part. You can't sleep in?"

I try not to grimace. Can't go there. "Well, no, but—"

Just then, someone cuts him off, and we jerk forward in our seats.

A growl escapes his throat, but then he pulls a hand across the back of his neck, relaxing again. He's praying? I like him more with every minute.

"You okay?" I ask.

"Yeah."

I try to lighten the tension in the car. "You mentioned you bring a journal? To the pool?"

"Yes, I like praying by writing," he says. "It helps me crystallize my thoughts. Plus, I can check back and see answered prayers."

"I love that. When did you meet him? Jesus, I mean."

His eyes smile like my badgering is endearing, but something else lingers there. Weariness.

"Well, Veronica," he jokes, "It was my senior year of high school. I ... started looking for answers. Life didn't make any sense. I had a friend who seemed like the only one who wasn't miserable, and I asked him what his deal was. I wasn't buying it at first, but the answers are all there if you look into it." He pats the phone in his pocket. "Really, believing in God started as just the most reasonable answer, and now I know Jesus as a person."

The grin plastered on my face is going nowhere. I'm Buddy the Elf today. My favorite person is telling me all the things.

He turns to me at a stoplight, and searching eyes tour my face. "I love seeing you like this. You look ... free."

My mouth opens, but no words.

"Can I hear your story?" he asks.

"Oh, my story? I don't have that dramatic moment. The 'I was one way, and now I'm completely different, and the thing that happened in between was him.'"

"From *The Chosen*, right?"

"Yeah. I mean, I hope I'm different, but I grew up with Jesus, so it's hard to know which part is Jesus changing my heart and which part is just growing up."

"I've seen a lot of adults who act like toddlers. You can feel pretty confident that all the goodness in there is Jesus's doing." He motions to me. "I interrupted. Please, continue."

"Well, my parents are 100 percent Team Jesus—"

He chuckles.

"—and they raised me to know him. I knew Jesus loved me before I could even talk."

"What a gift ... Tell me more?"

"I don't know. I never know how to tell my testimony. To tell what he did in my life would be to tell you everything that ever happened to me. That would be sort of wordy."

"What's he doing right now?" His expression turns resigned, like when he invited me to join him today. Like he doesn't expect the whole truth.

What am I willing to share to keep him close? I won't tell the complete truth, not even in my moment of freedom, but there is something I can open up about.

"He's been helping me see that he loves me and that's enough." I tug a knee to my chest. "I tend to want to prove to people that they made a good choice keeping me around. It kills me when I can't." I'm telling him too much about my relationship with him by extension, but I'm Brave Kit. Braver than I've been.

He leans on an armrest as he glances over, caring and not judging. Like always.

I reach across the center console to play with the edge of his leather jacket. Buttery soft, so close to his hand. His pinkie twitches.

"I even feel that way about school," I admit.

"Because of your full scholarship?"

I snap up. "How did you know? I don't … tell people that."

"I noticed you at the scholarship competition."

A year ago? My hand falls from his jacket. Is that what this is? Just another guy seeing something he wants?

"I saw what you were like and … I may have formed a little crush. I asked my buddy on the student panel if you won."

I stare as doubts claw at me, but his eyes soften, swooping around my face with affection. Aiden never once looked at me like that.

"Don't worry," he says, "your secret is safe with me."

I shake the doubts from my head. He's earned my trust—with weeks of gentle patience, accepting no after no with kindness and understanding. Can this be real? He noticed me a year ago. He remembered me and wanted to know me. Enough to break down his own walls for the privilege.

"Imagine when you showed up on campus again and wouldn't even take a pen I picked up from the floor," he jokes.

I belly laugh at that memory in a new light, and my remaining tension slips away.

He smirks. Like Dad when he makes Mom laugh.

"Winning that scholarship? It's very impressive." His charming smile—the one that always gets me—spreads across his face again. I wish I could kiss it.

I bubble over. "Not as impressive as leaving everything you know to find something harder but better. You're amazing."

Bewilderment paints his face. "Thanks, Kit."

His gaze keeps darting back from the road.

My hands ache to reach for him, so I sit on them and turn to the window. I can't believe this is real—this drive, this guy, this ... us. I just want more. More details, more smiles, more time. I tuck my hands further beneath me as my nerves tingle with thrill and anticipation and ... hope.

"Hey, Levi?"

"Hey, Kit."

"Can I watch you swim sometime?"

Surprise lights up his face, and a crooked grin grows.

"You look proud," I tease. "You know I'll be impressed, don't you?"

A shocked laugh bursts out of him. "What's gotten into you?"

"I don't know. Stop changing the subject," I joke.

He eyes me. "Hey, Kit?"

"Yes, Levi?"

"Can I watch you dance sometime?"

Oh ... "It's been forever since I've really danced." I mean, almost daily ballet warm-ups lately. Stretching, plus the work on my rear *attitude* when Ayumi isn't in the room. But he knows none of that. Besides, with no hard flooring in the suite, I haven't done turns or leaps since fall break.

"You don't have to show me," he says. "But don't act like you forgot. I know it's still in there."

My heart gallops. "There's not really a place," I finally say. I'm not going to dance in the gym as basketballs bounce past.

"I have a spot." He drapes an arm over the steering wheel. "You can watch me swim if I can watch you dance."

I break into a grin. "Okay."

Eye crinkles, anticipation, affection. It's all there, and it's glorious.

I sink into my seat, soaking in this afternoon, treasuring it. I should have done this months ago. After this, I can never go back to Old Kit.

I won't.

CHAPTER THIRTY-NINE

LEVI PARALLEL PARKS in front of one of the historic brick homes that have been turned into businesses. The Thanksgiving-themed wreath sways on the door as he opens it for me. A bell dings, and a waft of lavender and sugar greets us.

An elderly woman with a gray bun makes a dainty beeline for us with a joy that radiates from her face. She's even shorter than me. "Levi!" she calls, with a Texan lilt. "And is this—"

He winces and she stops.

I almost laugh at his expression.

"So nice to see you again, Miss Evelyn. This is my *friend* Kit."

"It's lovely to meet you, dear." She pats my hand and leads us to a display case full of mouthwatering treats.

"Do you make all of these?" I ask, marveling.

"Sure do, for almost fifty years."

"I think I've tried some of them already. Safe to say you have a gift."

She and Levi chuckle knowingly.

"Miss Evelyn is inspiring. She wants to use what God's given her to bless the kids in the south-side elementary schools." He points that direction. "You contribute dozens of sweets to their bake sales, right? And you offer them free baking classes in the summer. Sometimes you bring cookies to the baseball field on Saturdays just because."

Evelyn shakes her hand at him. "Now, Levi, stop making me blush. I just do what I can. It will never be near as much as the Lord has done for me."

I grin.

She loves you.

"Pick something out?" Levi tilts his head toward the case.

I bite my lip and assess. The shop is old and snug, but the delicacies themselves are lovely and sophisticated. It's no wonder Levi considers them suitable. I choose a giant white chocolate peanut butter cup, giddy and spoiled. After paying, he holds his hand toward the door and guides me out of the shop.

I wave goodbye.

"As always, an honor, Ms. Evelyn," he says.

As he opens the door for me, she covers his other hand with hers. I continue through the doorway and pretend not to hear her whisper.

"She's beautiful, Levi. And you were right—she really is a delight."

Levi murmurs something to her before catching up to open the car door for me to climb in. A sudden wind whips his white button down around his chest as he controls the door to a gentle close. I clutch the bag in my lap, kicking off my shoes to pull my feet up. He gracefully sits to drive, fingers combing that enticingly wavy hair back into place.

"I wish I could talk to people like that," I say.

He glances at me in question as he pulls out of his parking spot on the street.

"You learned so much about Miss Evelyn in a few visits. And

you've talked to her about her faith. I would never know what to say or how to start."

"I've just had a lot of practice. I can't tell you how many stuffy parties I've had to attend."

I shake my head at him. He's being humble.

This time it's Levi who looks over like he might get away with something. "Can I ... take you somewhere? Like a real date?"

I adore how he waits for my yes, even for this. He works so hard to respect my boundaries, to make me feel safe. I'll never find another guy as perfect for me as Levi, even if I'm "all better" someday. This is my chance. A chance for a relationship like my parents—the like with the love, the crazy attraction with the trust. The Noah to my Allie. I have to be brave, to see what happens. Maybe I can be free.

"Yes ..." Yes? Yes.

Yes?

His smile gleams, thrill back in full force. A fire ignites in my chest knowing that I can put that kind of happiness on his face with one word. That's what he does for me.

"I know just the place," he says.

I close the gap between us, stretching my seat belt, to whisper in his ear. No consequences last time.

"Thank you for waiting," I say against his ear. It's even better this time. My lips tingle like they've found new purpose. They like the feel of him so much they'll get carried away if I let them. I shift back a few inches, but they're about to try a kiss on his jaw. So tempting.

Light shines in his eyes. His mouth moves but doesn't form words. The blinker clicks. Is he pulling over?

Rain falls sudden and intense.

I jerk back in my seat. No. A gaping pit forms in my stomach. I can't breathe. I have to warn him. "Levi?"

He snaps over quickly, but I don't get to finish.

At a burst of thunder, I snap. Black fear rushes in, consumes me. I clench my hands over my face and try not to remember.

Aiden shouting. His hand slamming the wheel. Rain pounding. Wipers manic. A vicious grip on my arm. I need out, but all I see is my terrified reflection. He grabs my neck—

I rub my eyes like it will erase the images. The hurricane of fear is slow to fade away. I'm still drowning. I try to breathe, to be present, to fight it. I sob into my knees. My chin, my stomach, my whole body shakes.

Help me. Please, make it stop.

I'm always here.

When I am afraid, I put my trust in you.

When I am afraid, I put my trust in you.

When I am afraid, I put my trust in you.

"Kit? What can I do? Are you alright?" The softest voice, the lightest touch on my knee.

I flinch so hard that I jump in my seat and sob even harder. I can't face him. I cover my face and hide behind my hair.

Why? I hate this. I hate that I'm like this. That I can't be with Levi. Why won't you take it away?

He could. But he won't. And once again, I've let Levi down. I clench my fists until my nails dig into my skin. I can feel Levi's care, almost tangible, but I curl up tighter, avoiding him like one glance would turn me to salt.

When we're parked, he rips off his seat belt and bends toward me. "Kit, I want to help." His voice is soft but filled with urgency. "Please just tell me what's going on."

I'm still barefoot. I can't bear another second in here. Don't look at him. Just get it out. "This was a bad idea. I'm sorry. I know"—my voice breaks with emotion—"I know better."

Seat belt off. Grab my shoes. Door open.

I run all the way to my room, lungs burning, tears mixing with the rain. Rocks prick my feet. Water sloshes. Like an extension of my flashback.

I'm okay.

I'm okay.

CHAPTER FORTY

I'M ON A MISSION, embarrassed of this half-baked plan but proud of my newfound courage. Yesterday needs to go away. I ignored Levi's text checking on me, and I'm in dangerous territory. If I don't act soon, things will turn unbearably awkward.

After breakfast, I borrow Sophie's curling iron, swipe on mascara, and zip leather boots beneath my white long-sleeved dress. Books dropped off in the classroom, I bolt across campus.

Sophie didn't push for details yesterday when I came barreling in, just held me there on the sofa like a drenched cat. As she rhythmically smoothed my hair, I let something slip about ruining things with Levi. Without hesitation, she said, "Then go get him back. Put on that white dress he likes and get him back."

I'm not sure about the logic or wisdom of that advice, but I'm following it out of desperation. I never had him fully, but I had some part of him, and getting back to Before Us might still be an option. Joking and confiding and reading his eloquent, caring eyes is worth almost anything to me. I can still choose to be Brave Kit. So I'm run-wandering around campus, panning my head around, hunting him down. I'll hate if I curled my hair for no reason—it was a big step. I know he's frustrated that I won't tell him anything, and he deserves to be, but an argument would only push us further apart. Maybe a pretty dress and a smooth-over will be enough of a Band-Aid, just this once. Enough to keep him from insisting I tell the truth.

A far-off car door slams, and a spike of fear stabs through me —proof that this is necessary. Two weeks after prom, I couldn't hear a door shut without flinching, nightmares every night. I couldn't stand another word of Mom's consolation, so I told Tess everything, thinking I wanted her level-headed advice. Now I can hardly stand the memory ... Squirming in that armchair in the church atrium, throat aching with hidden tears. Her sheer contempt. She said I was asking for it, that I should be happy, that I didn't even deserve flashbacks because nothing happened. She said it wasn't fair I was spared when worse things happen to girls who don't walk right into it. Her derision, her flippancy. I shiver. Enduring a sequel with Levi? Never. I can't, and I won't.

A cool wind blows the final leaves off a tree. I hold down the skirt of my dress while my eyes bounce around my surroundings.

There. Levi's dark-green sweater. A favorite of mine. I can't wait to see the hazel above it. I stride up to him and his Jesus backpack with all the confidence and calm I can muster. This ridiculous plan might work. I need it to work.

He sees me coming, but he doesn't start like I expect. He straightens to perfect posture and avoids my eyes. "Are you okay?" I've never seen him so walled off.

I motion past the corner of the engineering building, ensuring the privacy he'll want so we can get back to normal. He follows silently, stops at the wall, and pivots to face me without meeting my gaze. I thought he'd be stubborn, insist that I explain. What is this?

My skin chills. Are we done? It's only fair. He should distance himself from me and my crazy—especially without a word of explanation.

"Levi?" I try.

When his eyes finally meet mine, they soften instantly. They're every bit as green and gold and dreamy above his sweater as I anticipated, but I can't enjoy them because I caused the hurt there, the concern. I want to kiss him until he sees how much I care about him. No! Not the k-word. I can't think like that. I have to stay on task.

"Friends?" It's not actually a question. I'm channeling my mother—only a yes will be acceptable.

He doesn't answer, so the plan is on. I step close to him, as close as possible without touching, and look way up.

He holds perfectly still. The ghosts of his eye creases are visible this close. He'll have wrinkles there when he's old. He watches me intently, hopefully, affectionately. The hurt isn't visible anymore —I've distracted him thoroughly, at least for this moment—and I can take him in with delight.

"Friends." His voice is like gravel, almost a whisper, more of a question.

His full attention, that brilliant laser focus, all for me. It warms me like a fire. He doesn't blink. He doesn't fidget. His breath smells like wintergreen flavor ... I want to taste it. No. I can't think that way.

I was planning to say something. Wasn't I? I force my eyes down from his intense gaze. Oh, and away from the lips I'm one impulsive moment from kissing. My fingers find his backpack straps, not quite touching his sides. I have to keep my arms still. No pulling or my suggestive stance will become a full-body hug. No pushing or he'll hit the brick wall. Can I touch him at all? What can I get away with? Nothing more. Anything else would be ruined, and no one needs a repeat of yesterday. This is all I get.

I return to his eyes and melt into the pebbles. Levi. He lifts a curl, running his fingers over it with an unspoken question. He opens his tempting mouth—wintergreen again. I wonder if his breath always betrays the flavor of Tic Tacs in his pocket. I have to get out of here before I do something I'll regret.

"Um ..." I swallow. "Can I have a Tic Tac?" That was not the plan.

He tucks the hair behind my shoulder, his calm accentuating my disarray. I hear him lift the box out of his pocket without touching me, suave as ever, eyes squarely on mine.

I release his backpack straps and reach down blindly. My hand grabs his in a jolt of electricity, and I hesitate. I hold his warm fingers around the Tic Tacs for a full second before I jerk away. It's as good as I always thought it would be.

The nerves in my belly mix with the black wisps of fear swirling. I might be sick. I drag my eyes away from his and my body too, squeezing his Tic Tacs as I turn around. I'm instantly colder, stiffer. I rub my temples with nervous energy and try to walk normally until I'm out of sight, my heart beating wildly against my ribs. The fear doesn't materialize into a flashback. Are they getting less frequent?

I shake my head at myself. I tried to distract him, but I'm the one who lost my mind.

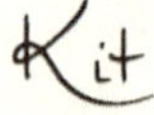

CHAPTER FORTY-ONE

RIGHT, left, side, attitude. And pivot around. Even with the sofa wedged out of the way, I can't fit my *grand battement* combination within the lounge without kicking the walls, so I aim diagonally toward the hallway. My biggest muscle groups have me breathing heavy, and the exertion is cathartic. I did this combination a thousand times in ballet class. With every kick I'm more in tune with my body, more hopeful, more freed from worry.

"Woah!"

I jump at Sophie's voice.

"You almost kicked your nose! You can do the splits standing up? Like a circus acrobat?"

"Ha. Kinda." I weave my fingers behind my back. My ballet workouts had gone undetected until now. Her near constant singing usually announces her presence. "Hi. You're back early."

Sophie cackles. "You look so guilty right now. If I didn't know you better, I'd think you had a boy in here. What was that?"

"Uh. Ballet. Center work."

"Cool. Did you see Mr. Dreamboat today?"

I confirm, gnawing on my lip.

"Well, did you get him back?"

I shrug and nod, unsure which precisely.

"Yay! Well, your hair looks obnoxiously perfect."

I choose to ignore that. She seemed to mean it well enough. "Thanks, Sophs. For yesterday."

"Duh. Okay, carry on with your super-secret acrobatics. I want a ballet lesson sometime." She bounces off to her room, graciously leaving me the lounge, and I notice a Bible clutched under her arm. I close the suite door and transition to *promenade* and *arabesque*. Quitting midway through the progression of a ballet class feels wrong, even after two years. Besides, this is the best way to burn off those Levi nerves. I can still feel that warm hand in mine.

⁕

Ayumi is here. I can't see her face, but I feel her shaking me gently. "Wake up, Kit. You're okay. You're okay."

I'm clammy and breathing raggedly, dragging myself out of the fog. My terror gives me away, but she already knows. Just a nightmare. Just another nightmare. I nod at Ayumi reassuringly. She pushes my hair back from my face and goes back to bed. She's used to this. Poor Ayumi got the worst roommate.

I stare at the ceiling. I'm fine. I jumped out of the car at a red light. I ran faster than I've ever run. I heard his car door slam, but I hid inside a gas station bathroom. I got there in time. The guy at the gas station called the police. I was fine. Except I'm not fine.

The dreams never end like that. I know how that night was going to end. I just endured a vivid rendition of it again.

Why? Why do I have to live with this? It was one bad guy, one bad night, and now I'm broken forever? Please make it go away. Please take it away.

I'm always here.

In the morning, I run a brush through my hair, working out the knots from the night. I try to do the same with my thoughts, but the nightmare's tangled mess keeps snagging. I circle back to the same memories—not the worst ones, but the ones from before, when things were still fixable. Why can't I let it go? Why must I obsess?

Trying to pull away from another kiss. Hand held too tight. Everything too fast, too soon. Ownership. Three months of what he wanted. Another human trophy, another win, another notch for his belt.

I saw it happening, but I didn't see. Why didn't I see?

CHAPTER FORTY-TWO

Kit

LEVI PULLS open one of Saga's doors as I drop off my lunch tray. He sees me coming and slows to a stop. Sweet Levi. Our not-relationship is running on the fumes of false hope, but I won't just give in.

He flicks the top of a new box of Tic Tacs. The last one is sitting on my desk, half-full. His smile grows as I reach him.

This is the first time I've seen him since our not-conversation yesterday. I study him for awkwardness or judgment. None. Maybe yesterday actually worked. Maybe we're back to Before Us. Except, I'm not Before Kit. I'm Brave Kit. I'm doing instead of just thinking all the time. The car ride after Miss Evelyn's was a train wreck, but I won't be derailed.

Awe and amusement surface in his eyes again, joining the fatigue and concern. "Hey, friend," Soft, lazy.

I deteriorate into a goofy grin. "How was Jesus class?"

"A worthwhile endeavor."

"Speaking of an endeavor, did you decide about running for student body president? I meant to ask ... the other day."

"I think I'll throw my hat in the ring."

"Yeah?"

"I've been praying about it. I feel like he might want to use it."

"Of course you have. You're amazing."

"Thank you. And thanks for remembering." He taps my notebook affectionately. We're getting better at this no-touching thing. I should rewatch *Pushing Daisies*.

"Of course," I say. "I want to help with your campaign. If—" I drop his gaze. "That'll be next semester, huh?"

His head tilts. "Yes. March."

He'll have given up on me by then. At least I bought myself a few more days.

I bend to check his watch. I have to get to lab early today.

He about-faces. "I'll walk you to class?"

"You sure? You must be starving from all that swimming."

He nods, like *Definitely*.

"The lunch prospects won't please you. Probably a sandwich day. One of your Goliath sandwiches with half a pound of grilled chicken and hummus and every vegetable available."

He shakes his head, amused.

I'll have to check for rain clouds or open car doors. Just this morning the wind from an open window slammed a classroom door. I blink hard. That was humiliating.

When he opens the door for me, it stirs up the memory of when our eyes locked across Saga that first time. He's so much more than my assumptions. He isn't at all how people said he'd be.

Oops, I missed what he said. "Sorry, what was that?"

"I saw you from there the first week of school." He motions back at the doors, like he read my thoughts. "Do you remember that?"

"Oh, I remember. You caught me staring."

"Glaring, actually. We hadn't even met."

I shift my books. "You had quite a reputation. Everyone said you were untouchable."

"You still don't touch me," he says, trying to make me laugh.

Instead, I adjust my armful again. He holds out hands to take my books and tucks them under his arm. But then his Tic Tacs make another appearance, and he sucks in a breath. Uh-oh.

"I told you I saw you last year. I was drawn to you in a big way. But the reality is, I would have just joked around a little and left it at that. Except ... when I finally talked to you, you were so different from other girls. So unimpressed and self-assured. Zero interest in me or what I could do for you. You blew me off so many times"—he sends a teasing sidelong glance—"and, oddly, it helped me trust you. You didn't care about the impression I give off, the things I'm sick of being known for. You finagled your way into knowing the real me."

I blink at him, dreading how this speech will end.

"I've gotten to spend so much time with you," he continues, "and every minute makes me like you more. You take care of your people whatever the cost to you. You have this certain smile when you talk about your family. You're wicked smart and so motivated. You ... you love Jesus in a way I've never seen before."

My head spins, and I can't hear anymore. I stop right there on the path. I'm not a normal girl doing normal girlfriend things. I've given him such a hard time. I don't deserve any of this.

"Thank you," I mumble. "So many compliments."

He presses his lips together before turning serious again. "I'm not the kind of guy who does situationships."

He lets that hang in the air while I scramble for a not-stupid reply. I've got nothing.

"I'm in this, Kit. I've been trying to be patient and give you space, to give you time to trust me too. But I need to know if you don't want a relationship with me. A real one."

"O-of course."

"Okay ..." he says. "Yes, you want a relationship with me? Please?"

I gape. The paragon of manhood included a please.

What do I say?

"Look, I know you're not ready to tell me everything," he says. "That's okay. We can figure it out. Together."

"I ... I just ... can't."

I hold my breath for his response. This is it— *We're done.*

Instead, he gestures limply, as if I sucked the energy from his Olympian body like a vampire. "Will you at least tell me why not?"

The king of the school humbled himself, put his heart on a platter. He deserves the truth. But ... how? Nothing could be worse than Levi finding out how crazy I am, how broken, how stupid and vain and careless I was last year, how it's all my fault. If he knew the whole story, I'd fully lose him. I'd lose the way he looks at me, the way he bends to listen like I'm the only person in the room. I'd lose every bit of the high regard he holds for me.

He thinks the truth will help, but it won't. He'd say I deserved what happened and far worse. Hearing that from him? To see the light go out of his eyes, the affection replaced with disgust? ... It would be unbearable. The cruelest torment.

"Is it something about me?" he prods.

"No!" He thinks I'm being all weird and crazy because of him? "No, you're ... No."

"Something about you?"

I study my feet and force them to walk again. He follows. Maybe I'm brave enough to tell him some tiny part of the truth.

"I'm ... broken." I said something. I said *something.*

"Did something bad happen to you? Something scary?" His voice is low and ragged, like the thought pains him.

I should have known he'd figure out that much. He's a smart guy. He knows most of my symptoms now. But he doesn't know the whole story and he won't. My throat grows thick. I wish he could give me a hug and tell me it's going to be okay. But he can't. And it isn't.

He continues with me all the way to the lab building, but I

remain stubbornly silent. I can't tell him. I can't. Handing back my books, he tries to catch my gaze. Finally, he nods curtly and spins back the way we came.

I track his hunched leather jacket before dragging my feet to class. Have you ever been in a room where every last person hates your guts? That's how my body feels. My ears and eyes and skin and hands and lips and gut and heart—they all hate me.

I wish I had said yes. I wish I had blurted out a laundry list of every beautiful thing I see in and on him. But I couldn't. It would have been selfish, confusing. I tried to be honest, at least to the extent I could. I have no idea what I'm doing. I don't know how not to hurt him.

My eyes fill. I pray with a sigh that shakes as I release it.

I am your comfort and strength, a very present help in trouble.

Very present.

I plod down the hall, set up my experiment in a zombie state, sit obediently on my stool. The professor starts talking, but I don't hear any of it. I'm just here for my attendance record.

I'm trying to stop convincing people that I deserve their love, but I don't have the courage to be fair to Levi. So which is it? Stop trying to deserve kindness or stop leading him on?

I press hands to my face.

I want to lean into the joy of Levi's words today, the affection in his eyes. Despite everything, he wants to be with *me*. He's better than a dream, the best guy I've ever known, growing-old-and-wrinkly-together material. But I can't be that for him. I can't even give him a hug when he has a hard day.

CHAPTER FORTY-THREE

TWO DAYS LATER, I make my way from chapel to the library. A universally beloved former football star appears next to me, shuffling down the sidewalk.

"Hi, Austin."

"Hey, Kit." He scratches the back of his neck.

"What's wrong?"

He jerks up. "Ah—nothing. I just ... I wanna make sure you're doing right by Jeeves." His voice has a rare earnest quality. "You know, not messing with his head."

I deserve that. My hands tighten into a ball, mirroring my squeezing conscience. Samwise is just looking out for his Frodo. I've thought so many times that they have something worth imitating.

"He doesn't know I'm here," he says. "He'd murder me in my sleep for this, but he's my buddy, you know."

"I don't mean to be messing with his head," I say. "I've tried to be super clear that I can only be his friend. I guess he can tell that I *really* like him." I wince. Too much emphasis.

"If you don't date, that's cool," he says, "but he needs to hear that."

I hesitate. Austin's warm, reassuring presence pulls the truth even closer to the surface. I force it down.

"'Kay ... He's a really good guy, Kit. Gives player vibes, but he's not like that. He'd treat you right."

"I know." My eyes threaten tears. I try to squash down the emotion, but it's full in there—like sitting on a suitcase to get it zipped.

"His faith is rock solid," he says.

"Yeah. He's amazing." It's terrible.

"Amazing," he repeats.

I expect he'll cave and tell Levi all of this. At least I've already said that to Levi myself.

"Well, uh, mind if I ask why you won't date the guy? You obviously have the hots for him."

Yikes. Expressiveness strikes again. "It's ... complicated."

Austin groans, exasperated.

Join the club, bud. "You're a good friend. I'm glad Levi has you."

He frowns.

"Hey, Austin. Sophie, huh?" I smile.

His breath releases.

"Holding out for the Leo thing to run its course?"

Odd. He doesn't usually hold back.

"Sophie doesn't know I'm here," I mimic. "She'd murder me in my sleep for this."

That earns a chuckle.

"I won't blab on you." I don't blame him for needing reassurance. My loyalty lies with Sophie, but keeping his confidence is what's best for her.

"I can't promise the same," he says with a sideways glance.

I confirm that I knew as much.

"It's not the right time. And also, I'm not sure we're on the same page yet." He tilts his head. "Sophie would be ... she'd be ..."

"End game?"

He agrees with a slight movement of his head.

I knew it. "Not on the same page about that? Or something else?"

"Ah ... When I pray about it, I always feel like I need to wait. I think it's 'cause she's still sort of working out what she believes. I just wanna end up with somebody totally obsessed with Jesus, and I don't see myself staying all casual with her if I open that can o' worms. I need God's enthusiastic go-ahead before I tell her—" He stops.

I nod quickly to spare him. "He's working. Stay tuned."

Bless him for his commitment to you. Give him all the good things.

The line Austin is holding is impressive and important. But I can see Sophie diving in, and I wish they could just be honest with each other. The secret-keeping is making a mess. I internally face-palm. Then again, I'm Hypocrite of the Year.

Austin laughs suddenly. "You're trying to out-wingman me, aren't you?"

I chuckle.

"Uh-huh," he says. "One point, Kit. Okay, I don't think this is against bro code." He pushes his sleeves past his elbows and studies the sidewalk. "Yeah. You're gonna be downright impressed."

I stare. *Spill already!*

"There's this girl Ada. She's ... ah ... you'll see."

My stomach drops. Who is Ada?

"She follows Jeeves after our Bible class every time. We have it today. Not this next class, but the one after. The humanities building. The door over here." He points. "Come see for yourself."

"Okay," I get out.

"And Kit?" Yikes. Austin's stern voice.

I turn.

"Don't torture him."

Guilt glues my lips shut.

"See you tonight," he says.

The moment we're dismissed, I'm the first one out of class and running next door. I can't not. Like a complete creep, I step behind a tall bush in the landscaping, my nerves going haywire. Austin emerges with Levi and whacks him on the arm as they part ways.

And then she appears. Perfect brown curls bounce down her back as she jogs to catch up with Levi. Flawless olive skin and natural lashes that could star in a mascara commercial. A fitted jumpsuit shows off her gorgeous figure. She's perfect—like if Esther walked out of the pages of the Bible. The first time I saw her badging in at Davidson Hall I did a double take myself. Now I know her name. Ada.

She tugs on Levi's hand to stop him and drops her books on the grass without a glance—bold move. And then she slides her hands up his chest.

My whole body tenses. My jaw clenches so hard my teeth might shatter. *Get your hands off him.*

I can't hear what she says, but her eyes are all desire and playfulness. He shakes his head and drags himself away. No wonder Austin used the word *torture*. Ada seems undeterred. She waves and calls something after him as he walks toward Albert Hall.

I watch him with a hand covering my mouth. I can't believe who Levi is rejecting in my favor. A gorgeous girl all over him— and so persistent. It would be easy with Ada. Not complicated, not frustrating, not unworkable.

Last week I stood so close to him, touched his hand. It felt so intimate to me. But he has a girl closer than that three times a week. Humiliating. How could I be so stupid?

At a standstill with my mind in overdrive, I slog a few steps to park on the nearest bench. I'm intolerably jealous of Ada's hands on him, but I channel all my concentration—I can't blame her. I know how likable Levi is. She and I have that in common. And I don't have any claim on him.

I don't want to hate her. That's not who I want to be.

Help me think clearly, to see things the way you do.

As a loop of that moment plays in my head, what stands out isn't Ada's hands on him, but Levi stepping back and walking away. He's opting for a slim possibility with me, rejected multiple times over, in favor of certainty with her. Someone straightforward, uninhibited, assertive, more beautiful. I know, I hate when other girls compare themselves like that, but I can't unthink it. And it's a bizarre and tremendous relief that I'm convinced of her superiority. It means Levi's been choosing me for *me*.

I swipe happy tears from my cheeks. How I look isn't interfering like I feared. That doesn't measure my worth—not to Levi. He's so good, so disciplined, so focused to decline such an offer, and repeatedly. Affection for him bursts and sparks inside of me like bubbling lava. For the first time, that whisper of paranoia on my shoulder is quiet.

My parents flash to mind. Mom's beauty didn't keep her from finding the perfect guy or building a beautiful life. They've always said their relationship was God's gift—of course it is. I've been trying to play God, trying to control everything myself. I thought beauty could only be a curse because I didn't trust him to intervene, to provide like he did for them. But Dad loved Mom for who she is. He still does.

I'm sorry. You've given me everything I've needed my whole life, but I didn't trust you with this. It doesn't matter how I look. You're the one who would provide just the right partner, the right person to grow old with. You're the only one who can control anything.

I pull my legs up on the bench.

So now what? I can't keep confusing Levi. You haven't taken my freakouts or even my nightmares away. I'm still as broken as when I came here.

I can't go out to celebrate with him when he finishes a coding project. I can't squeeze his hand when he needs some encouragement. I can't even give him a high five after a football game.

Levi proved himself to be everything I want in a guy, but I can't be the best girl for him.

$$\sim ele \sim$$

I bowed out of Sophie and Austin's plan tonight. I have to think. Something has to change. Ever since I left the scene of Ada's not-crime, I've been ruminating.

I could take Levi up on his offer to be with me without all the facts. But the daydream requires so much creativity. There could be no lifting and twirling. No kissing or hugging or holding. But I could bring him something. A present. A letter. Or ... I don't know, something worthy of him. I could tell him how amazing he is and how I want every minute I can have with him. I could tell him I'll take whatever he's willing to give and I'll give whatever I can. I want that desperately. I could soak in our talks and our closeness and those eyes on mine. He could comfort me through this awfulness, even if he doesn't know its cause.

Or.

I could let him go.

I could cut the thread tethering us, let him find something fulfilling. Something good and sweet and complete. Someone who can be for him what I can't. I swallow thickly.

Ding. It's him.

Sorry about Austin. He means well.

He tattled on himself?

He did.

He's a good friend.

He is.

If I don't say something, I'll feel like I'm keeping the Ada thing a secret. I will not keep a single other secret from him.

> I saw Ada.

The dots remain for a few seconds. My thoughts tornado.

I push her away, but she keeps coming back. I guess I'm her Kit.

My mouth falls open.

Should I have told you about her? I didn't want it to come off as coercive.

Three dots.

There are others.

There are others.

> No. I have no right to be jealous.

That right is still yours for the taking.

I ALMOST CHOKE on the last bite of my oatmeal when Levi shows up at my table at Saga. Almost no one else on campus is awake so early on a Saturday morning. His hair is still damp, but he's dressed for a fall photo shoot—jeans, laced leather boots, Jesus backpack, and a solid charcoal flannel buttoned up. He sits with an expertly crafted yogurt parfait, Exhibit A of his well-rounded nutrition.

Dissonance hums between us. Things have gotten so complicated and yet so clear. We're not just friends. We're exclusively, non-casually not dating. Last night I ripped myself to shreds in a tug-of-war between what he asked for and what he needs.

"I thought I might find my favorite morning person here," he says, cutting through the silence.

I manage a sheepish smile. "Oh look, it's my favorite early morning swimmer."

"Up for a walk today? An off campus ... date walk?"

What would Austin say? A walk isn't torture, is it? "Are you sure? ... Considering."

"Yes." Is that a challenge in his eye?

"What's in the backpack?" I ask.

"A thermos. I got some mochas for us from Copper Fox." He glances at the mug in front of me. "For later."

The best coffee shop in Pinecrest, and he prefers tea. I shake my head at him. He's impossible.

He rests his arm on the table, and I tilt his watch toward me, avoiding his skin, to read it upside down. Bible, swim, shower, and coffee run before 8:30 a.m. I give him a pointed look. He smirks.

"Thank you," I say softly.

When he's politely downed his yogurt, he tilts his head toward the door in invitation. "All set?"

For weeks I was stuck in the cycle of *Like Him, no, Can't Like Him*. Now that it's a forgone conclusion, I'm stuck in *Be Brave, no, Be Kind*. Sorry to Live-Action Cinderella, but I can't seem to do both. I'm sick of it. Nothing I do feels right anymore.

As we drop off our trays, his gaze drops to my go-to pointed-toe flats. I huff in annoyance. I thought I'd be safe putting zero effort into my outfit this morning, just threw on jeans and a T-shirt.

"What's wrong with my Rothy's?" I grumble. "Not everyone can afford Ferragamo."

He recoils. "I was going to offer to stop by your room to grab your sneakers, since we'll be walking awhile."

Oh. Oops.

"Is that what you think of me?" He opens the door for me, still chivalrous even when hurt.

"I mean, look at you." The words tumble out, sharper than I intend. My lack of filter and exhausted frustration is a terrible combination. "I'll never keep up. How could any of us plebes?"

He scowls at me. That's a first.

Whatever you wish that others would do to you, do also to them.

I cringe inwardly. *Okay, I see the glaring hypocrisy.*

I hate when people treat me differently because of how I look. And I just did that that to him, but with his money.

"I'm sorry," I say. "Can I have a do-over?"

His face relaxes, instantly forgiving. A huge credit to him. "Sure." His expression turns mischievous. "I know you don't like to be complimented about your appearance, but may I please have an exception today?"

I half laugh, alarmed that I'm so pleased. "If you must."

"I see the need to state, for the record, that you always look lovely. Timeless and elegant, understated. Same story today." Then, with quirked lips, "Emma Watson wants her vibe back."

I'm giddy, fourth-grade style. A full 180 from my reaction the first time he complimented me. Like the day I found myself brushing my hair to go see him, like the day I put on that white dress, this is oddly revolutionary. His reaction to Ada has freed me, not only to accept how I look, but to want to be beautiful to him. It's just one part of me. He sees beyond it, just like he trusts me to see past his money. My head spins with the reworking of so many thoughts. Energy zings in my veins. I've finally come back around. I'm finally comfortable in my own skin again.

"I love when you wear white or blue," he adds. "Your eyes ..."

"Okay, okay." I push his backpack.

He checks to see if I mean to stop him, but my stupid smile tells him otherwise.

"So many favorites." He loops thumbs around his straps. "The white silk tank top you wore in summer. The navy sweater that wraps around. The denim skirt with the white button-down tucked in. Mm. So classic." He's fully flirting now and enjoying himself. "My favorite is that white dress—but you knew that already." His sidelong glance is cheeky, like I might be mad.

"You're impossible. I fuss at you, and you compliment me?"

He grins, then it softens. "I still remember what you had on when I first saw you."

My brows shoot up.

"White button-up, sleek gray skirt, black heels," he says. "Ring a bell?"

"I do have a woman-crush on Rachel Zane from *Suits*," I joke. "That was for my interview with the panel."

"You looked bummed, in your own world."

I nod and kick a rock back into its place in the landscaping. "Their last question was what animal I'm most like. I blurted out 'zebra,' of all things."

We chuckle.

"But then the next girl was heading in," he says. "She looked terrified, like she was about to lose it. You stopped to encourage her, held her arm. Whatever you told her ... she walked in there like a new person." He shakes his head. "I'm still blown away that you'd do that for your direct competition. You're incredible."

I study him. He liked me for me—from day one.

"I really wanted to talk to you then, to see you smile. I was so close to coming over there, but I had this feeling I shouldn't. Now I know that chat would have been a crash and burn." He grimaces to be funny.

But, actually ...that was pre-Aiden, when I was trusting, whole. I would have jumped at the chance to talk to Levi, and anything more than a hard pass would have scared him away. Timing really is everything.

Timing is usually your thing, God. Did you give me that crazy zebra answer to get me here? Did you give me these months with him? Why?

"I prayed that you'd win the scholarship."

I snap up. Like he heard my prayer.

He twists his lips, embarrassed. "Now I know you earned every bit of it. You're just like a zebra, after all," he teases.

I roll my eyes to cover an flattered smile.

"But I did—I prayed for the enchanting stranger, and here

you are, stunning and selfless, and also brilliant and fun and inspiring. You're so much better than I'd hoped."

I try to breathe. He prayed for me and here I am. Why would God say yes just to let this disaster with Levi blow up in my face?

"In conclusion—"

I laugh at his official tone, and it melts the tension growing in my chest.

"— you are exquisite. And I don't want to hear any more comments about Varas, or whatever you said."

Exquisite?

I tug his backpack strap. "Thank you."

As we step off campus, Levi shifts between me and the street, a silent shield. I dart a glance upward, half-expecting storm clouds. Instead, blue sky and wispy clouds greet me—a profound relief. But the road we're on is risky, unpredictable. Hopefully there won't be any alarming interruptions.

CHAPTER FORTY-FIVE

"WHERE ARE WE GOING?" I ask.

"To a playground," Levi says. "It's a mile that way."

"Only if you'll swing with me."

"Only if you'll show me your best jump off."

I spurt out a surprised laugh.

"I'm not half as cocky as you seem to think I am," he says.

"Maybe I think you deserve to be."

He lights up.

Our walk winds down quiet neighborhood streets to a deserted playground nestled in a thick pine forest. I let out a happy sigh. Just what I needed. Birds chirp, and the branches sway with the cool wind.

Your creation ... It's beautiful.

In one smooth motion, Levi sheds his backpack, clutches it in an arm, and jogs backward, pine needles crackling beneath his feet. He glances behind him to avoid running into a tree. "Think you can beat me? I'm giving you a handicap." He grins.

I scoff and take off as fast as I can. He spins forward when I catch up and runs casually, matching my sprint with ease. I push him on the arm without thinking, and he pretends to fall over, letting me win.

I shouldn't have done that. But no darkness appears.

He rolls onto his back in the pine needles, refreshingly uninhibited, and pulls up to his elbows to watch me. I wiggle in a silly victory dance but stop shyly when his eyes widen in enjoyment. He pats the ground next to him, and I join him there in the pine needles, no care for the cold ground or the poky pinecones. I get to be close to him.

"Velociraptor," Levi says, pointing at a cloud, moving his head to see around the tall trees.

I clap my hands together and point at a different cloud. "Blender?"

"Great Wall of China."

"Magic carpet."

He twists toward me, offering a hand. "Do you trust me?"

I spark at the endearing *Aladdin* reference—until my arm drops midair. My face falls, and so does his. I can't grab his hand.

I lock into his eyes and nod seriously to his joking question.

"Just not enough to tell me the truth." He stands abruptly, snags his bag, and brushes off pine needles as he heads for the playground.

Levi was a wild stallion before I came along—all grace, strength, and raw energy. He would be a sight to behold in a reciprocated relationship, a beautiful force of tenderness and passion. He'd be free to run concurrently. But I can't be the one. To be close to me is to remain in my cage.

Watching him pump his legs on a swing tugs at my cheeks. I join him on the next one and oochy-scooch into proper position. Closing my eyes, I revel in the freedom of flying through the air. Back and forth, hair blowing in the wind.

"Favorite color," I say into the quiet.

"Today, blue." Frustration leaks into his charming reply.

"Today, green and gold."

We silently adjust to swing in sync, side by side.

"Favorite place," he asks.

"The creek at our usual trail. One of my favorites, anyway."

"Tell me about it."

My chest warms. "Okay, close your eyes. Picture a bright blue sky, weirdly blue. Dry, clear-tasting air, and pines everywhere. They're taller and thicker than these and, I don't know, happier looking."

He peeks at them, chuckling.

"And aspens and spruces. Fifty-foot spruces you can't even see the top of. And so many rocks, like God ate some red marbled cake and different sized crumbs fell everywhere. Some so big they'd crush you if they shifted. And some so small they crunch under your feet. Depending on the season, there's grass or leaves or snow or flowers on the ground. And then, if that wasn't perfect enough, there's a wide stream—crystal clear water, with that perfect falling sound. And if you keep walking, you'll see layers and layers of mountains, grayish blue at the front and lighter in the distance."

He opens his eyes to send a wistful smile. "I'm sold."

"What's your favorite place?"

His gaze drifts to the horizon. "The Sound. On a boat."

"Your dad's sailboat?"

He brightens. "You remember that?"

"Duh."

"With Everett. And a couple grinders."

"Grinders?"

He half laughs. "I'd be almost unrecognizable to my friends growing up, but I can't remember how to say a sandwich. A grinder is like an Italian sub."

"Was that a daydream or a memory?"

"Memory." He hesitates. "A daydream would probably include you."

My shoulders curl in. Sweet Levi. The familiar pang returns—I'm not being fair to him.

"You'd be unrecognizable?" I ask.

"I ... adapted when I came here. Some differences were an asset. Others, a liability."

We share that inner terminology, that perspective. His upbringing has been a hindrance for him like my appearance has been to me. We have more in common than I realized.

"No need to adapt when you're with me." I try to sound casual. "I like all of you." I mentally face-palm. Real casual. I catch his tender gaze through my blowing hair and brush it over my shoulder. "I'm surprised you didn't choose a school near the ocean. I could see you chillin' with the surfer bros in California. Or you could be a Pacific Northwest crunchy guy. You're already deep in a love affair with whole foods. Or the Deep South with your impeccable manners."

"Trying to get rid of me?" he teases. "I do miss the ocean. I tried setting a sound machine to waves crashing, to no avail."

"Aw. Is your house close enough to hear the waves?"

"Right on the water. I can hear the waves lap when my windows are open."

"The sound machine couldn't fake you out?"

"No. Those waves sound like Hawaii. On the Sound we have puny waves." He lifts a finger. "But huge egos."

I giggle. "What a slogan."

"Remember the guy I told you about who introduced me to Jesus? He had a list of Christian schools, and I admit I decided to enroll at whichever had the lowest acceptance rate, as long as it was far from New England."

"Mayberry won."

"Mayberry won." His face clouds with an unreadable expression. "I always plan ahead. But coming here was impulsive, very unlike me ..." His voice trails off.

"Impulsive."

He gives his head a half shake, as if to reset. "Your turn."

"Pets growing up?"

"Killed a couple fish by accident. My parents aren't really pet people. But when I grow up," he says like a kid, "I want a dog. A big one."

"Poor dog," I tease.

"Hey!" he jokes back. "Maybe someone will take care of it with me."

My happiness sinks as I grieve the future I want. Resting my head against the chain, my swing falls out of sync with his.

"Let's see what you got," I say, propelling myself higher to change the subject.

Never one to back down from a challenge, Levi swings high enough to rock the swing set's supports. We both laugh.

"One, two, three," he calls.

We jump, but I hesitate before takeoff.

Levi lands an Olympic-sized jump and lifts his arms in victory. He is handsome beyond excuse. It's unlivable.

"Show off." I shake my head with endearment.

He saunters over, digging Tic Tacs out of his pocket, but stows them again to pull a pine needle from my hair.

Levi. I long for the best for him. I am the obstacle.

He slowly, intimately pulls fingers down my hair. Like I'm precious to him. My eyes close in pleasure, but they flutter open full of tears. The fear is absent—only my guilt threatens. *I'm not good for you. I can't keep you trapped.*

"I'm sorry," he says gently. "I won't do it again."

"That's not why ... I liked it."

He works his jaw around.

"Levi?" I barely made a sound. "This is really fun."

His sad smile matches my own.

"You're my favorite," I whisper sadly, unwisely. My greedy fingers grab the bottom of his shirt. The thick flannel is soft and warm and so close to his skin.

"Let me be there for you, Kit," he almost begs. "Tell me what you need."

Give him good things, God. Please fix this mess I've made. Take care of him.

"I don't know what I need. But I know you deserve better than this."

"Better than you? She doesn't exist."

My stomach ties in knots of confusion and honor. Surely he knows what I mean. "It's time," I blurt out. "I'm not getting better." My throat tightens. "I care about you too much to keep on like this."

"You're not getting better from what? You mean about being broken?"

I tug his shirt and try to wordlessly explain, to say I'm sorry, to tell him how much I like him, admire him. This time, he turns away, dragging a hand through his hair. His raised arm pulls the shirt from my grasp. He stands there, hand still on his head, lost in thought or prayer.

Tell him what to do. Help him, God.

He spins back—calm, collected, determined.

I huff. He is impossible. No self-preservation. As rational as he normally is, logic won't do the trick here. I won't be able to talk him out of this.

Tic Tacs peek out from his pocket. I could grab them without touching him, and he'd make that inviting face I love. What am I thinking? No. That would not be kind. Or consistent with what I just said. I clasp my hands behind my back to keep myself in line.

He pulls the Tic Tacs out. "Are you going to steal these too?"

Before I know it, I'm grinning up at him, bending closer, smitten.

Help.

CHAPTER FORTY-SIX

Levi

I STEP into the night air, alone. Usually Kit is with me when I wander campus in the dark, but tonight I need to run off this energy, funnel my thoughts. I couldn't swim right now—my breathing has to be perfectly timed. With the chaos in my head, I'd probably drown. For a few liberating seconds, the sound of my feet hitting the sidewalk dam it off. I need to sort my thoughts, though, so I let them rush in.

Austin didn't hear me when I brought up his serial dating. The weirdness on the floor is no better. And I still have no ideas for another prank prep spot. I should be studying for my Linear Algebra test or working on that architecture project. But the debacle that crowds out all the others is Kit's hobby of tearfully trying to quit me.

Meanwhile, Ada's escalating. Every time after Jesus class it's harder to walk away, and she's picking up on my hesitation. To be touched, wanted ... I like it more than I'd ever admit. But that's not what I want. I want Kit. She's the complete package, the one worth keeping. I can't let Ada's persistence—or her hands—wreck this for me.

Maybe I should ask Kit to meet me after class on Friday. If Ada saw how lovable Kit is, she might finally drop the antics. I'll have a dessert from Miss Evelyn's ready, some flowers too. I'd hire an orchestra if I thought it would help. I'd commission a sculpture. Anything to deliver the perfect *Sorry, I'm with her.* Even though I'm not. Even though Kit's assured me that it's never going to happen. I press my fingers to the ache behind my eyes. I'm pathetic.

At first, I thought a little encouragement was all I needed to stay patient, but that was way off. The past few weeks, Kit has given me more than enough reasons to hold on—finding time for us to be alone, her heart-stopping grin, finally accepting my date invitations. That alluring look she let slip in the car. The Kit-level compliments. The way she keeps almost touching me. I can't be imagining all of that.

She said I'm her favorite. She said she likes all of me.

I avoid the loop where the couples walk. That's the last thing I want to see right now. My legs push harder, burning through the pent-up energy. I won't be able to keep this pace for long.

I can't take care of her if I have no idea what she needs. But I can't cut ties while she acts like she really wants me.

My lungs strain for air. This is helping.

Her secret-keeping grows even more unbearable every time those big blue eyes hold affection, admiration, even longing—

Kit, magnificent in that dress, so close the air crackled. Hair and skirt blowing around, sending whiffs of the orange-scented shampoo I've grown to crave. Those eyes taking me in like she wants nothing more. I really thought she was going to kiss me. I can't stop thinking about it.

I'd give up Tic Tacs forever if she'd so much as touch my hand again. I let out a grunt. She's robbed me of my heart, my mind, and now my cool too.

Skidding to a manageable pace wears me thin, but I start with my feet as I eye the stars in question.

When I can hardly take another step, I scale the two flights of stairs to my room, sweaty and spent. No lights. Austin's already in bed.

Pray for Kit.

I need a shower, but I pause in the dark.

Help Kit with whatever is going on with her. Comfort her. Take away whatever is hurting her and give her good gifts. Give me words to encourage her. Help her, please, Jesus. Guide her to what you have planned for her. You know what she needs.

CHAPTER FORTY-SEVEN

IT'S the night of the last Flooders intramural game before the championship. No official football team or field here, but the top teams on campus get to a compete on the official Mayberry soccer field, complete with bleachers and floodlights. The cool metal of the bleachers seeps into my skin and my mood. The lights aren't enough for Haymitch to play. I'm missing home. And that conversation with Austin still weighs heavily on me.

Dreamy Athlete Levi catches an important pass—of course he does—and lands hard with a thud. He barely moves.

Levi.

I jerk up, ready to run to him, but he hops to his feet. My lungs inflate again. He's fine.

I drop back into my spot as Sophie starts singing. "You should take it as a compliment that I ate your sweets and made fun of the way you nod." Modifying a Taylor Swift song on the fly.

Impressive. "You should think about the consequence of your magnetic smile pulling a little too strong."

Her impromptu performance is rewarded with a burst of laughter from Mia and giggling from Ayumi. I try to purse my lips at her, but it's far more of a grin. The other girls scoot closer to listen.

"I got no boyfriend, you're older than us. You're on the field doing I dunno what."

The whole floor cackles, and I miss a line. From noise or humiliation, I couldn't say.

"Long walks at night. Your eyes so kind. Favorite part of life. But I won't say you're mi-i-i-i-ine."

I hide my face with my hands. It's painfully accurate. And apparently premeditated. How else is she doing this quick lyric swap?

"You're so gorgeous. I can't say 'I like you' to your face. 'Cause look at your face." Sophie holds her arms toward Levi to illustrate as the guys come out of a huddle.

He's too far to hear what she's singing, but it's clear the girls are laughing about him, and he points at me, like a wink from afar.

"And I'm so mortified when people say I feel this way. But I keep at my games. You're gorgeous."

My games. My head droops.

Maybe bravery isn't flashy or exciting. Maybe it's simple self-lessness. Maybe bravery is doing what's best for Levi, even though it hurts.

Sophie startles our giggling floormates when she suddenly bolts up and cheers Austin down to the end zone. The guys chant "Samwise," and despite my imitation of Sadness from *Inside Out*, I'm so happy for Austin and the boys. They'll be in the championship after Thanksgiving break.

After the G1 team tunnel—already fully tradition—and their final huddle, Levi beelines to me. I know it's a sacrifice. His friends will disapprove that he's not heading back immediately to celebrate this big win.

His text flashes to mind. He's Ada, and I'm Levi. He managed to walk away from her, but I can't "walk away" from him. Not in the long run. My actions prove as much. Still, I've reached the end of what I can manage with my unreliable mind. I can't be what he needs. I can't manipulate a happy ending. The only way he's going to let me go is if I force his hand—if I tell him the truth.

My friends poke and prod me toward him as they leave the field.

I haven't had the resolve to protect my own heart, but I can find it for him. I can't let him continue on this path for another day. My mind swings from ecstatic to unsafe in a split second. This isn't fair to him. He won't move on, do what's best for him. He won't do what makes sense.

I ache seeing Levi up close. He's rolled a black bandana around his forehead in honor of the playoff game. Flushed face, messy blond hair. He's triumphant, like an adorably harmless warrior. But with every step, his shoulders fall, even more weighed down than yesterday.

"Great game, Levi. You really killed it."

His smile doesn't reach his eyes. "I need to talk to you about something. Can I walk you back?"

We wander off the field, but I'm only half present as my mind churns. I've thought for too long. I have to do something—no more thinking, just doing. When we get to the woods by the pond, he motions for me to stop. His compassionate, worried eyes aren't helping. I avoid them. An angry red scrape stretches across his forearm, dried blood visible even in the dim light. I reach for it and lift gently, wanting to take the hurt away. We should clean this up, get ice from MSC, use Neosporin. I have a first aid kit in my room. That fall must have really hurt. I feel a gentle squeeze on my arm and jerk back, dropping his injured one.

Darkness looms. My stomach drops.

"Sorry," he whispers.

I shake my head. It was my fault.

I squeeze my eyes shut, arms wrapped around my middle. It's too much that a kind touch from him can't be relished—it's always accompanied with fear of flashbacks, fear of fear itself. I'm not trustworthy, at least my mind isn't. I'm a ticking time bomb.

The black claws of fear grip me, wrenching me where I don't want to go.

Aiden shouting, his hand switching between slamming the steering wheel and gripping my arm. "You got what you wanted, now I'm getting what I want." Speeding toward the hotel he booked, the one I said no to so many times. I beg him to let me out. I try to secretly call Mom, but he yanks my phone away and rolls down his window, flinging it out. He grabs my neck and squeezes. "You did this. Don't go out with someone if you don't want to act like a girlfriend. Don't say yes to prom if you're not going to give me what I earned."

Trapped in this bullet speeding into the darkness. Searching frantically for a way out. Slipping my heels off. Silently releasing my seat belt. Tumbling out of the slowing car. Running as fast as I've ever run. Rain pouring down my face, sloshing over my legs. The car door slams. He'll catch me any second. Something keeps me moving. Falling, scrambling up. Gas station lights.

I lurch back to the present, scrubbing my eyes as if it will remove the darkness. I refuse to cry. I refuse. "What do you need to talk about?" I force out.

"Are you okay? What can I do?" His concern washes over me.

"You can start talking. Please, it will help if I can listen."

"Alright ... My father called yesterday. Something has ... come up. He needs to borrow some cash." He looks like he could be sick.

"Something bad?"

"Yes, bad. This has never happened before. I'm not ... I'm having a hard time." Like a lost little kid.

I gently nod him along.

"I ... I thought it would be easier if that money were gone. And I've tried to pretend it is." He swings his head away and studies a grove of sullen oak trees. "I tell myself it's not even mine —my grandparents set up the trust when I was born. But Granny is the trustee, and my father knows I could convince her to pull the principal if I wanted." He starts pacing. "But when I committed to Jesus, I gave him everything, including that money. So I have to decide where it goes as if he's here to authorize every expenditure. I've been praying constantly since yesterday, and ..." He deflates.

"And?"

"I don't think I'm supposed to give it to him."

"If you're sure it's not what Jesus wants, you can't do it."

"But he's my father. He needs me. He'll never forgive me if I betray him like this."

"May I ask why he needs the money?"

He studies me. "Why?"

I lift my hands. "You don't have to tell me. It's okay. God wants our hearts, not just our money. It sounds like this is more about loyalty."

Levi's eyes drift to the pond, avoiding mine. "Easy for you to say."

I shrink back. "It's hard not to say the wrong thing if I have no idea what you're talking about."

"Fine." His voice drops. "My father's being blackmailed."

My jaw drops.

"It's more common than you'd think." He drags a hand over his face and behind his neck. "Most of these situations go unreported. Image is everything," he says bitterly. "His assets—and Everett's—are rather illiquid at the moment, whereas mine are two business days from a wire."

"That's terrible, Levi. I'm so sorry. May I ask ..."

He steels himself. "Go ahead."

"May I ask if the secret needs to stay that way? Will this continue to be an issue if he covers it up?"

"You don't understand." He says it gently, like my suggestion pains him.

"I don't. But I'd like to. If you want."

He pulls in a breath. "I can trust you?"

I confirm with a wobbly nod. I should have left this alone.

With a glance around, he lowers his voice. "He has a history of mental illness."

I go still.

"If the details leaked, it would be humiliating to him. He's convinced it would destroy him, our whole family. It's not … minor. He's been stable for years, but that doesn't—" He finally meets my eyes and frowns. "Kit?"

"Mm?" It's a gurgle, like a moan from cornered prey.

"What?"

"Nnnothing."

"Just say it." His jaw clenches. His eyes turn to stone.

"Nothing. I'm so sorry." I don't recognize my own voice. My head swirls. I step back.

I didn't think we could be together, but I had no idea to what extent. Even if I get better, this darkness will always be part of my past. Here he is finally cracking open, but I can't stay. I can tell him the truth though. He deserves to know, even if it breaks me in the process. I'll go back and gather my words, write him a letter. I can give it to him just as soon as the family turmoil resolves, when he has the emotional bandwidth.

Thank you for my time with him. Take care of him. Show him what you want from him, and help him obey you.

"I need to—to go." My limbs are lead.

"You need to go," he repeats. His Adam's apple bobs as he swallows. The wall in his eyes cover his whole body, like he's hardening into a statue.

"I'm sorry. I can't—"

"I trust you will care for my father's situation—that you

should *not* have asked after—with the complete privacy it warrants."

I nearly crumble to the grass. "Of—of course. I would never—"

"We're finished here." He holds an arm in the direction of my building to dismiss me.

CHAPTER FORTY-EIGHT

Levi

THE NEXT NIGHT, I slip into the former storage room and click the door closed behind me. My hand hovers over the light switch, but a glance at the upper corner reminds me of the security camera I reluctantly agreed to. I'll leave the light off. No sound on the recording, so I can speak freely.

The quiet settles over me, lulls my eyelids closed. After two sleepless nights of praying, I could pass out standing up. I shake it off and pull out my phone—two missed calls I need the strength to address. At least I'm alone here. I grimace as an incoming call flashes onto the screen.

Give me the words. And the patience. And the guts.

"Yes?" I wince. Terrible start.

"Excuse me? Were you raised in a barn?"

I pinch the bridge of my nose. "Hello, Mother. How are you this evening?"

"Much better now, thank you. I'm calling with an update. Is that of interest to you, or are you too busy with a tent revival?"

I half smile. Teasing is progress.

"Don't worry," I say, "I've stepped out of the tent to take your call."

She chuckles.

"How is he?" My feet carry me toward the chair I recently unboxed, but I freeze as hurt and loss hit me with a one-two punch. I'll stand by the door.

"He's hired a reputable PR firm. Past time, of course, but you and Everett were too well behaved to warrant media intervention." A pause. "Your early-life crisis has long since cycled out of the rumor mill, you know, but the neighbors are holding out hope for more intrigue in your twenties."

Remarkable. She's teasing me again. And ... was that a hint of gratitude?

"Caldwell Sterling is crafting a narrative of resilience as we speak," she continues. "Thus far, they seem perfectly competent, if not promising."

I digest the news and jerk up. "He refused?"

"He refused."

I lean against the door to steady myself as the pieces fall into place. "What changed his mind?" His team has offered a thousand alternative maneuvers, though they still don't know a single detail about the people threatening him.

"I like to think I made him see the value in this course of action," she says. "Of course, he'll insist it was his own idea—a simple necessity for a family like ours."

I press my head to the door as a chuckle escapes into the dark. The wave of relief is so strong it brings tears to my eyes. After all these years, he's done hiding.

How did you do that?

Thank you.

TISSUES ARE STREWN ABOUT, as Levi would say, and my eyelashes have been constantly swimming for two days. Let the Lego guys know to change their song—actually, everything is awful. I wrote that letter, but I ripped it up. He can just misunderstand and hate me forever. It'll be easier for him to move on this way. A clear path forward. I've spent every minute since that conversation wallowing, even in my classes, which I couldn't make myself skip. I've experimented with Taylor Swift songs of every era that might succeed as a heart first aid kit. Spoiler: they don't. Ayumi has graciously given me a lot of space. I gather the tissues around me and drop them into the trashcan, hiding the shredded remains of my letter. Curling back up in bed, I hug my knees and stare out the window.

I waver between crying and scowling, despondent or angry. When I'm angry, it's at Levi for existing, for being excessively lovable. At Aiden. At the criminals tormenting Levi's family. At his father for taking out his difficulties on his sons when they were young and vulnerable. But mostly at myself—for my carelessness last year, for being broken, for dragging Levi around, for missing him so much.

Then I cry because Levi is everything I could imagine wanting and I'm too broken to manage a little trip to Miss Evelyn's. I can't stop thinking about his laugh—warm, rich, and unguarded. But if it wasn't impossible enough before, now I know I'm far too much of a liability for his elite family. I stare at the ceiling and daydream about what it would be like if I could just say yes. Yes, hold hands, yes, dates, yes, honesty, yes, girlfriend, yes, hugs, yes, closeness, yes, kisses. I just want to say yes. And then I'm angry again.

I slide off the bed and settle on the floor with my back against the wall under the window. Cooler air seeps in, and the light is fading, a reminder of how long I've been here. Two days have crawled by since the impossibility of our relationship was doubly confirmed. I'm still stuck. I know an answer is right there in my Bible, but I can't bring myself to open it.

My phone rings. Mav on FaceTime. I'll call him some other time.

Answer it.

My chest warms—God and I are still on speaking terms, even when I'm being a brat.

Okay.

I wipe my face and answer the phone with a perky-ish "Hey, Mav!"

"Kitty Cat!" He's not fooled. "Hey, talk to me."

"I broke up with my not-boyfriend." Sort of. Close enough.

"Oh no. That sucks, Sis. I felt like I was supposed to call you. Guess that's why."

That was you, huh?

"I'll be okay." Maybe. Probably not.

"Why'd you break up with Not-Boyfriend Dude?"

"I'm too much of a mess to keep him." He gets more honesty

than most because he never sugarcoats the truth. He couldn't tiptoe if he needed to get by a sleeping dragon. Plus, he already knows something happened with Aiden. Not the specifics, but he lived with me all summer. For a while he'd silently appear in my room and sit in the corner until I fell asleep. Actually, he's the perfect person to talk to right now.

Thanks for that.

"Because of whatever happened last year?" he asks.

"Yes." I slump against the wall, resting my phone on my knee.

"So rough. What happens now?"

"Nothing happens now. I'll lie here until my body is covered with tissues like a hoarder with newspapers. They'll excavate the room in May and archaeologists will tell the story of my downy prison and overall dysfunction."

"Bleak," he says. His Hawaiian shirt has chili peppers all over it. I may have dragged him to one too many thrift stores. "So, you're bawling your eyes out, and I hear old school Tay Tay in the background. It's time to—"

"I know, I know. Do something. But this time there's nothing else to do."

"Oh, so you mean you're waiting on God. Even better."

I blink at him. It's hard to hear wise things from a sixteen-year-old covered in chili peppers.

"What are you hoping God will do exactly?"

"I need him to fix me."

"Cool."

"But he won't," I say.

"You mean he hasn't yet."

I squeeze my legs closer. "Right."

"Okay." He nods confidently.

I glare at him. That's not what I wanted to hear. At least now I have someone else to be mad at.

"What?" he accuses. "I hate that you're so bummed. I kinda want to beat up Not-Boyfriend Dude just for being related to you being this bummed. But I'm not worried about this, and you shouldn't be either. I've been watching God take care of you my whole life. If this guy's supposed to stick around, God'll make it happen. If he's not, you can trust that God's plan is better."

My little brother's faith is surpassing my own at the moment. I think the chili peppers just shook their heads at me.

"News flash—Tay Tay isn't going to tell you anything helpful right now."

I huff.

"Too preachy?"

"No. You're right."

"So ... are you gonna trust him?"

A chuckle sneaks out. "I'll try, Mr. Leadership Qualities."

He grins. "Can't wait to see what God does with this."

"Glad my life can be so entertaining for you."

"Tune in next week ..." Great, it's his TV narrator impression. "To see Kit realize how incredible her eldest brother is and lavish praise on him rather than sarcasm." He sits up, and I know he's about to imitate my voice. "Mav, you're a stellar brother. I wish I had shared more Halloween candy with you. I left you with only Laffy Taffy and Starburst when you had braces, and I'm all torn up about it. As penance, I'm going to come home every month and do your chores and write your papers and fan you with a palm leaf."

I shake my head. His antics have erased my scowl. I love this crazy kid. "In your dreams. I have enough papers to write. Hey, pray for me?"

"Duh. I wish you were coming home for Thanksgiving. Or that you had warned me. I could've bought you a ticket with my chicken money." Mav works at Chick-fil-A. He dodges questions about his post-high school plans by saying that he'll climb the ladder at "the chicken store" until he can be the "Eat Mor Chikin" cow.

"Me too," I say. "And that's why I didn't."

"I figured. Later, Sis. Sorry it sucks right now."

"Thanks, Mav."

I rise to the bed and eye my Bible. My fingers inch toward it, almost on their own, driven by need. I pull the worn leather cover onto my lap and silence the music with a mash on the space bar.

Hey, God?

A verse about peace waves at the edge of my mind. I can't remember where it is or what it says, so I search the concordance in the back of my Bible for verses with the word "peace" in them. Dozens, but I know the one the moment I turn its soft, crinkly page.

"You will keep the mind that is dependent on you in perfect peace, for it is trusting in you. Trust in the Lord forever, because in the Lord, the Lord himself, is an everlasting rock!"

Keep me in perfect peace. Teach me to trust in you.

Like a broken compass, I've been erratically pointing at where I think is North. Avoid Levi. Warn him. Be brave for him. Push him away. But what use is an unreliable compass? I can't be the mastermind of my life. The desired dominoes don't cascade anywhere. God has to be the mastermind. But ... to put away my defective compass, I'd have to step off a blind edge and fall, trusting that the descent is part of His design. I shudder.

Trust. Trust you with my friendships, with my next steps, with my future and Levi's. Trust you to heal me, in all the ways. I've done such a terrible job trusting you. I'm sorry. I'm so sorry.

As far as the east is from the west,

so far do I remove your transgressions from you.

I suck in a breath that sounds like a sob. *Thank you.*

I wedge a pillow behind me and scribble the windstorm in my head into prayers in my journal.

For those who love me, all things work together for good.

My vision zooms out and comes into focus. Not only did God help me escape that night, but he used it to spark a longing to hear his voice. Since that pivotal moment, I've been chasing him down, head buried in my Bible every morning. His voice has gradually become clearer as I've prioritized him, attentively absorbing his words. Is this what I needed to make him a priority?

I rub my temples. God is able to stop bad things from happening, but he doesn't always. Still, he never wastes the bad parts. He doesn't waste anything.

I write,

<blockquote>
You didn't waste this. You've proven yourself over and
over. But
</blockquote>

I rest my head on the wall and risk a glance out the window at the field to Albert Hall. No Flooders. Some brotherly A2-ers shove each other on their way to their building.

This trust thing. I wish I could sneak in an asterisk. Like, "Yes, God, I'll trust you.*" And at the footnote comes a list of demands: *So long as you keep me from too much pain. So long as you let me have him back. So long as you heal me soon.

But there are no asterisks with trusting God. Just an outlandish declaration and that terrifying free fall.

I'm always here.

I feel his presence, but I don't have next steps yet. I just slump in a puddle of blankets and insights. He never gives up on me. He's been here the whole time. His plan really is the best one. It has to be. I was never meant to be the mastermind of my own story.

"Levi asked me to give you this." Ayumi holds a package skeptically. "Unless you don't want it?"

I stare at the cookie as if it will speak up and explain itself before I finally pull out the note—boy cursive.

CHAPTER FIFTY

Kit,
I'd appreciate the opportunity to apologize before my flight
tonight.
I'll be at Common Grounds until 7 just in case.
—Levi

HE WANTS TO APOLOGIZE. I crumple the note and then
smooth it out on my knee. The clock says 5:30. He's going to sit
there all through dinner? Ayumi slinks back to the lounge.

*This is my next step, huh? I don't think I can talk to him again.
What if I undo my progress?*

Right. Trust you with it. Trust, trust, trust.

I splash my face at the sink, knot my hair, and shuffle to the
lounge to ask the girls about dinner. They walk with me to Saga in
solidarity, crushing me with squeezy hugs I desperately need.

I scarf down a bowl of cereal before assembling one of Levi's

Goliath sandwiches and wrapping it in a napkin. Maybe he already got fried chicken next door at the Hive, but I doubt it. Canola oil is not his jam.

Now to Common Grounds. Just because I'm emotionally handicapped doesn't mean I should treat Levi badly. I can say goodbye like a big girl. It's the least I can do for him. I try not to squish his dinner as my hands clench with nerves.

There he is. I roll to a stop in the doorway. He's at the same table of our first meetup, somber but not spiraling. What happened with his dad? His Bible lies open, and he loops letters in his journal, careful not to knock his tea. I stand motionless, like a loon, jumping to life and out of the way each time someone walks in. It's creepy to watch him like this, but I'm hooked on the expression on his face while he prays—focused and earnest and at peace.

My sheep listen to my voice; I know them, and they follow me.

Look at him. He gets it. He loves you. I wish things were different. I wish I could keep him.

But I trust you. I trust you to take good care of him.

I square my shoulders, tighten a lock around my heart, and force my legs to move. They slow-mo an exaggerated step out of the doorway and catch some weird looks from a group walking past me. *Don't mind me, just getting my lunges in.* Just a few more steps.

"Hi." I thrust my arm out with my protein-packed offering.

Ever the gentleman, he stands in greeting. He takes in the sandwich eagerly, but my face more so. "Thanks, Kit. I've—I'm really glad you came. Can I get you a mocha? Decaf?"

"No, thank you." I sit, and he follows suit.

He gulps down the beastly sandwich in sixty seconds flat. My lips twitch. He really is hungry to forego his impeccable table manners. I'm relieved to have a last minute to stare at him uninterrupted. I won't let myself do this after today.

He finishes swallowing sheepishly. "Excuse me for that. Samwise recommended two-a-days."

I try not to picture him at the gym, all sweaty and strong, hair doing that thing, dragging around his favorite water bottle. This is not helping. I shouldn't have come. Wait, no. I'm not calling the shots, right? And this felt like the next step. But I want him to go first so I can escape after my part. My head swims. Whatever that is. "How is—" I shake the sentence away. I can't really ask, can I? He said we're finished. "Never mind."

"Do you mind if we walk?" he asks.

I stand, careful to ooch out the dangerous metal chair.

He collects his things in the Jesus backpack before leading me out. "My father put out a press release about his experience with Capgras syndrome. It's a delusion disorder."

"A press release?" It just slid out, as if shock greased up my throat.

"It's part of the PR firm's elaborate plan. He is who we thought he was, but this is a turning point. On his terms, of course. His symptoms are well managed with consistent antipsychotics, so it was past time he let go."

"So, the blackmailers ..."

"Deflected for now, and the FBI's problem. You know, it was my mother who managed to convince him that we can't live this way anymore. This ordeal has been oddly healing for them." He meets my gaze and swallows thickly. "But I'll get to the point. I'm sorry for being harsh with you. I shouldn't have snapped like I did, even out of protectiveness. I'm disappointed, to be frank, but Samwise made me see that I expected too much from your original reaction. I should have given you time to process."

He wasn't cagey. He told Austin the whole truth.

"Pushing you away was a serious error in judgement." He glances at me sheepishly.

I hesitate. "You said protectiveness ... of your privacy? You thought I was going to tell someone?"

"No, protective of my father. I really didn't expect disgust from you. I love him, flawed as he is."

"Disgust …? Not at all. I can't believe you thought …" But of course he did. I rub my forehead. It's time. I have to do it. But how?

Give me the courage.

"Are you open to continue discussing," he asks formally, "or would you prefer to complete our conversation here?" Before I can reply, "I ask because I'd like to share another piece of information—unrelated to my family. It isn't fair for me to have kept it to myself when I insisted you share your own."

I bob my head.

"I was … serious with a girl in high school. It took me too long to realize that she was only with me for my family's reputation, our opportunities. I was raised to be on my guard for that kind of thing, but"—he shrugs a shoulder—"it felt real. That was almost three years ago. Maybe it seems small, but it's … embarrassing to me. Mortifying."

She was only with him for his family's reputation? I flash back to the first time I saw Levi. He seemed so invulnerable, so strong. I remember assuming he was someone who would make a trophy out of a girl, never that someone had once made a trophy out of him. I've been too caught up in my own story to see him clearly. I know too well what it's like to be used, tricked.

I send him a gentle glance. "So you swore off girls." Shared secrets have always drawn us close, but that's not what this is for. I'm here to maintain the separation but more peacefully. I was right to be afraid of losing my resolve. I shove my hands into my pockets, pull them out, rub the back of my neck.

Help.

"Until you," he says. "I never knew who I could trust, and dating leaves both people a mess."

"No kidding." I mean to lighten the mood, but the words fall heavy between us.

He opens Arma Chapel's creaky door for me and flicks on a

light. It's cold but peacefully empty inside. So much for a sanctuary. My favorite building on campus might be ruined for me after today. He positions two cushioned chairs to face each other behind the pews, angles his backpack against his chair, and motions for me to sit in the other. "God used the thing with Genevieve. In the aftermath I started searching for something else. That's when I found Jesus. I moved here and eventually met you." That light flickers in his eyes. "It's wicked frustrating that you won't tell me what's going on, especially after I've been so vulnerable with you, but I deeply regret that I ended things the way I did, and so suddenly. I didn't give you any time to rethink or explain. I care about you too much to let you go over one mistake. Will you forgive me?"

The lock around my heart loosens another notch as he humbles himself to ask for forgiveness. Again. That's a relationship green light if I've ever seen one. But it doesn't matter. And this is only making moving on harder.

He squeezes his Tic Tac box, and a rush of affection crashes over me.

"I can't believe that girl," I blurt. It makes no sense. How could someone not like Levi for everything he is? I rub my eyes. Focus. "Yes, I forgive you. But as for your dad, it's safe to say you have no idea what was going through my head on Thursday night. But how could you?" Panic wells in my stomach. I can't. I can't do it.

For everything there is a season ... a time to keep silence, and a time to speak.

CHAPTER FIFTY-ONE

I SIT CROSS-LEGGED on the chair like a kid, gripping my hands as I gather the courage to obey. I've already lost nearly all of my self-preservation. I already put my lips on his ear, rode in his front seat, touched his hand, very nearly kissed him. My rules of protection have been evaporating one by one. But maintaining my secret—my dignity—is my most important protection for myself. Can I really let it go? I squeeze my eyes shut.

I can be brave because I trust you. My mind is dependent on you. I'll do what you say.

Something whispers that maybe Levi will understand. Maybe his experiences will sway his response.

I cover my face but force my hands down. "It's time I tell my secret too."

Surprise and curiosity leap to his eyes.

"I haven't talked to anyone but my mom ... and one other person ... about this."

He nods once.

Okay, give me the courage. Give me the words.

"When I learned that your family's reputation would suffer if your dad's experiences came to light, it was clear that I'd always be a liability."

"A liability?"

I fill in the gaps for him about my change in appearance, Aiden's sudden interest in me, and my relationship with him. Levi watches me carefully, resting his forearms on his knees. I try to speak in a quiet, businesslike voice, but his look of compassion makes my voice wobbly. When I started I just wanted to spit it out, but the act of sharing is a salve for my wounds. His expression shifts subtly, his eyes revealing more than his still posture—care morphs to grave concern, then flashes of anger as I tell about Aiden's disinterest in my boundaries, and then about prom night. My nerves somehow calm with every sentence. I wrap up my story to explain that my brain is stuck on that night, that it haunts me still in nightmares and flashbacks.

All those words hovering in the air, my nails dig into my palms as I await the fallout. I'm nauseous with dread.

"That—" He stops, his eyes flaring with raw anger. The Tic Tac box creaks under the pressure of his fist. "I could just—" His jaw locks tight, the muscles flexing as if he's barely holding back.

My hands tremble, and I press them against my stomach.

"I wish I could have protected you. I wish I could make him pay," he spits. He drags a hand behind his neck and shuts his eyes. Deflating, he says, "Kit, you deserve so much better."

My mouth falls open. He's angry *for* me. A heavy, shaky sigh releases, and the lock on my heart mutinously melts off. The burden I've been carrying is now shared. He understands my brokenness—the brokenness I don't even deserve to have—and he doesn't hate me for it.

When I shiver, he absentmindedly slips off his favorite leather jacket and holds it out. I drape it backward over my shoulders and pull my knees under. Almost a Levi hug. It smells just like him.

Uncharacteristically, he slumps in his chair and stares at the wall behind me. He's silent but his eyes speak for him, morphing to horror. My favorite light in those eyes fully extinguishes.

"Levi. Please talk to me?"

When he finally speaks, his voice is barely above a whisper. "Do I ... do I remind you of him?" He won't look at me. "Is that why you never ride in my front seat? And the time you did—" He manages to glance over and then away again. "Is that why you hated me before you met me? I thought you were nervous around me because ... Is that why you don't want me to ... to touch you?"

I don't have words.

"All this time." His voice wavers. "I've been making this worse for you?"

Uh, God? What do I say? I don't know what to do here.

I shrug his jacket to my legs. "Levi, look at me. You're nothing like him. You're kind and gentle and patient. You listen—You listen when I say no. You're not like him."

With effort, he holds my gaze.

"When I first saw you ..." I'm not sure how to say any of this. I want to get it right, for his sake. "There were some broad similarities. Confidence, popularity with girls, that sort of thing. That's why I avoided you, even though I was immediately—" I shouldn't finish that sentence. "Uh, even though I normally would have wanted to talk to you. I don't know if it would be different with someone else. I haven't so much as shaken a guy's hand since ... since that. I don't ride in any guys' front seats. Except with family. There are other ... triggers. Rain, doors slamming, yelling, that kind of thing."

He nods slowly. He's been paying attention.

"But I do have more flashbacks with you." I study my hands. "If someone brushes by me in the hall, I'm fine, but if you touch me ... sometimes it's really bad. I've wondered if ... strong attraction was part of all of this. That's why I considered going out with Matt." I squirm in my seat.

On one hand, the dam of secrecy has finally been smashed to

bits, and a flood of relief splashes into every crevice inside me. On the other hand, dragging Levi into this mess is unbearable. I don't want to leave him with my burden. I won't let him take an ounce of blame for my pain. It's my brokenness, my dysfunction.

"I hate this part of me," I say. "I hate that I'm broken."

That light bulb is back above his head. "You didn't tell me because you're ashamed?"

Ashamed. That feeling has never been named in my head. I'm ashamed? "Um. Maybe. That sounds"—my voice catches and answers my question—"right somehow. About what happened and about getting stuck."

"But none of that is your fault."

"I mean"—I fight the tears threatening to make this awkward for everyone—"it is though. And I deserved much worse."

"No." His face is stern, his voice indignant. "It's not your fault. You deserved—How can you say that?"

"I take responsibility for my actions. I knew I shouldn't date him. My parents had a bad feeling about him. I knew deep down. I didn't know that would happen, but I could have prevented it. I could have done so many things differently. And my dress. I—"

"Kit, no. No. You cannot take responsibility for"—jaw clench—"for his choices. It's not your fault. No one could ever deserve that. No."

I swipe frantically at the spilling tears. "It's not fair that God spared me. So many girls deserve better and suffer far worse. It's not fair."

"I don't know. I don't understand it either. But they don't deserve that and neither did you."

The jacket falls to the floor and we leave it there. I hang my head, cover my face, and sob. I can't manage to do anything else.

I finally brave a glance up, wiping my face. His expression full of care makes me think maybe it's okay. I bend down for his jacket and squeeze it like a teddy bear, clutching the soft leather.

"I'm so sorry that happened to you." Levi's face scrunches up.

"That you have to remember it all the time. I'm so sorry I've been showing up everywhere, asking more of you ..." He trails off.

I shake my head as my chest aches. I wish I could take it back. It was better to struggle with it myself than to be the cause for the pain on his face. I thought if he understood he would leave for good, not that he would leave for my good.

"You said it was impossible. I should have just listened."

"No, I was being so confusing. I loved spending—" The chapel door creaks.

Levi dons his imperial look for a split second before thinking better of it. He sends me a rueful smile and turns. "Come on in, man. We can head out."

"No worries. I'll come back later."

And the coast is clear again. Good thing we're not trying to have this conversation at Common Grounds.

"I wanted to spend that time with you. But ... your dad worked so hard to keep his difficulties under wraps, and look at me. I'm a mess."

He shakes his head slowly. "You are far more important to me than my family's attempt to control the narrative. I wish you knew that by now. Besides, knowing you, hearing your story, it would be such a benefit to my father. It would be helpful to so many if you chose to share it."

I'm speechless again. How could Levi transform my darkest secret so thoroughly?

My eyelids flutter closed. *I hate this. I don't want him to be hurt. I want whatever is best for him. Help?*

Be still before me and wait patiently for me.

Okay.

I open my eyes.

"Praying?" Levi asks.

"Yes. 'Be still before the Lord and wait patiently for him.'" I have no other answers.

He jerks forward. Wordlessly, he pulls his journal out, opens to the bookmark, and turns it to me. The same verse is scrawled there in his dear cursive. God had said the same words to Levi.

I hear you. Thank you.

"You had that memorized?" he asks.

"Mom had us memorize Bible verses as part of bedtime. A lot of them stuck. Sometimes God brings one to mind."

"What a gift," he murmurs.

I give a half-smile, like *Now what?*

"Now we obey."

"I'll have a lot of space to be still and wait next week." I'll make use of it to the best of my ability. "You're going home?"

"Yes. I need to be there. And it's past time I attempt a Thanksgiving with my own family."

He holds a hand on his head, fingers through his hair. I want to fix the weight in his posture, the dejection drawing his face.

I can't fix it. Will you?

I cast my anxieties on you because you care for me.

I'm always here.

"Alright." He winces. "We talk again after break."

I respect so much that his choice is to obey God's prompting even though it's not what he would have picked.

"Levi ..." It hurts to say his name. "Thank you for understanding. I'm so sorry for ... dragging you around. And for being" —my voice breaks again—"such a mess."

Forearms move to his knees again. "You are a *delight*, a *treasure*." His eyes are wet? "Whatever God has planned, he's got this. He's got you."

Yes.

"Can I pray?" he asks. "Right now?"

I nod eagerly.

"We love you, Jesus. Whatever you have for us, we're in. Whatever you don't ... we follow you still. Give Kit what she needs. And me too. Amen."

"Thank you," I whisper. Rising to my feet, I fold his jacket and allow myself a last longing look before he meets my gaze. Reluctantly, I hand it back. As I close the chapel door behind me, he's hunched over in his seat, watching me go.

But the tiniest match strikes, and peace glows in my heart, a peace beyond all understanding.

CHAPTER FIFTY-TWO

Levi

RENDERED motionless in the back of the chapel, I reel with the verdict that I'm poison to Kit's wounded mind.

A merciless image sears through my mind—Kit finding someone else. Her carefree laugh. Her contented silliness. Her brilliant mind at peace. She's happy and whole. With him. A vice crushes my stomach. Acid burns up my throat. Samwise. He's the only one who could deserve her—the only one good enough, pure enough. He can nurture and protect. His happy, loving family will adopt her as one of their own.

Jealousy claws, but something deeper rises to meet it. I will do anything to give her the best. Anything. If that's what she needs, I will put every ounce of my will and determination into making that agonizing image a reality. I will make any sacrifice for her wholeness, even if it means watching her with him. Even if it means enduring a marriage like my father's.

It's in that crushing moment that it hits me—I love her.

Does this mean "pay attention?"

This story smacks me in the face, but I don't know why. Today's reading in my Bible-in-a-Year plan led me to 1 Samuel 1. With my head in my hands, elbows planted on my childhood desk, I pore over the passage. What am I supposed to see here?

Hannah wanted a child so badly. Her husband insisted that she had enough in him. Her sister-wife rubbed it in her face. But what she needed was surrender. She got there—Hannah said that even if she got the child she wanted, she would give up raising him, that it was enough to see that God remembered her. She found peace, she felt better, even before knowing whether God would grant her request.

The child she longed for was a good dream in itself, but it had become her identity, her deepest longing—her soul's anchor. She had to surrender it so it wouldn't eat her alive.

Am I like Hannah? Have I made Kit the anchor of my soul?

I scoot my chair out and kneel.

She's not my savior. You are. You're the only one I worship. I accept your decisions, whatever they are. I accept what you have for me. You're the only one I need.

Emotion grips me. My legs move under me until I'm sitting, arms resting on my knees. I sit in surrender, eyes closed.

I finally open my eyes, taking in the familiar surroundings from a new perspective. This imposing mahogany desk. My four-poster bed sitting on the antique rug I'm not allowed to eat on, the ornate crown molding, my antique dresser. Thumbtack holes on the dresser serve as relics of a fort Everett and I once attempted with blankets. That did not go well for us. My floor-to-ceiling bookcase is still crammed with old books and yearbooks, sports trophies and piano awards. Childhood stuffed animals and books hide behind the cabinet doors on bottom. On the other side of the room, the fireplace beckons with its crackling fire and my cozy leather chaise. This bedroom is monstrously large and opulent compared to my dorm room. I don't need all of it, any of it. It doesn't satisfy. But neither does economy.

My knuckles rap against the desk. I had to leave when I graduated, to see what it would be like to live differently. A huge blow to my pride, to start—I was pitiful when I showed up on campus. Laundry, vacuuming, shopping for shampoo, even making a sandwich were skills I never knew I lacked. Austin taught me everything I needed to know and never once ratted me out for my ignorance, never treated me like I was obnoxious. We've been like brothers ever since. He had his own skills to learn. Winning friends and girls' attention had come easily on the varsity football team, but at Mayberry, Austin had to begin anew. We helped each other.

It's weird to be back here. Growing up, menial tasks were a rarity for me, yet the expectations that remained nearly crushed me. Here, I was never enough. In Texas, I'm some kind of fascinating specimen. To blend in enough but not too much is exhausting. But my reputation isn't my job, here or there.

I surrender that too.

I raise myself to the chair and my journal.

> I'm your son, wherever I am and however my life looks.
> Whether I have a lot or a little, teach me to be content. Like
> Paul said.

My empty stomach pleads to be addressed. After swimming this morning—a luxury in my family's heated outdoor pool—I'm already ready for lunch. Undoubtedly, premade delicacies fill the fridge. Another perk of being home. Plus, I'm sure my parents are downstairs now, and I should see how they're faring after everything this week. I place a hand on the open pages of my Bible, as if to maintain memory of what I've discovered. I will accept what God chooses for me. I worship him alone.

CHAPTER FIFTY-THREE

I TURNED down Levi's offer to pay for my trip home, but God surprised me. Yesterday fellow G1-ers Rosemary and Savannah told me they're driving to Utah on Sunday and offered to drop me off in Denver. It's last-minute and out of my control, but I accepted. This opportunity is a gift.

Please keep rain away while we drive.

I'm packing a few things—I won't need much—when I see storm clouds out my window. A terrible idea hits me. I couldn't, but I should. I should have done it a long time ago.

Is this your idea?

I steel myself in preparation, in surrender. Maybe I finally have the courage to face my fear head on—to stop squashing and start fighting.

> Hey, Austin. I really need a favor

> What's up

> Can you please drive me somewhere?

> Feeling ok?

> I'm being serious.

> If Jeeves is cool with it

> We're not talking. I can explain on the drive.

> Not gonna step on his toes like that sorry

I need this, and only Austin can do the job. I trust him. And ... don't judge me ... he's really cute. That's important here.

"Sophs." I peek my head into her room. She's panic-packing before heading to the airport.

"Kinda busy. Super late."

"I know, but I really need your help. Two minutes or less."

"You're being weird. What is it?"

"I asked Austin to drive me somewhere. I ... I need to figure something out. But he won't do it."

"Uh, yeah, he's Samwise Gamgee—loyal to a fault. And you never ride in the front seat with a dude. I mean, call me Captain Obvious. What's up with you?"

"I need you to convince him." *We both know you can, Sophs.*

"You're not gonna explain it to me either, are you?"

"There's not time, remember?"

"Sure, that's it." She steals a nervous glance at me. "You're not going after him, are you?"

Well, my instincts were right all along. I wring my hands. Am I actually capable of this? "Of course not," I say.

"You're insane. But I love you."

I breathe an almost-laugh. Yep.

Stuffing socks into her boots, she murmurs, "What would Jesus do if Jesus were me?"

Woah. This is new for Sophie. I'm so excited to hear her asking that. I want to know so much more.

Her frantic hands still inside her suitcase. "You and Levi? I want this for you." She's saying so much more than she's saying. "I'll do it."

Thank you, I say. But my words don't make a sound.

Sophie works her magic. Two minutes later, Austin texts me.

What time

A glance outside tells me it's going to rain any minute.

Now if at all possible?

Meet me at the parking lot in 10

Can you drive over to the library? So people don't see us?

K

If this gets back to Levi your gonna call him and fix it

And when he gets back your gonna tell him so I don't feel like I'm keeping secrets

Levi must be sick of secrets.

Deal.

Again and again, I run over how I'm going to explain this. The task helps distract me from the panic boiling in my stomach.

There's Ethan's truck at the library. Can't have small-school rumors starting over this, so I slide in with my best Sydney Bristow moves and double over in the seat. I crack into a laugh at the absurdity of my covert op, releasing some of the stress.

Austin snorts as he turns the ignition. "Okay, Crazy. You have some explaining to do." He and Sophie really are cut from the same cloth. "You used Sophie against me. This better be important." Gray-blue eyes intense, bushy brown brows raised. His stern look again.

I wince. "Sorry. It is. So, you might have noticed I have some ... quirks?"

"Yup."

I hide my hands under my legs on the old cloth seat. Gritty like I'm used to.

"I don't want to get into the specifics, but things between Levi and me have been really complicated because I have"—I pull in a breath to steel myself—"Because I have these awful memories. Flashbacks. That's why I won't ride shotgun. Or share a couch. And I avoid rain. This ... is an experiment."

Austin must see the darkening sky. "An experiment?"

"To see if I have flashbacks with you too."

"And if you do?"

"If I do, that will suck for me today, but I'll know it's not just with Levi."

"If you don't?"

"If I don't, then he's the catalyst. That wouldn't be good for me and him. It would make things very ... impractical for us."

"What makes it more likely for you to have a flashback?"

I half smile. He's trying to rig the experiment. "Yelling." I won't say touch. That's past the line. "Loud noises."

Austin glances over with a soft look.

I avert my gaze to the window. No rain yet.

"What should I do if your experiment works? What will happen?"

"If it works you can head back. I'll ... freak out, feel scared. I always cry. It's embarrassing."

"That's why you jet out of a room sometimes?"

"Yeah."

"How much of this does Jeeves know?"

"I told him everything yesterday. But not about this." I motion to the truck.

"Finally," he says dramatically. "Mind if I ask about y'all's 'not talking' status? I didn't see him before he left."

"We're going to pray. And talk after break."

"Good. Where am I driving exactly?"

I shrug. "Doesn't matter."

"Music or no?"

I shake my head, and we ride in silence.

Finally, the rain begins. I pull my legs up to my chest in preparation—no concern putting my shoes on Ethan's crusty seat. The harder the rain falls, the heavier the fear drips into my mind. I stare at my window, streams of water disguising anything outside. With Levi, there was thunder.

Here goes. I'm adopting quite a personality transplant for some unreliable information. "Right before you picked me up ..." I'm just loud enough for him to hear over the rain pelting the car. "I told Sophie what you said before, about you and her. She cried. Said she's done with you."

"You did what?! How could—"

And the blackness rushes in.

⁓ℓℓ⁓

Austin parks at the library, brows pressed down.

I wipe my face for the billionth time this week. "She didn't. I would never."

"I realized," he says with chagrin. "You were very believable. I'm sorry I yelled."

"No, I'm sorry. I really appreciate this."

"Sure thing, Kit. I hate that you're living with that."

I attempt a smile and open the truck door.

Okay, I did it. Now what?

⁓ℓℓ⁓

Levi

Feet slipped into slides, towel around my shoulders, I carry my goggles and water bottle up the frosty path. My breath clouds the winter air. Around the outdoor seating, through the back door—stifling heat. I might go back out with a snack. Down the main hall, through the dining room, into the kitchen. I drop my things on the island to open the refrigerator door and—

Levi.

Yes?

Love your enemies.

My fists curl.

CHAPTER FIFTY-FOUR

I NEVER TOLD my family about the last-minute road trip and take the light rail home from I-70, avoiding an hour in the car with telepathic Mom. When I push through the front door, I nearly collapse from the wave of comfort that crashes over me. My shocked brothers lift me onto their shoulders, parading me around the house like I won the Super Bowl. I laugh until I cry.

On my bedroom floor, I push my laptop out and fold into a butterfly stretch. When my chest meets my feet, a rush of nostalgia hits me—I used to spend hours in my room just like this.

It's my first full day at home, and I'm trying to finish a paper so it's off my mind. I have a lot of praying to do, and I don't want this springing to mind every ten minutes. I meant to do it last night, but I was busy with my brothers. I tried to apologize to Mav for not calling enough the last few months. He fussed—he and Mia should start a club—and insisted my being here was better than twenty phone calls. Later, my brothers and I practiced catching popcorn in our mouths while rewatching Grey's favorite SNL scenes, laughing until our sides ached. It's so good to be home.

"Hey, Kit girl." Mom's in the doorway. "Can we talk for a second?"

I save my draft and shut my laptop.

Mom slides to the floor with me. "I've been thinking. And praying. I know you value your privacy about ... what happened this spring. I've been taping my mouth shut to give it to you, but I want you to consider something."

I blink at her.

"You went through a traumatic experience, and you've never ... you won't talk about it. Not to me or anyone, to my knowledge. I want you to reconsider seeing a counselor, someone who loves Jesus and can speak words of wisdom and grace over you, give you strategies. Someone who you think will 'understand.'"

I gnaw on my lip. "I'll think about it."

She squeezes my hand and stands to leave.

"Mom?"

She turns back.

"Thanks."

She sends her enveloping Mom-smile, better than any hug. "I love you, sweetie." And she closes the door behind her.

A counselor? Do I have to?

I hem you in behind and before, and I lay my hand upon you.

Sophie. She mentioned a counselor out of the blue ... originally a trauma counselor. I feel unworthy to call my one-time scare *trauma*, but Sophie thought God wanted her to say it. I grab my phone to ask her for the counselor's contact info. There might be a last-minute opening. I have so many questions. Maybe I finally have the courage to ask them.

⸺ ℓℓ ⸺

Time at home is like a steaming bubble bath on sore muscles. I've been doing *pique* turns across the hardwood, choreographing languid mini-routines as I move from room to room. On a mountain trail, fluffy snow squeaks and crunches under my boots. The dry chill nips at my nose, but the fire's warmth melts it away. In the kitchen, I help peel potatoes and roll out crust.

I set aside hours a day to wander the neighborhood and to curl up on the porch with the heater and my knobby blanket. Sometimes I read a psalm. Sometimes I write my own. As rest and silence seep into my bones, God's whispers grow louder and more frequent. But even when I hear nothing, sitting with him in the quiet is enough. He's always here.

The loss of what I wanted with Levi sits like a brick in my stomach, but it coexists with cranberry and pie and the best sweet potatoes on earth. I'm talked into a snowy game of touch football, and my brothers argue about technique as they teach me to kick it to a precise location on the field.

⸺ ℓℓ ⸺

Another early morning on Friday, so I sneak downstairs for some Bible time and ballet practice while I have the living room to myself.

My mind calms and clears as I practice my *fouetté* turns. Shoulders relaxed and body tired, I fill a glass with water at the fridge. Dancing is the best respite from my own mind. Free and weightless, I'm distracted from my incessant worries, but the relief is fleeting.

Do not be anxious about anything,
but in everything

by prayer and supplication
with thanksgiving
let your requests be made known to me.

I'm reminded of what Mav said to me over FaceTime. "I'm not worried about this, and you shouldn't be either. I've been watching God take care of you my whole life."

He was right. You have.

And what else did he say? "You can trust that God's plan is better." It's that mastermind idea again. I won't need to be anxious if I really trust that his plan is better than mine. I sit on a stool and cradle the glass between my hands.

My plan isn't working. I need yours. I want yours. It's better, right? Yours always is. I'm scared, but I trust you. Thank you for taking care of me year after year. Thank you for this house, my family, a perfect place to go to school, and the scholarship to pay for it. Thank you for protecting me in April. Thank you for Mom and Mav and friends who make me laugh and tell me what I need to hear.

I imagine shoving cardboard boxes of worry out the front door, leaving them for God to take away. Worries about my mind, my nightmares, my safety, my sanity, my friendships, my family, my major, my future.

Here. I can't manage all of this. It's crippling. Take it. Please. You take it.

I've got this.

Another box looms, demanding so much brain space. The Levi box. It's full to the brim of anxious questions, hopes for his present and future, missing his closeness and friendship, shame for hurting him, fear that I'll never find someone like him again.

You'd better take this one too. I don't want to give it up, but I've only made a mess with it. You handle it. You take care of him. You'll have to be the one.

I've got this too.

Mysteriously, miraculously, I'm lighter. I've shed hundreds of pounds of mental weight. Something tells me I'll be doing this again soon.

Remember.

Yes. The freedom of ballet—whenever I can make that happen—will be a reminder. I don't want to let these boxes accumulate in my mind again. I have to lay it all back down. Again and again and again.

CHAPTER FIFTY-FIVE

"WANT SOME COMPANY?"

Later that day Mom catches me in my left splits—they're finally back—while I finish my schoolwork on the floor. Tomorrow afternoon my friends will pick me up for the drive back. This time they're splitting the drive into two days.

"Yes, please."

Snow floats into a pile outside my bedroom window. Mom grabs her crochet basket and settles against the bed beside me, looping her red hair into a knot.

I ease out of the splits and open Spotify on my laptop. "Walker Hayes?" I ask. "Rich Mullins?" Mom and I share some favorite artists—her old go-tos are surprisingly good, and I keep her up to date.

"Let's do some Walker." Her needles find rhythm on a blanket she's making for her friend's new granddaughter. It's weird that she's crocheting now. "Don't laugh at my old lady activity," she jokes.

Reading my mind like she always does. Now I know she's been cheating in her telepathy somewhat. Levi said my face is expressive.

"It helps me slow down," she says. "Hurry must be fought."

When "Fancy Like" comes on, we do a sitting version of the TikTok dance and deteriorate into giggles. She asked me to teach it to her back when the song came out.

I'm nearly done with my work when she goes still and rigid. Her eyes turn glassy. It isn't precisely what I do when I freak out, but maybe a miniature version of that.

I bend toward her. Is she okay? Did something happen to her too? "Mom?"

No answer. She appears to be listening. I turn my attention to what's playing. "Delorean." I know the song. Mom would say it's inappropriate, but that's clearly not what she's upset about.

She tries to swallow her tears. "It's so hard as a mom to know how much to share. Maybe I should have told you a long time ago, but I didn't want to burden you with my past mistakes, with information that is ... too much."

The song is about triggering happy memories, about falling in love. What kind of bad memory could this be?

"I need to tell you more about dating your dad." Her eyes remain unfocused and aimed at my side table.

"I've been wondering how you knew that Dad was The One." Oops. Outside voice.

That drags Mom's mind back to the present as if I tied a rope around it and yanked. Her red-brown eyebrows shoot up. I think I gave her mental whiplash.

"Well," she starts, "I could imagine building a life with him from early in our relationship, but we weren't ready for that until we got our priorities straight. We had to break up to learn some hard truths."

"Break up? I thought you've been together since you were

teenagers." How could I know so little about my parents' story? Looks like I'm not the only one who hides things.

"We met when we were sixteen, yes. It was a whirlwind. I loved him so much, so soon, but things were rocky, to put it lightly. Your dad made me incredibly happy, but happiness wasn't enough. Like I've always told you, marriage exists to make us better, not to make us happy. And a relationship that becomes an idol can't make you better. I'm thankful we learned that before we got married and not after." She tilts her head, knowing I have something to say. She always knows.

"So, if happiness isn't the metric, how does a girl know when she's found the right guy?"

She squeezes my arm and considers. "To answer that I'd want to know *what* she's falling in love with. People fall in love for all sorts of reasons that don't make their person marriage material. But, is she falling in love with his relationship with the Lord? With his loyalty and devotion to her? With his commitment to growing as a person? Attraction and fun and humor and intelligence and personality are wonderful, but they aren't enough on their own."

"What if you had to make, like, a list? A deal-breaker list?"

She considers. "A guy who One"—she holds up a finger—"worships Jesus with everything he is, which should imply that he, Two, wants to grow. Three, loves you more than he loves any other human. And Four, believes divorce is not an option. That's the absolute ideal. Most anything else can be sorted out along the way because of One to Three, and the time for that to happen exists because of Four."

I trace the keys on my laptop. I shouldn't torment myself with thoughts about Levi like this, but I can't not. He's all of that. He checks every box.

I wish things were different. I wish I could have him. I wish I hadn't gotten so attached.

But I'll trust you. Your plan is better.

"Tell me about falling in love with Dad? You never told me about the breakup stuff."

"Is all of this about Levi perhaps?" she asks.

"You first, then I'll spill."

"Deal. Let's take a walk."

Dad ambles in when we're on our feet. "Hey, sweetie. It's so good to have you home this week." He scratches my back in his way and kisses me on the head.

I squeeze his side and step back to analyze him. His brown hair has more gray in it since summer. The laugh lines around his mouth tell of his years smiling at Mom. I can almost imagine him when he was my age.

He wraps an arm around Mom's waist.

"Archie." Mom smiles flirtatiously at him. "Kit and I are going on a walk so I can tell her about falling in love with you."

His eyes sparkle. He grabs Mom's hand to twirl her in a circle and dip her. She laughs and snuggles into his chest for a hug. He squeezes her tight and kisses her head.

These two ... This is nothing new, but the bone-deep ache when I see it is. I wish I knew how to—

Nope. I shove the mental box back onto the porch. This isn't for me to mastermind.

For those who love me, all things work together for good.

"God knew," Dad says to Mom. "He used it all. His gifts are better than anything we could dream up." He winks at me and leaves us to our walk.

I suck in a breath and let it out. Downstairs, I slide into my warmest coat, hat, and boots and open the front door.

Your gifts are better than anything I could dream up. I can trust you with this.

"I'LL START FROM THE BEGINNING," Mom says. Her shoulders square with her determination to help me.

I've been pushing her away when I need her most. And what has my secrecy bought me? Nothing but isolation. I can't do without two-way openness with my people. I crash into Mom with a bear hug, parka squished against parka.

"Oh, my sweet girl." Tears are in her voice. "I love you so much."

"I love you, Mom. Okay, go."

"Your dad ... I fell for him so fast. He was charming and affectionate and thought the world of me. He liked my strong opinions and all my words—things others had no patience for. He was a go-getter and climbed the ranks of the Blockbuster we met at in no time flat. Such a hunk."

"Got it, Mom."

"Right. I was crushing so hard. So when he finally asked me out, I was all over him." She winces in apology.

Parent romance is so cringey. And that ache is back.

"I knew I wasn't going to go all the way, but—Here's the thing. Kissing is like a snowball rolling down a mountain. It can't help but grow. More and more snow accumulates, and it explodes at the bottom. That's how it's set up, and that's how it goes. I was under the impression that I could just stop somewhere on the mountain, where I felt was a good idea, and move on with my day, but that wasn't what I experienced."

That checks out, but ... where is this going?

"It was a beautiful time of falling in love and feeling so deeply, but also, I was a wreck. I felt so guilty. I knew I was doing things I shouldn't, things God didn't intend for me until after I was married. Hence my reaction to that song. That was us, except I don't remember it fondly. I still fight shame over those memories." She rolls her shoulders.

I forget that she has a tough inner critic behind the feisty exterior.

"The Bible doesn't cover those in between things. Now, I believe that's because none of it is kosher—ha, so to speak—but at the time I scoured every verse I could find and just felt confused and overwhelmed and helpless to stop. Our relationship kept growing—faster than it probably should have because of the physical bonding—but also emotionally and spiritually in really special ways. Even though we were so young, I knew so soon that he was the love of my life, the one I wanted to marry, you know, when we were older. But our constant fighting about the Snowball Effect was enough to implode our relationship. I broke up with him after senior year because I couldn't take it anymore. We could never find a way to fix it, and I couldn't live that way until we were old enough to get married."

I shake my head. I can't imagine any of that. "Is that why you went to a different college at first?"

"Yes. I almost followed him to Mines, but it's good that I didn't. I had a lot to learn apart from him first."

"Did you date other dudes?"

"I did."

So weird. "And?"

"And none of them were Archie. We were apart for a year, and it was torture. I cried myself to sleep so many nights. It felt like half of me had gotten amputated. That half was walking around in another state, dating I didn't know who. Thankfully it was pre-social media. All that would have made it so much worse. Anyway, the middle stuff—the stuff between kissing and the finale—it's part of the glue that God gave for a husband and wife. To cement them together." She grimaces at the expression I'm making. "It's a lot to stomach. That's why it's taken me this long. Should I stop?"

"No, I want to hear the end."

"Okay. We'd been apart about a year when your dad wrote me a letter." She chuckles to herself. "I walked to lunch with my friend as I read it and nitpicked every misspelled word and missed comma, just trying to cope with my mind exploding. I really never thought I'd talk to him again. And I wasn't going to just jump back into something that had hurt me. But a lot of prayer and long-distance calls later, we came to a solution—a strategy to keep God first in our hearts, never ever second. One way I did that was by spending time with Jesus before I spent time with Archie each day. And we quit kissing till we were engaged. We also quit watching TV together, since that was a big temptation spot for us."

"Wait, you quit kissing? Like, completely?"

"Yep."

Woah. "That's a big commitment."

"No kidding. Considering how much chemistry there was—"

"Got it. Say no more."

She nods quickly. "Our experience with the Snowball Effect taught us that not kissing was the only way we could maintain the boundaries we were committed to. So we did it. And that practice of putting our commitment to God's way before our affection for each other was really good for us, in retrospect. All of the self-discipline and daily choices were preparing us for marriage in a way I didn't expect. Never kissing him was crazy hard, but actually easier than trying to jump off the snowball mountain mid-roll."

"Is that why you got married while you were still in college?"

"No, not really. I'm pretty convinced we would have gotten married during college either way. I knew who I wanted to spend my life with, and I wanted to start it already. It's hard to wait around simply because other people want that for you."

I half laugh. Mom still refuses to do things because other people insist.

"The people we respected were on board with us getting married but not about the timing. It would have been different if they had concerns about Archie himself. Anyway, getting married that young is hard, but it's just a different hard from waiting. We can talk about that more if it comes up." She eyes me with an obvious question.

"Okay. A deal's a deal," I say. Time to spill about Levi. It's long overdue.

Dread pulls in my gut as I feverishly type questions.

What will she think of me? What will she say? What if it's like the first time? Do I have the courage to try this again?

It's not my job to figure it all out. This is the next step. I just know it.

Okay, God. Here goes. Help me trust you. Make sure I only retain what's true. Protect me from anything that isn't from you.

Sophie's counselor replied. She has a spot from a cancellation this afternoon.

Sharing with Levi unlocked a door for me. His response to

the truth astonished me. Like Mom's, actually, except for some reason I always thought her opinion didn't count, that her motherly love prevented her from seeing my fault in it all. But my heart holds a spark of hope that someone else might see my story the same way as Levi, or at least kindly—kinder than I have. Kinder than Tess did. Levi's response made me feel lovable, like I still deserve dignity, even when I didn't make the decisions I wish I had. Like I can fail and still have value. Like I can trust God more and surrender.

And if I have the courage to share my brokenness with him, of all people, I have the courage to share with a perfect stranger. The risk is worth the possible reward.

Cozied under two blankets for a final front porch prayer time, I turn up the heater and spot Stella on a walk with Judy. A spruce tree hides my view of the driveway and the sidewalk beyond, but just before they disappear behind it, Stella stops. Judy tugs on the leash lightly, then firmer, persuading her with a gentle voice. Not having it, Stella plops her long body down on the icy sidewalk, unwilling to move another inch.

That's me. I'm Stella.

God's been calling me, pulling me, coaxing me "home." He's showed me in a thousand ways that I don't need to be the mastermind or to protect myself, that he's got it. There are beautiful things waiting for me if I'll just follow along. I've been so resistant! Like this basset hound, I've been exerting so much energy dragging my feet, avoiding the hard part. Every step was a challenge against my stubbornness. God has had to pull me by the leash the whole way here.

My chuckle turns into a laugh and then into full blown hilarity. I kick off the blankets. My socked feet chill on contact with the icy path to the driveway, but I don't slow. Judy gapes as I come barreling down to the sidewalk with arms flailing, and I remember to pull myself together.

"I'm sorry. Did I scare you? I just would love to pet Stella here."

"Oh, surely! Back from college?"

"Yes. It's so good to be home." I kneel on the sidewalk. "Stella. Hi. Do you remember me?" Her droopy eyes squint as I itch around her ears. "I understand, sweet girl. Sometimes I have to get pulled along too. It's so warm in your house though."

"And we'll have breakfast," Judy adds.

"Ooh and breakfast. If you'll trust Miss Judy to get you home, you have so many good things waiting for you. You can do this." I stand. "Thank you. She's precious."

Judy chuckles. "She's a character, that's for sure. Okay, Stella Bella, come on. Almost home."

She begrudgingly rises to her enormous feet and takes the smallest step.

I PERCH on my dorm room bed, chewing a hole in my lip and eyeing the box of Tic Tacs sitting on my desk. What should I text Levi?

At a soft knock at my window, I pull back the curtain. It's him, with a big white box under his arm. Gold script and his blond hair glimmer in the sun. That favorite face of mine is a sight for sore eyes. So much concern, so many questions are etched into it.

"Kit."

I can't really hear him, but I may as well. I've heard that scrumptious murmur enough.

"Levi," I whisper back.

"Meet you at the bench?"

I grab the paper-wrapped package on my desk and cram the stolen Tic Tacs into my pocket, running through the hall to the stairwell.

I heave the door open and motion for him to come in for Open Dorms. He follows silently. He's never been in my suite before. My suitemates aren't around, but they could be back any minute.

When I finally told Mom everything, she had to remove her jaw from the sidewalk. To her, there was an obvious thread of God's orchestration throughout our relationship. I tried to tell her how impractical things were for me and Levi. "Then keep praying," she said, "and definitely ask Levi what he heard this week. If he heard a no, that's it. But it sounds to me like God's been setting this up all along, like he's gift-wrapped this relationship for you. I really think it's time you make your choices and let Levi make his own."

I prop open the suite door as required and whip around to him. "Hi." I shyly grin at Levi and his box. "For me?" I mean both.

"For you." He opens the big box with one hand so I can see the macarons of every flavor inside. This doesn't look like a no.

The box has attitude, like it hails from a fabulous bakery, folded by hand by someone French with excellent posture and perhaps a sneer of superiority. I want to dive in and transport myself there.

"Did you fly back from Connecticut with these?"

"I did. I dragged Everett with me to a patisserie in The City." Not something he'd do if he'd heard a no.

I snag a pink one as he closes the box. Strawberry bursts in my mouth with a perfectly delicate bite. A moan escapes. "Bless you, cosmopolitan New York."

"They were my 'personal item' on the plane," he says. "Very nearly stepped on. I'm clearly under the impression you're open to bribery." His face changes like he regrets the joke, and he sets the box on the coffee table.

My heart beats not a no, not a no, not a no.

Not a no?

I can't answer until I swallow but give a closed-mouth smile. Then, "What am I gonna do with you?"

"I hoped we could cover that topic," he says seriously. "What do you have there?" He motions to the package still in my hand.

"It's for you. Later." I set the handmade leather-bound journal I found for him next to the bakery box. Unable to wait another second, I take a step closer, almost touching, and look way up.

Anticipation and hope replace his hesitation. So much is different from the last time I stood like this. I have answers, strategies. It's scary—terrifying—but I'm ready. He can help me. I'll let him, teach him what I need.

"Kit." That gravelly, soft voice. "I've been praying, and—"

"Did you hear a no?" I blurt.

"No. I didn't."

"Me neither. It's not going to be simple, but ..." Let him make his own choices. "I'm in if you are." I'm resolute. I'm not my own protector. This is the new Brave Kit.

I don't have everything figured out. I don't have much of anything figured out. But I won't be Stella another day. I think this is the next step, so I'm taking it with gumption, with enthusiasm, with hope. God's got this. God's got me.

Levi rocks his head side to side like he isn't sure. He's clearly messing with me because my favorite hazel eyes lock onto mine, full of awe and amusement and growing wet.

Is this really happening?

Oh, I'm so thankful. I can't do this without you. I can't do anything without you. You're right here with me, right?

I study Levi's drumming hand. He knows why I never hold that hand, and he wants me anyway. But I want to. What if I can? I lurch out and slip my fingers into his palm. His fingers close around mine, and the dark clouds in my mind swell and cut a pit of dread in my stomach.

When I am afraid, I put my trust in you.

My breathing turns ragged, but I refuse to despair.

Help me. Protect me. If you won't take this away, teach me to fight it.

I'm always here.

Though the surging fear, I fight the instinct to run, to cower.

You want good for me and you never waste the bad. You "put my tears in your bottle." You care. You love me. I can trust you.

I shuffle a step back, still gripping his hand, retrieve the Tic Tac box from my pocket with my free hand, and concentrate on it. My counselor taught me about using grounding objects.

Set my shoulders. Time to face my fears and try what I learned. I pull in a shaky breath and focus on the feeling of the plastic on my fingertips, the sound of Tic Tacs falling, the texture of the label, the weight. I picture the day I stole it from Levi and ran off, undone not by fear but by closeness to him. An okay undone, a good kind, not the same as before. The darkness consuming my mind dissipates. Relief and gratitude flood into its place. A shuddering sigh tumbles out.

Thank you, God. Thank you ... thank you.

I intertwine my fingers with Levi's and sheepishly peek at his reaction to it all.

Surprise and tenderness mix in his expression. His warm hand squeezes—he's gentle and attentive as ever—and his thumb moves down mine, sparking a zing along its path.

"So ... can I talk you into a date tonight?" I ask playfully. "I want to hear about your week. And I have so much to tell you." I hold up the Tic Tac box to imply its relevance and hide it in my pocket, embarrassed to be copying his habit.

The creases at his eyes reappear in the dreamiest way. "Absolutely."

"Everett has the 'grinders' on the sailboat memory, but I was thinking barbecue in a canoe might be a fun Texas twist. I found a good place."

He's been pursuing me with vulnerable abandon. I hope he can see that I'm in this too, that it's not going to be one-sided between us.

"Sounds like a daydream," he says.

You made this possible. You said yes to all of those prayers. Thank you.

He slowly lifts his free hand to tuck my hair behind my ear. I close my eyes and feel his thumb brush down my cheek and under my chin. Tingles down my spine. My lips part.

When my eyelids flutter open, his head is moving toward the side of mine. He moves inch by inch, looking for a yes which I provide nonverbally though wholeheartedly. He kisses my temple, my cheek, my jaw, my neck, and back up. My heart hammers. All I can think is Jane's line in *Pride and Prejudice*, "Can you die of happiness?"

My free hand goes rogue and combs through his waves. It feels as good as I thought it would, soft and thick with the slightest stiffness. It's all I can do not to destroy his hairdo. His eyes drop to my mouth.

Ohhh-kay. I'd better tell him before I sabotage my own plan. Or maybe I shouldn't. It suddenly sounds like a terrible idea.

With a little sigh I pull my hands away and wrap them around his back, noting the Tic Tacs at my hip. They're ready just in case. He pulls me close, nestling his head on mine. My shoulders relax as I hear his racing heart slow beneath his sweater. My new favorite sound. In his arms I'm safe, known. Perfect contentment.

This strong back ... Keeping myself from escalating is my new full-time job.

"Your hair smells so good," he says.

I chuckle and look all the way up, chin on his chest.

I'd better tell him now. Now that I know that I can touch him —and it's amazing—this is what I want, what I need. It's okay because I'm not earning my place. Deep breath. "So ... I have a request you might not like."

That light in his eyes I adore beams recklessly from his whole face. "Anything."

CHAPTER FIFTY-EIGHT

I ARRIVE in my suite lounge that night in a half-float, half-panic.
Is a person supposed to be this happy? Is this even healthy?

Sophie is sitting in the dark, typing up a storm.

"Sophs, hi!"

She lowers the cover of her laptop and squints up at me. "No.
Way. I know that look. You've been with Mr. Dreamboat."

I bite my lip and bob my head.

More bravery required. But these three have earned my trust.
Two-way openness. Am I ready to brave a Tess repeat? Not really.
But I think I can trust Sophie. And either way, I don't have to
hold so tightly to my friendships. God will provide.

Right?

Right.

"I want to tell you some things," I say. "If you have time. And
... I have some juicy news."

She discards her laptop like a frisbee and bounds over.

"And I want to hear about your—"

But she crashes me into a hug and bounces around until she pulls back with a jolt, hands on my shoulders. "But we need ice cream. I've found the inverse to Ben & Jerry's heartbreak pints. Have you had Blue Bell? Austin introduced me. And I don't know your favorite flavor. And Mia's not back yet. And it's your bed time." She shakes me.

A buoyant laugh bubbles out of me. "I'll sleep when I'm dead." I step around the corner to crack open our door. "Ayumi, come get ice cream with us? Please? I need to tell you guys something."

Curiosity transforms her face. "Okay."

Mia bursts into the suite. "Is Kit back?"

"Oh, she's back," Sophie says with meaning.

"Mamma Mia!" I call.

She turns the corner to find me. "What are you doing with jeans on at a time like—" She gasps, and I'm yanked into another hug.

"Thank you." I squeeze her tighter. "For everything."

⁓ℓℓℓ⁓

Levi

I spent hours this week listening for Jesus's voice. He felt so close —in front of my fire, on the dock, walking the shoreline at Greenwich Point Park. He knew I'd need time to lay down my hatred for Kit's ex before it congealed to venom in my veins.

As I read about Jesus's life in the Gospels, he whispered to me about surrender and sacrifice and love. He reminded me that love isn't just one life-altering decision. It's an hourly commitment to put another first, to long for their best good, to pray for them and cry with them and delight in them. He assured me I could trust him, and then I had to keep waiting to see what he was doing. But what he was doing was even better than I could have imagined. He's been answering yes, yes, yes to my prayers.

I thought love was comfort, a fireplace on a cold day, and I have hope that mine will grow into that. But it's also danger. Starting with a single spark, it's grown into a wildfire. I played a part—I've been feeding it. Every minute with Kit nourished the fire until I was helpless to control its spread. The flames grew in intensity and threatened everything I held dear. Now, I couldn't reverse love's impact on my life if I wanted to. But I don't want that. Not for a second.

It's not time to tell Kit I love her. I want to take this slow, do it right. She likes to be eased into anything new, and I can do that for her.

I slide out my phone. I can finally text her whenever I want— one of a thousand perks of finally being a couple—but this particular text has my fingers drumming against the back. I don't know how she'll react to my surprise.

As long as she knows she's cared for, seen, it's served its purpose. Now is the time.

> Free after class?

> I'd like to show you something.

Hey, boyfriend. :)

Yes. I'm intrigued...

Is she making fun of my old nickname for her? I laugh aloud. Good thing Austin isn't here. He'd have a field day.

> Meet you at the bench at 4.

> If I may ask a favor, wear leggings?

I twitch in my desk chair. She's going to think I'm a creep until she understands.

> I'm surprised. Mr. Put Together wants me to wear leggings?

> You look amazing in them, but I have a different reason.

> Hmm.

It's time. I could puke. Or run a marathon.

I shouldn't be this nervous. Worst case, she doesn't want it and that's fine. No, worst case she thinks I'm over the top. I am, too. I went out on a limb, took a risk. Tenacity.

I squeeze the tiny hand I get to hold. Everything is better when Kit's next to me.

Part of me is relieved it's finally time. Austin and Haymitch helped me out so much—both with the execution of my plan and by backing me up when I repurposed the prank prep space I found. Anything for Kit. Besides, there will be plenty of time for our prank next semester, and I have months to figure out another spot.

A pack of the guys walk from the gym to an early dinner. When they spot us, they gape. Kit and I were off campus till late last night—word isn't out yet.

I push my sleeves up, keeping hold of her hand. Here we go.

"Dude. Jeeves."

"Right?" Kit stops when we reach them. "I gave him a tough time for a bit there." She cozies up to me, wrapping around my arm, running a finger down it. She gives me a face that's at once apologetic and alluring.

This time the awareness that she's putting on a show sends a rush of adrenaline surging through me. She likes me enough to set the record straight. She looks out for my reputation, on top of everything else.

They react like the rowdy bunch they are, with "Oh, it's like that!" and "Look who's off the bench!"

"Nothing he couldn't handle," Calvin flippantly replies to Kit. He's a good guy, but his role as RA this year has done nothing good for his ego. "Glad to see it's working out though. 'Lit' has got to be the coolest 'ship name ever."

A genuine laugh bursts from Kit.

"Congrats, bro," Noah says.

Mateo looks impressed but would never admit as much.

"Never doubted you, man" from Ethan.

Sure …

Pats on the shoulder. Fist bumps. And just like that, I'm back.

It wasn't even about the prank? I suppress a head shake at their fickle respect. Good thing I was ready to trade it all permanently for a chance with her. "Thanks, guys."

As they move on, Calvin says beneath faux coughs, "Someone's getting showered later." Hoisting a fully clothed Flooder into the communal shower when he wins the girl is floor tradition and a thorough endorsement. Note to self—keep my phone and keys out of my pocket for a day or two.

"Those guys gave you a hard time about me?" Kit asks, insightful as ever. She releases my arm and brushes both hands down on the way to hold mine.

It's a slower movement than I expect, and I catch her eyes darting down to watch, relishing what's under her fingertips. In stark contrast to a minute ago, that was completely for her. I croak a "yes" and shiver in pleasure. Those hands on me … it feels even better than I thought it would.

"All better," she says with a cheeky smile.

I eye her and joke, "It's very selfless of you to date me to save my reputation."

"At complete sacrifice of my own comfort." She covertly

points at a scowling girl several feet away. I recognize her but don't recall her name.

I squint at Kit in question, and she references our intertwined fingers. "She's the third one on this walk. Tom Holland wants his popularity back. Oh, new rule. You hand deliver any gifts."

She's talking a mile a minute. I've never seen her so cheerful, so at peace.

Thank you.

"Happily," I say. "But why?"

"I can't handle any more awkward handoffs. Those poor girls don't need any more reminders that the best guy on campus is taken."

I smirk at her. I'm thrilled that the compliments are still in full force, but dirty looks? Poor girls? "I appreciate the ringing endorsement, but I'm pretty sure you're imagining a lot of that."

"I'm relieved you're not half as cocky as I thought you were," she quotes with a flirty undertone. She knocks me with her elbow and I reciprocate.

Kit.

It's all so much better than I imagined. I had no idea how much she was holding back for my sake, trying to be fair to me because she was convinced our relationship couldn't go anywhere. I had no idea how much strain she was under before, at the mercy of her own mind. I can't believe I'm holding her hand right now.

I check on our walking progress. Only a couple more minutes and we're there.

"Should I be nervous too?" Oh, she's reading me.

I brush my thumb down hers to reassure her. "No. Nothing to be nervous about."

"Okay ..."

I push my Tic Tacs farther up my palm so my fingers can pull the key out of my pocket and hand it to her. She blinks at it.

"I've been working on something. For you. I want to explain before we get there."

She stares at me with brows raised, but she's still walking, so I haven't completely freaked her out. She finally plucks it from my hand and studies it like it's the key to a puzzle rather than to a door.

"First of all, I want you to know that Samwise and Haymitch and I did most of it ourselves. I didn't want you to feel uncomfortable about me spending too much on it."

"Did most of what? Spend too much on what?"

I squeeze her hand in anticipation, and she reacts with a jolt, yanks her hands away, balls them at her chest. She stops in her tracks on the sidewalk.

Oh no. The squeeze? "I'm so sorry." It's been less than a day. I have no idea what's risky and what isn't.

"I'm okay." She hesitantly grabs my hand again and continues walking. "Go on."

"Please tell me, Kit. I can't bear to scare you again."

This time she squeezes my hand. "It's going to happen sometimes. I'm sorry."

"Can I have more guidance than that?"

"Gentle is good. So just be you."

Please keep me from triggering her. Heal her mind. Show me how to take good care of her.

"No hand squeezes?" I ask.

"Um, maybe no squeezes while I get used to things. Now spill. What is this key for?"

No hand squeezes. Must remember. I hold her hand like it might shatter. "You'll see. So, listen, I did this to show you that I care about you ..." See? I can tone it down. "So it's about to serve its whole purpose. There is no pressure whatsoever to use it. It will benefit people after you, so it's completely up to you whether you want to use it or not." I'm repeating myself. At least I'm not speaking like my father.

Beautiful dimples reappear on her face. "Levi. What's going on?"

I open the door and guide her into the gym, down the hall with the multipurpose rooms. Here's the door. Her door.

She holds up the key in question, biting her lip. Resisting the urge to kiss that lip will be excruciating. I kiss the top of her head instead. She shrugs her shoulders in that delighted way that makes my heart pound, and I'm overwhelmed that Jesus said yes. That she's mine to care for.

Thank you.

And I motion for her to unlock the door.

CHAPTER FIFTY-NINE

A DANCE STUDIO, right here on campus. To my right, a barre. To my left, a pristine mirrored wall. I'm greeted by my own shocked face in the reflection, blue eyes wide and thrilled. I step onto the polished wood floor and kick off my shoes. Dance floors can't have dirt on them. Levi chuckles—I don't know why—and maybe follows suit. I'm too busy gaping at this magical place.

He did this?

When I glance over, he's sheepish, but at least his posture is relaxing. I run my hand along the brand-new barre, smooth and bolted firmly to the wall. I can't resist a *glissade* as I cross the room —"I didn't help it." Film on the back window blurs a swaying pine outside.

Matte black walls, speakers mounted discreetly. A cognac leather arm chair is nestled in the corner on a sheepskin rug. Levi's fingerprints are everywhere, so to speak. It's the most modern, elegant studio I've ever seen.

Oh—and on that cozy chair proudly sits a red box topped by a white satin bow as big as the box itself. Broad white letters scream "Capezio." I know what kind of present comes in boxes like that. I spin to Levi.

"Open it." He tips his head toward the prize.

I sprint the rest of the way, nearly slipping in my socks, and tear into the box like it's Christmas morning. Lyrical dance shoes in the perfect size. He remembered every detail.

"Do you remember at IHOP when you told us you loved ballet?" he says. "You had the most beautiful look in your eyes. Like pure joy." He arrives at my corner with uncharacteristic shyness. "It was obvious you were going through something, and I just wanted you to have, well, your version of what swimming is for me. I had this feeling that it might help. But like I said, no pressure."

Wow. So many gifts. Thank you.

I drop the shoes and reach to hug Levi but flinch, remembering the risk. I spot a Tic Tac box in his pocket and give it a try. His arms fold around me and I settle into his chest. Maybe hugs are okay. Could I have been hugging him all this time?

Every one of my muscles slackens until I'm floating in comfort. Even Levi's hugs overachieve.

"You have no idea how good this is," I say. "How helpful, how perfect." I'll have so many opportunities to remember to let go, to give God my worries. I lift my chin to his chest. "What do you mean you and the guys did it yourself? What was this before?"

His arms loosen to motion. "It was a multipurpose room. They were only using it for storage a few months ago. The wood floors were already in, but we refinished them. Haymitch taught us." He beams. "We installed the mirrors and barre and speakers and everything. And painted."

I shake my head. I can't believe he did manual labor to keep me from feeling guilty. "And the school let you?"

"Yes." A mysterious look. "I made an arrangement. I'll tell you another time if you want."

"Okay ..."

I enjoy his back and sides as I pull away. How can someone so solid give such delectable hugs? More research is warranted.

I ditch my socks and try on these beautiful new shoes. Soft tan leather, a perfect fit. My feet arrive in first position with a will of their own. Leg out to *tendu* in front of me. Those toes are so happy squeezing into a hard point. My leg circles around in *ronde de jambe*. I can hardly stand still. Something in me begs to be unleashed.

"It's yours until you graduate."

I whip my head to him. "Mine?"

He confirms.

I'll wrap my head around that later. For now I push up my long sleeves and twist my hair into a tight knot. I need a hair tie, but the bobby pin in my pocket will do. Ah, and the leggings make sense. I hope he's not expecting me to show off right now.

"Should I get out of here?" he asks. "Or do you want to take me up on our deal?"

"That does make for some excellent bribery." I return his flirty smile.

I step into him, and his strong arms wrap around me again. He smells even better from here. Clean laundry and mint and boy smell. His heart beats a contented slow beat. What a dream.

"No, get out of here," I say. "I need to acquaint myself with my studio." Sending him out while squeezing him close—a new kind of mixed message.

He leans toward the side of my head but abruptly stops.

"It's okay. Those don't seem to cause trouble."

A kiss on my temple. Bliss.

"Thank you." I feel that old tug to pay him back, but I fight it. Appreciation doesn't feel like enough, but it'll have to be.

"For the kiss?" he jokes. "They're on unlimited offer."

I send him a goofy, transcendent smile. "Yes, please. But really, you're amazing. I can't believe this place. It couldn't be more perfect."

He brushes a wisp of hair back with whisper-soft fingers. And then he strides away with a swoop to grab his shoes. "Let's talk Wodehouse later," he adds. "I did my homework." A wink, and the door clicks shut behind him.

I relish a now familiar flutter in my stomach. I can't believe this is my life. I pan my surreal surroundings. And my studio.

Share it.

A dream floods into my mind and courses through my veins. Mayberry girls stretching before class in a circle on the floor. A Bible study before ballet instruction. A theme for each week. One for hope. One for surrender. One for courage ... A floor combination with steps to echo the theme. Faith made physical.

Is that you?

A combination for hope lays itself out in my mind. Arabesque with a forward reach, step forward, drag turn. Slow fifth relevé with port de bras and eyes to the sky. Piqué turn, chassé, grand jeté. The beauty of those precious girls acting out their faith with their bodies.

Wait, I can't teach. And that's too much to cover in a beginner class. And who would even come?

Right. I glance at the ceiling and breathe out a half-laugh. *I'll let you be the mastermind.*

For now, it's time to warm up. I'm dying to try that grand jeté across this glorious floor.

EPILOGUE

____

Fourteen Months Later

____

A DOOR SLAMS down the street. My heart lurches. Levi runs a thumb down my hand as he checks my reaction. My sigh of gratitude puffs visibly into the cool January air. It's been months since my last full-on freakout.

Thank you, God.

Of course, life didn't magically turn fluffy and straightforward when my flashbacks subsided. Sweet Levi is still an alien. Everett's been spiraling. Grey's dating a girl I don't trust. People keep judging Levi for his money, and lately I've been lumped into that too. The whole thing with Sophie and Austin. I'm not sure if I should stick with all these math classes. Levi's pushing Colorado after college—he's amazing—but his family needs him, and he misses the ocean.

I straighten to reset. Nope—not my job.

You take it. I'm just following you.

Levi squeezes my hand and leads me through a door into a sleek lobby with framed prints of the Dallas skyline. He releases me to step to the receptionist at the desk. That man is a vision in his tailored navy suit. I can't believe he's mine. He turns to wink at me and I nearly swoon off my heels. Someone bring me some smelling salts from Regency England.

I twist around to take in my surroundings. Is this a fancy museum of some kind? Why are we dressed like this? Finally, he arrives back at my spot.

"Tom Ford should put you on a billboard," I say.

He formally offers the crook of his arm—I love when he does that—and guides me down the empty hall to a well-polished elevator. A blurry reflection of my black velvet dress stares back at me. It's easily the most beautiful object I've ever owned ... and the first formal dress I've worn since Prom. With Levi, beauty can be an asset rather than—

Oh. His hand presses on my lower back, pulling me close.

He angles down to whisper in my ear, "You in this dress. Mm. Audrey Hepburn wants her elegance back."

This guy. My blissful grin is interrupted by a demanding *ding* from the elevator, and it falls to a pout. Up, up, up we go until I'm thoroughly confused. How high are we going? There are only two buttons—for the lobby and one other floor—but the whir of the ascending elevator continues.

When we finally step out ... Wow. City views for days. Floor-to-ceiling windows afford a glorious view of the sun poised to set behind the Dallas skyline. Soon the city lights will glow. This must be Reunion Tower, five hundred feet above it all. I tug on the crook of Levi's arm. Mystery dances in his eyes. This dim restaurant drips with chandeliers and elegant diners. Clinking forks, and soft, tinkering laughter melds with the distant notes of a piano.

"Levi," I whisper. "Is this too much?"

"I'd like to spend a little bit of that money on the girl I love."

Okay. I need Levi to know that I love him with or without his trust fund.

Protect him from relying on it and from being hurt again because of it.

He glances over with a question. Oh, I quit walking. The hostess continues to a semi-private window-side table on the far end of the dining area. Of course Levi would plan ahead and finagle the best spot in the restaurant. But that means this isn't a spur of the moment dinner after all. Could it be ... No. I overheard Austin imply that it's next weekend.

Levi thanks the hostess and pulls out my chair. "What do you think?"

"Maybe we keep the fabulous dinners to special occasions?"

He agrees with his most kissable smirk. Let Ben Folds know—I'm the luckiest.

This afternoon he brought me an enormous box filled with this magnificent dress—for no reason at all—and said we needed a place for me to wear it. Then he whisked me off to Dallas with barely an hour's notice. I don't love surprises, but I'll grant that this is well worth a change of plans. To think I could be eating at Saga right now.

Levi

My eyes keep drifting past Kit's shoulder, thumb drumming my fork as I fight to stay present. Her head tilts, catching every slip of my attention. This is the night.

"Spill," she says. "What's going on behind those obscenely attractive eyes of yours?"

I sheepishly crane my neck to search the restaurant. It should be coming any minute. "I'll share with you over dessert."

I've guarded this surprise for months, but the widening of her eyes tells me that her curiosity is shifting into realization. My heart pounds and mouth dries. It's not like we haven't discussed this, but I want it so badly. I'm dying to know that she wants it too.

The sampler platter I arranged finally arrives—five desserts, but all I see is the tiny white wedding cake in the middle, her ring right there in plain sight. I press my leg to stop the bouncing.

Her eyes fill. It's go time. "I spoke with Archie and—"

"Yes," she blurts. "Yes, I really want to marry you." She grabs the ring off the tiny cake, removes the icing with a swipe of her napkin, and slips it onto her left ring finger herself.

My resulting laughter releases the tension in my body like a pressure valve. Her response couldn't be better. I couldn't be any happier. She wants me too.

Thank you. Thank you.

The ring sparkles magnificently in the light of the chandeliers. She toggles back and forth between me and her finger. She likes it.

"It was Granny's," I say.

Her eyes widen with compassion, and my gut tightens—I miss her. Kit got to meet her over a year ago, a couple weeks before she died. They're so much alike. "Another time you've jumped the gun and missed my speech," I tease.

"Ooh, a speech." She sits back in her seat. "I'm all ears. Please go on."

Kit. Every aspect of her is achingly beautiful. I sink into her deep blue eyes and long to give her everything she could ever want. For the ten-thousandth time, I wish I could—

I jerk up and bolt to her side of the table, managing to rebutton my jacket midstride—I'm not a barbarian. "In a bit," I spit out. "We're engaged. I get to kiss you now, right?" Overeager as a puppy, but I don't care.

I chose this table because the curtain separating the dining room from the kitchen bends into a corner here—we'll have some privacy. I offer her a hand to stand and lead a step back behind the wall of the curtain. That breathtaking smile. I get to kiss it just as soon as she agrees. Hands on my chest, she leans in with enthusiasm.

Finally.

My hands find the sides of her head, and I kiss her like I've waited over a year for the moment to come.

Fervor builds in his kisses and his arms wrap around my lower back now, holding me close. Euphoria. Fireworks. Perfection. He's gentle and decisive, softly leading, attuned to my every movement. Just like him. He's already reluctantly slowing. *No! Stop stopping!* He touches his forehead and nose to mine, lifting his hands back to the sides of my head, through my hair. I savor the closeness with him, eyes closed, and I tug on his jacket, releasing a little moan.

Someone give this man a medal for providing a secluded spot for our first kiss. His kissing is blissful, intoxicating, ardent. Now I know what I've been missing, so I'm fully grumpy with him when he releases me and steps back. My heart races, head swims—the snowball is officially rolling down the mountain. Breathing is difficult, like I just hiked to a high altitude. I frown delightedly at him, craving something good, precious, sacred ... a bit ahead of schedule.

Thank you for him, for this. Keep us on your timing.

With wonder, I take in the broad shoulders and blond head of the guy in front of me. God planned this all along. God knew after my scholarship interview. God knew at that first look at Saga.

You knew.

For I know the plans I have for you. Plans to prosper

you and not to harm you. Plans to give you hope and a future.

Job offers have been streaming in for when Levi graduates in four months. He's serious about living his own life. His trust fund usually gathers dust except to give lavishly and anonymously to charities God puts on his heart. I don't love that money looming, but I trust God to guide him with it.

I'm set to graduate a year early. Beyond that, I don't know much. But God used my fear and reticence to earn the trust of the perfect guy for me. If he can use that, he can use anything. He is the ultimate mastermind.

"I'll need another kiss later." I eye Levi, prim and testy.

Longing pulls his face. "Yes, please." His hands find mine.

"You can finally make full use of those Tic Tacs."

His serious expression dissolves into laughter. "Mm-hm. And what do you call it when you go up on your toes? Elevé?" His excellent French is handy for the ballet terms I mention from my classes. "You can finally make full use of those elevés. Good thing you're the resident expert."

I rise up and plant a playful kiss on his lips.

As his resulting grin calms, he lifts my left hand to brush a thumb across my ring. His eyes shine with honor and thrill, and his fingers intertwine with mine.

I grab his left hand and touch his ring finger. "Still want a tattoo for yours?"

"Absolutely."

I bet he's thinking of his parents. He prays for them so faithfully, and God keeps saying yes.

"Can I ... copy you?" I ask. "For my wedding band?"

His mouth falls open. "Are you sure?"

"I'm sure." I can be brave. This is worth it. He's worth it.

"I would love that." Emotion fills his voice.

Levi releases my hands to squeeze me into a hug. "Thank you, Jesus. We need you every minute. We love you. Thank you."

I nod in emphatic agreement as the reality of the moment settles around us. Do I really get to keep him?

We should probably sit now, but I don't want to let him go. He doesn't seem like he's in any hurry, and he knows what we can get away with in this fancy restaurant.

"I've been watching you bite that perfect lip for so long." His soft, lazy voice.

I release the offending lip and prop my chin on his chest. "Oh, have you?"

He bends to steal another kiss, checking my face.

The yes is all over it.

The End.

You made it!
I hope you're filled with all the satisfied, hopeful, giddy feels.
Thank you for spending your time with me and my characters.
I'm so very honored.

If you have a second, would you do me a huge favor and **drop a review on Amazon**? It doesn't have to be fancy—even a quick line about what it was like reading this story helps new readers decide if this is a safe place to invest their time. And if you want extra credit, recommend the book to a friend or two.

With your help, I can keep writing stories like these, where Jesus is a main character. Thank you for being part of this movement!

Next page: a **sneak peek** of the next book in the series: *Anywhere.*

Like **playlists**? Search for me on Spotify for "soundtracks" I made for my novels.

—Kristina

SNEAK PEEK OF ANYWHERE:
CHAPTER 1

Check out the first two chapters of *Anywhere*, the next book in The Mayberry University Series:

Sophie

Hugs haven't been a thing between us, but when I get there, I'm risking it. It's been two weeks, and I miss my friend.

Pasadena may be home on paper, but that penthouse with Mom is the exact opposite of campus with him. There, the yelling is over, but the oppressive quiet is permanent. She said exactly one positive thing to me over break—that the Chanel sweater she bought me for Christmas would look pretty on me. I won't be reliving that over spring break. I'd sooner subject myself to Kit's perfect little home sweet home.

His mini-smile comes into focus as I approach. It's not the same on FaceTime. I can almost smell his lumberjack scent from here. Hands in his pockets, back on his heels, waiting next to my favorite spot in my dorm's parking lot. I squeal into it, throw my Jeep into park, and nearly rip off the door. Jumping down, I ... screech to a halt. Some girl has stopped to chat with him. Red hair, delicate curves, short skirt. Right there on the sidewalk in front of my parking spot.

Already out of the Jeep, I 180 to the back to feign a fascination with my suitcase. Do the zippers work? Mm-hm. I can, in fact, access my belongings. I would trade every last one if she'd kindly remove her hand from his arm.

"What are you doing tonight?" she asks. Major eye contact, inching closer. Innocent eyes and a naughty mouth.

She could teach a master class on flirting with nonverbals. I have plenty to learn but no stomach for this lesson. I'm sure it would be great fun to watch her on a screen with my suitemates and a bag of tortilla chips. And—oh yeah—a different mark.

"Could you help me with my laptop?" she asks. "I know how smart you are. And handy."

Oh, verbals too. Cool, cool. He would have gone out with her anyway, but she phrased it like a favor, so now his plans tonight are set in stone.

"And helpful," she continues.

Suitcase, yep. Backpack. Some jackets I left in here a million years ago. Paper bowls, water bottles, more crumbs than make any sense ... I should really clean this out. Probably won't.

"I'll text you later, 'kay?" he says.

When I risk a glance around the passenger headrest to check on the happy couple through the windshield, she notices—yikes! —and sends me side-eye. I hop to pull my backpack out, like I'm way too busy to be spying, but I yank too hard and fall on my butt.

I let out a sigh as I wipe off my jeans. Wow. And the Klutz Award goes to ... me. I'd like to thank my parents, my severe inferiority to the girl in the skirt, and the Texas-sized guilt for my crush on the guy in plaid.

Shrug into one of the jackets, slide it off. It might be January, but my burning face is acting as a nice space heater at the moment.

I smooth my hair and straighten my shirt. In any other situation, I would prance over and make friends with Pretty Redhead. I bet she's fun when she's not hitting on this dude completely out of the blue on the first day back to campus. I wouldn't mind borrowing her boots either—boots that are standing obnoxiously close to the guy who was waiting for me. But I won't be going near her right now. I can only imagine us standing side by side for comparison, as if he has a rose in hand. *Which will he choose?* the narrator asks. Oof, the quickest choice in the history of reality romance shows. No rose for you, Blondie.

I'll stay back here with the luggage, thanks. I'm not a masochist.

Is Leo back yet? If he were, I'd know. He's learned to give me space, but he never leaves me guessing. No Open Dorms tonight, but we could do a field trip. Bowling? I'll text some friends, see who's in. Then suite movie night. Unless they'd be down to go to the lake again. I push the zipper around my suitcase, calculating the timing. Kit will be stocked up on sleep after break. The stars out there ...

A yelp escapes when my side is tickled, and I hit my head on Austin's hand. He had it braced along the edge of the Jeep, ready for my Tigger jump.

"Whatcha doin' back here?" That playful voice.

"Nothing! Something! Hi."

Redhead has vanished.

"Hey, Soph. C'mon." He tilts his head toward Saga. "Let's get you some dinner." He pauses with a hand on the tailgate. "Safe to say you're gonna leave your suitcase in here for a couple weeks?"

I grin. "You know ... in the event of a zombie apocalypse, I'll be really glad to have a few changes of clothes ready to go."

"Remind me to throw some things in there too. I don't wanna miss you fighting off a zombie."

"Don't blame you. Last semester I took—"

"Karate," he says with me, chuckling. "Oh, I remember. But I don't think you'll need it. Give you ten minutes and you'll have them committing to a vegetarian lifestyle and joining you for a nice night of laser tag." He throws my backpack over his shoulder and closes the door.

Ooh, laser tag. "Whatever. I'm super intimidating. Those zombies will turn vegetarian because of the terror I inflict."

I reach to tickle his side, and his giant hand gently grabs my wrist. "Nice try." Those blue-gray eyes smile at me as my blissful wrist calls a *bye, I'm going with him!*

I reach for a bear hug—just a friend hug—but he sidesteps with a practiced spin.

Right. Barely-there side hug it is.

"I missed you," he murmurs.

Yeah.

It's like this.

Sophie

THAT NIGHT LEO'S jacket smells like popcorn. I pull it tighter to keep out the chill and find a box of Nerds in the pocket. He nods easily, so I tear them open. The night sky is celebrating our first night back on campus with a rare lack of clouds. Austin would want to plop down right here and watch the stars—

I bat the thought away.

Rather than meeting up, Leo left his scooter on Flooders so he could walk beside me on his own two legs. He stuffs his goose-bumped arms into his pockets, framing today's punny shirt: an orange staring at a glass of orange juice saying, *Mom?*

With a chuckle, I tug the hem of his shirt. "I like this one. It's too dark for your personality—oddly adorable."

His nervous smile draws me in like the first time I talked to him on Flooders. After like three months together, he still gets tongue tied. He still stares when he thinks I'm not looking.

I grin back. "So, I bet your Great Danes loved having you home."

His eyes soften, almost reverent, as he brushes the edge of my sleeve.

But a for-sale sign catches my eye outside Davidson Hall. Spin a slow 360. One outside Turner Hall too. A phone number is handwritten in Sharpie at the bottom of each. "Leo, look."

"Yeah, there's one at Albert too."

"Whose number is on there? We should text it."

"Uh, not sure."

For now, I snap a picture. I'll ask Austin. He'll know the extent of the prank and who's pulling it. He'll probably know whose number that is. I bet it's already in his phone—

I straighten. No Austin. I'm with Leo.

Okay. Yes. Dating a guy who barely scrapes into second place in my heart might be a crime against basic human decency. A war crime, even. But Leo is exactly the kind of guy I should like. What am I supposed to do? Sit back and watch Austin casually date his way through the entire campus? I refuse to live out the lyrics of a tragic Taylor Swift song. If I'm going to survive this pathetic, messy, unrequited crush on my best friend, I have to act. So I'm aiming toward liking a guy who's more realistic. This is healthy, right? If I just give it some more time, this could blossom into something good for both of us.

The problem is, moving on is like trying to untangle a knot that tightens the harder I pull. Austin is a walking paradox, and that's part of the problem. A boulder of muscles on the outside hiding a soft, gooey inside. The sweetest smile laced with an edge of mischief. Gentle eyes that smolder—

At this exact moment, Leo halts at the chapel and jerks all 100 percent into a chicken-peck kiss—not the 90 percent Hitch recommends. I freeze, wildly unprepared for our first kiss. My first instinct is to lean in and help him aim this time, but something stops me.

Is that you?

An involuntary montage plays in my head. Jeremiah, Peeta, Jacob, Lon, Prince Maxon. The Nice Boys Club—sweet, cautious, predictable, tame. I've yelled at them all, "What are you doing with your life? Find someone who actually appreciates you!" Stepping away, I bite my lips together as the pieces fall into place. He deserves so much better than my nonsense. I can't steal another kiss from this sweet, oblivious guy. Leo is a dream. Just not mine. Yes, he's everything that should make this work, exactly what I should want. But my heart keeps skipping school, and I can't keep pretending. I lift my eyes to his vulnerable, boyish face. He's not staring into my soul. Not expecting me to be something I'm not. He's just... here. Quiet, sweet, uncomplicated. I thought trying on commitment with the tags still on would keep me free. But now I've set off the alarm at the door.

One thing is certain—I can't act on this epiphany now. Guilt prickles my skin. Dumping someone after an awkward first kiss? Cruel.

My gaze drifts to Griffin Hall. I have no one to process this with. Kit would blame herself for Leo getting hurt, and I don't need her puppy-dog eyes. I mean, Sir Levi himself decided "Oh, actually, I do date" with one glance at her. What does she know about not settling? Mia has no patience for romance woes. Jenny, Izzy, and the G3-ers? No way would I offer this as gossip fodder. And Austin. He's already the best friend I've ever had. I'd tell him almost anything. But not about this. Not one flying chance.

Austin is selfless, compassionate, generous, gentle—but never "nice." There's a wildness to him. A spontaneity. A force of will. Still, I've never seen a better friend, a more sacrificial floormate and son. He cares so deeply, gives so wholly.

My chest constricts.

If Leo is a dressing room mirror of my medium-ness, Austin's goodness is the fluorescent lighting overhead. Some people weren't built for that kind of exposure. I'll never not flinch under that glare.

With a swivel back to Leo's searching eyes, I blurt out, "Cool." What? I have to get out of here. "Thanks for the ... walk.

I'm headed to MSC, so I'll see you tomorrow, yeah?" I fumble his jacket off my shoulders and hold it out to him.

He droops like a puppet whose strings were forgotten. "I'll walk you over there."

"Thanks, but I'm ... going to call someone on the way over. Adios y vaya con Dios!" I call, Zac Brown Band–style.

Not helping. *Tone it down, Sophie.*

That sad smile. I know. I'm horrible. But I don't know how to fix anything right now, so all I can manage is to hightail it across campus. I'll break up with him soon. I will.

But a familiar ache settles beneath my temples, and my pace slows. What am I thinking? I have no business dumping a quality guy like Leo. I'm a hot glue stick person—shiny in the package, a mess of strings once the pressure hits, raised by a family that could stick things together just long enough to fool the neighbors. Not exactly an appealing résumé to an Austin type—even if dating someone like that didn't come with a side of slow emotional implosion.

I pull out my phone to call Mia.

"Hello?" She's all business.

"Hi, roomie! Miss me?"

"Absolutely, but why are you calling?"

"Just wanted to see if we could do the lake tonight instead of a movie."

"Kit's with Levi, so let's do tomorrow instead," she says.

"Should've known," I grumble. Behold the new normal.

"You sure there's no emergency? You text. You've literally never called me before."

"All good here! Oh—while I have you, is there a for-sale sign outside Griffin Hall?"

"Nope. Just the buildings with dude floors. I heard it's A1's prank and they covered their tracks with a sign outside their own building."

"What's with the phone number?" I ask.

"Don't know yet. You're gonna text it, aren't you?"

"Duh. Unless Austin can clear it up for me."

"Figured. See you in the suite later."

"See you in a bit!"

A punch of the red button. Phone call, check.

Our student center, a.k.a MSC, is three stories of fun, including a coffee shop, movie rooms, and The Hive, home of greasy chicken goodness that's free with meal punches. Austin is their best late-night customer. He looks like a bear—broad shoul-dered, with a curly brown mess of hair—and he eats like one too. Always stocking up before hibernating in his dorm each night, lest he wake up hungry midsleep.

But by this time, he's usually gone, which means my trip here has maybe a 15 percent chance of seeing him. Even if I do, I'll avoid the topics of his computer tutorial with Pretty Redhead and my epiphany kiss. Yes, I'm great at making a mess of things.

I haul MSC's door open and pan around the mostly empty first floor. He's not here—probably into some kind of dude mayhem on his floor, Flooders. Leo will join in when he gets back. This kind of social overlap is unavoidable on the tiny Mayberry campus. I guess it's part of the charm.

Maybe I'll text Austin. Just in case.

Austin

At a *ding*, I check my phone. Sophie.

> No chicken tonight?

I text back,

> On my way there

Jackpot. Love me some chicken, but if Sophie's there, anything else is just gravy.

DISCUSSION QUESTIONS

1. Kit struggles with PTSD and avoids situations that might trigger her flashbacks. Do you think her avoidance is a healthy coping mechanism? Why or why not?

2. Levi chooses to avoid the topics of his wealth and childhood experiences. How do you think this affects his interactions with Kit and his approach to following Jesus?

3. How does Kit's past trauma shape her interactions with Levi? Identify specific moments in the story where her trauma influences her decisions. How does her faith journey impact these moments?

4. Levi struggles with trust due to his past experiences. Do you think it's possible to fully trust again after being betrayed? Why or why not?

5. Compare how Kit and Levi deal with their past hurts. How do their approaches to healing and faith differ, and how are they similar? What are some ways you can seek healing through healthy, safe relationships and your faith?

6. Which character's faith story resonated most with you, and why? If you're on a healing journey of your own, are you still freshly wounded, feeling more balanced, or well on your way to healing? How does this impact how you view their stories?

7. What daily habits did you notice in Kit's and Levi's routines? How did they impact their faith, relationships, and growth?

8. How do you think Kit's relationship with her suitemates influenced her healing process? Discuss the positive and negative impacts they had on her.

9. What are some examples of safe relationships you saw in the story? How about unsafe? What are some ways you can be a healing and safe presence to friends of yours who have undergone dark experiences?

10. Do you like Kit's relationship with Levi? What is something you would imitate, and what is something you would do differently?

11. Kit tries to push Levi away for his own good. Do you think this was the right decision? Why or why not? Would this be the right decision in a different circumstance?

12. Kit created new dating boundaries for herself going into a relationship with Levi. Why do you think she did this? Do you agree or disagree with her choice?

13. Mental health is a significant issue. How does Kit's story join the conversation about mental health and faith? How can Christian communities better support individuals facing similar struggles?

AUTHOR'S NOTES

Kit and Levi are fictional, but the God in their story is the same one who has shown himself to me time and time again. He wants to do the same for you. He says to his people in the Old Testament, "You will seek me and you will find me, when you seek me with all your heart." (Jeremiah 29:13) If you don't know him yet, talk to him now—in your head or out loud. Tell him you're sorry for the wrong you've done and that you're ready for him to be the Mastermind, the Orchestrator, and the Boss of your life. That's all it takes for him to become part of your life. What does it mean to seek him? A great way to start is to read his word and talk to him about it.

Below you'll find each of the Bible verses referenced. In the story, I paraphrased the verses God speaks to Kit into first person to emphasize how he speaks directly to our hearts, but they are listed below as they appear in the Bible (English Standard Version, unless otherwise noted). They are all game-changers that I love to soak in.

Chapter 1:
1 John 3:1—"See what great love the Father has lavished on

us, that we should be called children of God! And that is what we are!"

Chapter 3:
Jeremiah 29:11—"For I know the plans I have for you, declares the Lord, plans for welfare and not for evil, to give you a future and a hope."

Chapter 4:
Proverbs 3:5-6—"Trust in the Lord with all your heart, and do not lean on your own understanding. In all your ways acknowledge him, and he will make straight your paths."
Psalm 46:1—"God is our refuge and strength, a very present help in trouble."
Psalm 62:2—"He alone is my rock and my salvation, my fortress; I shall not be greatly shaken."

Chapter 5:
Proverbs 3:5-6—"Trust in the Lord with all your heart, and do not lean on your own understanding. In all your ways acknowledge him, and he will make straight your paths."
Psalm 46:1—"God is our refuge and strength, a very present help in trouble."

Chapter 13:
Romans 8:28—"And we know that in all things God works for the good of those who love him, who have been called according to his purpose."

Chapter 15:
Ephesians 4:32—"Be kind to one another, tenderhearted, forgiving one another, as God in Christ forgave you."

Chapter 24:

Ephesians 4:32—"Be kind to one another, tenderhearted, forgiving one another, as God in Christ forgave you."

Chapter 25:
Proverbs 3:5-6—"Trust in the Lord with all your heart, and do not lean on your own understanding. In all your ways acknowledge him, and he will make straight your paths."
1 John 3:1—"See what great love the Father has lavished on us, that we should be called children of God! And that is what we are!"
2 Corinthians 12:9—"But he said to me, 'My grace is sufficient for you, for my power is made perfect in weakness.'"

Chapter 28:
Mark 12:30—"And you shall love the Lord your God with all your heart and with all your soul and with all your mind and with all your strength."

Chapter 29:
Proverbs 16:9—"The heart of man plans his way, but the Lord establishes his steps."

Chapter 33:
Matthew 5:8—"Blessed are the pure in heart, for they will see God."
Psalm 56:3—"When I am afraid, I put my trust in you."
Psalm 56:8—"You have kept count of my tossings; put my tears in your bottle. Are they not in your book?"

Chapter 34:
Romans 12:2—"Do not be conformed to this world, but be transformed by the renewal of your mind, that by testing you may discern what is the will of God, what is good and acceptable and perfect."

Chapter 35:
Lamentations 3:25-26—"The Lord is good to those who wait for him, to the soul who seeks him. It is good that one should wait quietly for the salvation of the Lord."

Chapter 36:
Haymitch references Luke 14:28-30 ("For which of you, desiring to build a tower, does not first sit down and count the cost, whether he has enough to complete it? Otherwise, when he has laid a foundation and is not able to finish, all who see it begin to mock him, saying, 'This man began to build and was not able to finish.'") as well as Jeremiah 42.

Chapter 39:
Psalm 56:3—"When I am afraid, I put my trust in you."

Chapter 44:
Matthew 7:12—"So whatever you wish that others would do to you, do also to them, for this is the Law and the Prophets."

Chapter 48:
Psalm 103:12—"As far as the east is from the west, so far does he remove our transgressions from us."
Isaiah 26:3-4 (Holman Christian Standard Version)—"You will keep the mind that is dependent on you in perfect peace, for it is trusting in you. Trust in the Lord forever, because in the Lord, the Lord himself, is an everlasting rock!"
Romans 8:28—"And we know that in all things God works for the good of those who love him, who have been called according to his purpose."

Chapter 49:
John 10:27—"My sheep listen to my voice; I know them, and they follow me."
Ecclesiastes 3:1,7—"For everything there is a season, and a

time for every matter under heaven ... a time to tear, and a time to sew; a time to keep silence, and a time to speak."

Chapter 50:
Psalm 37:7—"Be still before the Lord and wait patiently for him."

Chapter 51:
Phillipians 4:6-7 is referenced—"Do not be anxious about anything, but in everything by prayer and supplication with thanksgiving let your requests be made known to God.

And the peace of God, which surpasses all understanding, will guard your hearts and your minds in Christ Jesus."

Chapter 53:
Psalm 139:5—"You hem me in, behind and before, and lay your hand upon me."

Chapter 54:
Romans 8:28—"And we know that in all things God works for the good of those who love him, who have been called according to his purpose."

Chapter 56:
Psalm 56:3—"When I am afraid, I put my trust in you."
Psalm 56:8—"You have kept count of my tossings; put my tears in your bottle. Are they not in your book?"

Epilogue:
Jeremiah 29:11—"For I know the plans I have for you, declares the Lord, plans for welfare and not for evil, to give you a future and a hope."

Throughout the story:
When God speaks to Kit, he most frequently assures Kit of his

presence. "I'm always here." This psalm is one of many portions of the Bible that describe his closeness:

Psalm 139:7-18—"O Lord, you have searched me and known me! You know when I sit down and when I rise up; you discern my thoughts from afar. You search out my path and my lying down and are acquainted with all my ways. Even before a word is on my tongue, behold, O Lord, you know it altogether. You hem me in, behind and before, and lay your hand upon me. Such knowledge is too wonderful for me; it is high; I cannot attain it. Where shall I go from your Spirit? Or where shall I flee from your presence? If I ascend to heaven, you are there! If I make my bed in Sheol, you are there! If I take the wings of the morning and dwell in the uttermost parts of the sea, even there your hand shall lead me, and your right hand shall hold me. If I say, 'Surely the darkness shall cover me, and the light about me be night,' even the darkness is not dark to you; the night is bright as the day, for darkness is as light with you. For you formed my inward parts; you knitted me together in my mother's womb. I praise you, for I am fearfully and wonderfully made. Wonderful are your works; my soul knows it very well. My frame was not hidden from you, when I was being made in secret, intricately woven in the depths of the earth. Your eyes saw my unformed substance; in your book were written, every one of them, the days that were formed for me, when as yet there was none of them. How precious to me are your thoughts, O God! How vast is the sum of them! If I would count them, they are more than the sand. I awake, and I am still with you."

ACKNOWLEDGMENTS

Jesus

To my first and greatest love. What an adventure this has been with you! I'm flabbergasted that you care so much and that you provide so intricately. Thank you for your closeness, your whispers, and your answers at your perfect time. As always, this is your thing. I'm just along for the ride.

Brit

Thank you for so much patience, devotion, and support as I tornadoed, roller coastered, and shook my head at myself. As I wrote this story, and in every department, you've surpassed my wildest dreams. For encouraging me read it aloud to you (twice!). For all your insight about overachieving dudes so I could write Levi and Archie. For asking about my "next step" one billion times. Any rational husband would have told me that I don't have the time, qualifications, or energy to be writing a book right now, but you did nothing of the sort. You deserve the biggest trophy imaginable. Your next-level-ness is material for a thousand love stories.

My kiddos

You're the coolest, smartest, cutest kids around. Thank you for making space with me to cram this project into our lives. I can't wait to see what crazy projects Jesus leads you into.

Mom

Thank you for teaching me about Jesus and how to talk to him about everything, for helping me learn all those Bible verses, for telling tiny Kristina I could do anything I set my mind to (even be an astronaut!). For teaching me to take on projects just because and then to actually *finish* them. Turns out, your opinion *does* count, and yours brings me to thankful tears. I wouldn't be me without you.

Dad

Thank you for all those Barnes & Noble dates—I'd always find you with an even bigger stack of books than mine. For all the kitchen table debates growing up and for your profound patience as I disagreed with nearly everything you said for a decade. You never let me get away with a half-formed argument, and it grew me more than either of us realized. It taught me to love Truth.

Dori

Editor and coach extraordinaire, God sent you at just the right time. What a privilege to have your brilliant advice and profound encouragement. You understood! You treated me like a real author, and it was a self-fulfilling prophecy.

Gabby

For your invaluable advice and insight.

Kyle

For use of your studio and for your expertise. You made the audiobook possible.

REFERENCES

Crossway Bibles. *The Holy Bible, English Standard Version*. Wheaton, IL: Crossway Bibles, 2001.

Goff, Bob. *Love Does: Discover a Secretly Incredible Life in an Ordinary World*. Nashville: Thomas Nelson, 2012.

Holman Bible Publishers. *Holman Christian Standard Bible*. Nashville: Holman Bible Publishers, 2004.

ABOUT THE AUTHOR

When Kristina Welch isn't adventuring around the world with her husband and three little blondies, she's home near Denver, Colorado. She thrives on date nights, forest hikes, and peanut butter cookies. Her days include half-homeschooling her kids, thrifting for treasures, regretting DIY home projects, and soaking in the beauty of the mountains—and their Creator—from her favorite writing spot.

Let's Stay Connected

Did this story make you smile, cry, or yell at a fictional character? I'd love to hear your thoughts! These are my imaginary friends, after all. Email and links below. Also, inspired by Bob Goff's bold move in *Love Does*, I'm putting my number in the back of my book: (720) 224-2648. Feel free to text me about the story or Jesus —my very favorite subject. Just mention the book in your first text.

Want more Kit and Levi? Check out the Pinterest board and Spotify soundtrack I made for their story—perfect for all the feels after you finish the book. Find them on the Extras page of my website. And don't forget to subscribe to the newsletter on my website for freebies and updates on upcoming books. Links on the next page.

—Kristina

Website: https://www.kristinawelchauthor.com
Email: kristinawelchauthor@gmail.com

goodreads.com/kristinawelchauthor

instagram.com/_kristinawelch

pinterest.com/kristinawelchauthor

amazon.com/author/kristinawelch

www.ingramcontent.com/pod-product-compliance
Lightning Source LLC
Chambersburg PA
CBHW050514110726
47899CB00005B/1450

9 798999 233761 7